LONDON BOUND

LB

A Novel

AMY DAWS

Copyright © 2015 Amy Daws
All rights reserved.

Published by Stars Hollow Publishing
ISBN 13: 978-15-11933-85-8
IBBN 10: 15-11933-85-2
Editing by Heather Banta www.linkedin.com/in/heatherbanta
Cover design by Amy Daws
Cover photography by Megan Daws
Author Photograph by Megan Daws
Cover models Allie Sievert and Jacob Jay Nair

This book is licensed for personal enjoyment only. No part of this book may be reproduced in any form or by any electronic or mechanical means, including information storage and retrieval systems, without written permission from the author. The only exception is by quoting short excerpts in a review. If you're reading this book and did not purchase it, then please go www.amydawsauthor.com to find where you can purchase it. Thank you for respecting the hard work of this author.

This book is a work of fiction. Names, characters, places, and incidents are products of the author's imagination or are used fictitiously. Any resemblance to actual persons, living or dead, events, or locales are entirely coincidental.

Dedicated to my Mom and Dad.
As far as parents go,
you guys are the beez-neez.

PROLOGUE

He strides with slow, purposeful steps right toward me. I immediately halt my diva-power-squat dance move I've been perfecting for the past year. Hey, it's not as bad as the twerking I was attempting poorly only two minutes ago. His face is slack, serious, and completely focused on mine. His vision doesn't stray to any other girl on the dance floor—*only me*. What the hell does this guy want? If he's a bouncer and coming to yell at me for dancing like a fool, he can just piss right off! I'll Harlem Shake all over his ass if he isn't careful! I know this is a posh London nightclub, but fuck him. In fact, upon further reflection, I hope that's exactly what he's coming over for. He's going to get an earful from me because that shit's un-American! *Oh, shit. I'm in London. Duh, Leslie—moron.* Still though. Even for London, getting kicked out of a nightclub for dancing like a fool is bloody rude.

"Look, I'm just having fun. Piss off or I'll sic my friend Frank on you. He's a huge Irish demon and he'll rip your ass off if you don't watch it." I fix a pointed glare at him, preparing myself for battle.

His deep, soulful eyes hood briefly, and the intensity of his expression winds me. "Dance with me," he says, simply. It's a demand, not a question.

Well that's unexpected. I briefly shake off my initial feeling of indignation and shrug my shoulders nonchalantly, giving him an 'if you must' look. This could be fun. He's not bad looking—in fact, he's pretty hot now that I know he's not a bouncer coming to thump me. He instantly snakes his hands around my waist and pulls me up tight against him. I'm slightly stunned by the intimacy of his hold but am taken off guard too much to object. His right leg pushes between my thighs and my little black dress rides up scandalously high.

He eyes me closely and then begins swaying our hips to the erotic nightclub beats. Oh God. This feels a bit intimate with his leg positioned just so. But oof, it's quite nice if I'm being honest. I get that little zaza feeling up my spine, and it's not altogether unwelcome. I look around at the other people dancing, trying to get a better grip on myself and quit focusing on the squirming sensation happening in my under belly right now. *Ye gats, I hope to God Frank doesn't see this or he'll never let me live it down.* It's quite obvious everyone around us is pretty hammered at this point because they are all completely oblivious to our sensual motions. It's late enough now I suppose, even the Brits are behaving with a bit more bravado.

My attention is snapped back to my dance partner as he hitches his leg slightly. Goodness me, I drop my chin to my chest and shake my hair forward to conceal my face. Oh shit that feels good being tight up against him like this. I feel hot and flushed. Who is this guy?

His hand moves gently up my side and he crooks his finger under my chin, forcing me to look up at him. His eyes are boring down on me, intense and curious. Without even telling it to, my tongue slips out from my mouth and licks my upper lip leisurely. His eyes flare ever so slightly—his black-rimmed glasses making it difficult to see his expression properly. My eyes rove around the rest of him and take in his buzzed, dirty blonde hair and dark scruff peppered around his face. He's got a sexy, lazy-Sunday-morning-just-fucked look about him, if I do say so myself.

"What's your name?" he asks loudly enough to be heard. His British accent sounds a bit Cockney. Perhaps East London? I can't quite distinguish accents as well as Frank, but I've picked up a few regional signs. The feel of his vibrating chest against me when he speaks is nice.

"Leslie," I answer, taking quick note of his tight-corded muscles roping up his arms. Jesus, his triceps are huge! "Yours?" My curiosity is peaked. Any man that has the nerve to come right up and ask me to dance has some serious balls. Brits in general tend to keep to themselves at most nightclubs until the booze really starts flowing. But this guy doesn't appear to be drunk. In fact, he's got some serious dance moves that indicate to me he's stone-cold sober.

Suddenly, he shifts his leg snugger between my thighs and my eyes fly wide open as I panic, feeling my dress ride up nearly past my kitty-cat! Oblivious, he leans in close and murmurs, "My name is Theo." He stills, breathing deeply near the area just below my ear. His heady scent invades all of my senses and his warm breath sends shivers down my neck and spine. *Wait a sec. Did he just nuzzle me?*

My hands instinctively grasp his firm biceps for balance as a zinging sensation courses through me. Shit, this feels positively exciting! Wrong, but thrilling as hell! My hands stroke gently around his thick arms bulging through his tight t-shirt. He has a bulky, muscular build, and appears to be at least six-foot tall—easily dwarfing me. Though at only five-foot-five myself, that doesn't take much. Either way, I definitely wouldn't toss this guy out of bed for eating crackers.

"You looked like you were having a lot of fun just a bit ago, Leslie." He says my name like he's testing it out to see how it feels on his lips. His voice is smooth but deep. A timbre that reaches me everywhere it shouldn't. His comment is sweet and light, but his face is serious and contemplative.

"I'm here with my best friend, Finley. We were just having a laugh." I shrug my shoulders and smile, trying to earn a smile in return. He continues to look at me with a pensive expression.

"You're American?"

I nod. Just then, Finley grasps my shoulders and mumbles into my ear that she's running to the loo. I turn to reply, but she's already scurried off. I hope she doesn't have a bathroom emergency. There's nothing worse than pooing at a high-class nightclub.

"Americans are pretty good at laughing." Theo's voice interrupts my thoughts like he can hear them somehow poking fun at my poor friend. I gaze at him as his mouth drops open slightly. He moves his tongue to the side of his mouth biting the tip with his back teeth. He appears to be contemplating what he's going to say next. Seemingly deciding against saying anything at all, he pins me with a sexy smoldering look and I catch myself gawking at his thick bottom lip.

My coworkers give me crap all the time about being obnoxious and how utterly *American* that is. They say American like it's a bad thing! I just like to laugh and goof off! But this Theo guy doesn't seem to be saying it negatively. I decide to let the comment slide.

"Why so serious?" I ask in a low, creepy voice, imitating the voice of the Joker from Batman Returns. I pucker my lips out into a playful pout. His eyes lock on my lips and I giggle at his obvious lack of humor.

He shrugs his shoulders and answers, "Not everyone can light up a room like you, I guess." He looks off to the side and I bark out a laugh.

"That's a line if I ever heard one! I'm sure you say that to all the girls." I wag my eyebrows sarcastically.

He frowns and looks back at me confused. A dissatisfied expression ripples over his features. "I don't. I'm not…really *a line* kind of guy. I've actually never said that to anyone. Well, maybe my mum…before…" he pauses, smiling softly for the first time since he approached me. There's a sadness to it though. My heart flutters at the adorable expression on his face. He should do happy more often—it looks good on him.

I finally tear my eyes away from his face and look around at the people surrounding us. I forgot we weren't alone for a second and suddenly I feel self-conscious of our provocative dancing.

"I mean it," he says, pressing his chest into mine and speaking close enough that I can feel his lips tickle my ear. "It's not a line. You…" He pauses and exhales deeply. "You sparkle." He pulls back quickly, appearing to be taken aback by the words that just tumbled out of his own mouth.

I want to swat him sardonically and make some wisecrack about what a lying cow he must be. But his expression and demeanor feel too honest—*raw*. I can't explain it. I believe him now but feel uncomfortable with the compliment at the same time. I've never been good at compliments. The only compliments I ever seem to get are on my clothes.

"You must be referring to my keen fashion sense." I wink playfully.

His eyes dip down to my chest and he scowls briefly then returns his gaze to my green eyes. "Not the clothes," he replies simply.

I get the first proper look at his eyes when a blast of white light illuminates the dancers. *Wow.* His eyes are amazing—pale brown around the iris, and darkening slightly toward the edges. And of course they'd have to be framed with thick black lashes. As his gaze pierces me I'm struck with a feeling of mourning. His eyes have this beautifully sad look about them that I can't quite make sense of. I want to rip off his black-rimmed glasses and see if that reveals the cause of his obvious remorse.

He shifts his leg slightly and the friction of his expensive-looking tweed pants between my legs shocks my thought process. Oh my word, this is bad. This is much too intimate. *Get a hold of yourself, Leslie!*

I pucker my lips, attempting to contain the growing arousal in my body. Between his sweet words and his sensual movements, I feel myself losing control like a wanton floozy. I have to get off this man's leg. I have to. Why did I wear such lacey underwear? This sensation is just…too…much.

He brings his mouth to my neck and gently exhales along the skin below my ear. My organs wooze for England. I can almost feel the moisture of his lips on my skin. I press myself deeper into him, enjoying the feel of his muscular leg under my clenched thighs. I had no idea dancing could be this arousing!

Pulling back, he looks intensely into my eyes like he knows exactly what's going through my mind. His eyes squint for a second and then look down to my lips. *Holy fuck, is he going to kiss me?* Oh God, he is! He's going to kiss me—I know it. I should stop this. He's a stranger and my nearly-naked vagina is riding his thigh like a bucking pony. *Damn, his lips look soft.*

Before I have time to make some smartass wisecrack to break this sex-bubble we're forming, he leans down and confirms my suspicions. Yes—oh yes, those lips are as soft as I suspected. As soon as we make contact, my cheeks tingle with excitement, the sensation ripples down to my core. His lips are smooth, plump, and rocking my fucking world right now. He doesn't insert his tongue, which only makes me desperate for more. Like the sexually-deprived woman I am, I move my hands up from his chest to his cheeks and attempt to insert my tongue. Suddenly, he breaks our kiss and eyes me tensely. I can feel my eyes dilating with an aching need.

He bites his tongue again and moves his hands down to cup my behind. He pulls me onto his thigh even further. The friction and his hands touching me so intimately are nearly unbearable. Despite myself I thrust my hips into him and look up at his eyes with pure, unadulterated arousal. *Jesus, I am such a scandalous hussie!* My breath comes out in soft, shallow puffs. This Theo guy knows what he's doing—that's for damn sure!

He peers down at my crotch riding his leg. His eyes flash in a state of passion as his body catches up to mine. I moan softly. I feel like I've crawled out of my body and am watching it from above in perverted fascination. His previously controlled expression vanishes. His hands move from my butt to my hips and he rocks me back and forth on his hard leg.

I gasp, feeling stunned, and throw my head back. His actions grow frenzied and he pulls me flush against him. My head tosses over his shoulder. I hardly recognize what's happening before it's too late. A silent scream rips through me as sparks fire brightly behind my tightly closed eyes dancing with the bright club lights. I cry out loudly in shock, but my voice goes unheard over the roar of the music. But Theo's heard it. He's frozen in place, just like me. *He knows.* He recognized my body transitioning from a coiled, tight rocket, to a limp, weak noodle.

Holy tits on a bull, I just climaxed...on a stranger's leg!

I look up with wide, horrified eyes as my body settles back into reality. I chance a look at his reaction. He looks desperate—

awestruck maybe? His eyes flash to my lips and he kisses me powerfully, swirling my still-fully-satisfied state. Just as he inserts his tongue, I break the kiss, overwhelmed by everything.

"Leslie?" He says my name in a questioning tone through a raspy, thick British accent.

"I, uhh…I need to…" I breathe heavily. "I'll be right back." I try to pull away and he grabs my waist tightly, refusing to let me go.

"I want to talk to you." Did his accent get thicker or is it just me? His demeanor shifts to nervous and unsure—which for some bizarre reason only makes me want him more.

"I'll be right back. I promise." His eyes rove over my face, seemingly trying to determine if I'm trustworthy. He brushes my auburn bangs away from my eyes, assessing me further. He must see something because he releases me, albeit nervously.

"I'd like to walk you."

"No," I reply without thinking. I pause and smile reassuringly. "It's just right over there." He follows my gesture over to the women's restroom and contemplates for a brief second, then nods his head slightly.

"I'll wait right over there." He glances to an empty bench area on the side of the dance floor. I nod my head confidently and hold one finger up, indicating I'll be right back.

In a flash, I rush to the women's loo on shaky legs. As soon as I'm secured behind a stall door, I let out a huge breath and attempt to stop my trembling hands. Holy fuckity-fuck-fuck-fuck, fuck. What was that? Did I seriously just cum on a stranger's leg at a nightclub. What was his name again? Theo? *Oh my God. What is wrong with me?* I repeatedly bang my forehead on the side of the bathroom stall until it smarts and I flinch. *I fucking deserve it!* I rub the tender spot glumly.

How could I be so utterly pathetic? He probably thinks I'm a lonely, desperate cow who hasn't been laid in years…which, unfortunately, is true.

I sigh loudly and attempt to wipe my soaked panties. Deciding the panties are too far gone, I peel them off and toss them in the bin. I hate wearing the damn things anyway. I only did because Finley said we were going to dance wildly tonight and I thought it better to be safe than sorry. I pull down my little black dress, feeling completely exposed and raw below. Normally, going commando is no big thing for me, but doing it after an orgasm feels a bit more vulnerable.

I reluctantly exit the stall and get a glimpse of myself in the mirror. *Jesus.* I look like I've been properly fucked. My short bob is tousled and mussed and my green eyes are wide and dilated. Cheeks flushed. *Jesus Lez—this is just great.* I wash my hands as mortification blankets me the longer I stare at myself in the mirror.

This is just so inherently me that I could laugh. I *could* laugh, but I won't. It's too pitiful. I know one thing for sure in this moment—I sure as shit can never face that Theo guy ever again.

CHAPTER ONE

<u>*PRESENT DAY: 6 Months Later*</u>
FINLEY & BRODY'S WEDDING:

Watching my best friend Finley walk down a beach isle in a wedding dress on the coast of Mexico is blowing my freaking mind. *Mind. Officially. Blown.*

Two words come to mind…cat lady.

Behold, Lez…your future with cats has now been secured. My best friend is leaving me in the dust and there's not a damn thing I can do about it.

Finny and I have spoken in great lengths about her issues with marriage. She was always bragging on and on about how hot her sex life was with Brody when they were living together in Kansas City. She was once certain that marriage would just ruin everything they had going for them. I sure as heck wasn't going to correct her. I loved Finny as my partner in crime. We broke the mold together in

London Bound

our Podunk small town of Marshall, Missouri. This was my best friend.

And now she is getting married before my very eyes. *Cats…so many cats.*

Don't get me wrong, I love Brody, Finley's chosen suitor. And I think proposing was the best thing he could do to snap Finley out of her ridiculously selfish bullshit. She arrived in London over six months ago, tear stricken, sad, and broken-hearted, telling me she wasn't going back to KC. A small part of me…scratch that…a LARGE part of me, wanted to jump for joy. My best friend moving to London meant having a piece of home with me! It was great news.

But I knew the special relationship she and Brody had wasn't something everyone found. Hell, I don't know a single person that has the beautiful shit that they have. Saying *I love us* is their own personal endearment to each other. It's sickeningly adorable. *Almost as cute as my future cats will be.*

And now they've gone and wrecked everything. Getting married. Pff. There goes the neighborhood. A loud sniff distracts me from my far away thoughts. I glare at the guilty culprit.

"Frank, you better get your shit together! You're a dude for Christ sake," I bite at him, embarrassed at the spectacle he's making at my best friend's wedding.

"That's quite nearly the meanest thing you've ever said to me, Lezbo." He looks at me with a horrified expression. "You know better. I hate associating with the male species. They are all barbaric arses…hot, sexy arses, but barbaric all the same."

I roll my eyes and straighten his coral bowtie. Frank was in the middle of yet another tumultuous breakup. I don't think it had even been six months since the last one and he'd already found another to crush his spirits.

"I can't believe Finley's getting married," I whisper to no one in particular.

"I can't believe you didn't wear underwear to Finley's wedding," Frank whispers, turning his shocked, brown eyes on me.

I cut him a mean glare and reach up to ruffle his tall red hair because I know it'll piss him off. I pull my hand back, dramatically clutching it to my chest. "Ouch, Frank! What the hell kind of product do you have in that hair? I think it drew blood!" I shout in a whisper.

Frank smirks wickedly, delicately coifing his tall rooster-red puff of hair on top of his head. "That will teach you to try to ruffle a lion's mane," he states deadpan.

I giggle and turn my attention back to Finley and Brody, sighing quietly. Damn they look happy.

"Stop looking so glum, Lezzie. This is supposed to be a happy day." Frank drapes his long, slender arm around the back of my chair and rubs my shoulder soothingly.

I shake my head, attempting to clear my thoughts. Frank's right. Jesus, what's the matter with me? Finley's my best friend—this is a wonderful day for her. I need to be happy!

And she's stunning standing up there. And tall. Fuck she is so tall. Lucky bitch. Everything looks good on her. I'm a designer so I know how great clothes look on tall, curvy bods—and how dull they look on short, stumpy averages like me.

I mean. I'm not ugly. I can afford myself that raving compliment. I'm not entirely delusional. My green eyes are interesting because they have a tendency to change colors on me, which I find fun…from a purely fashionable standpoint. They are like a cool, unique accessory that plays nicely with my crazy clothing choices. But that's about where my uniqueness stops. My body is average at best.

I'm only five-foot-five and have very minimal curves. I like my hair for the most part I guess. It's a deep auburn color and super thick. It used to trail long down my back, but when I moved overseas, I did the unthinkable and chopped it into a super-short bob with pixie bangs. It was an extreme difference, but I needed it. It felt rebellious and bold. Cutting my hair felt like I was metaphorically cementing my big move across the pond. Makes tons of sense, right? *I thought so too.*

My bob has grown out considerably now. Even my bangs need to be cut. I have to swoop them dramatically off to the side because they are constantly getting in my eyes. I didn't really let it all grow out on purpose. Life just got kind of crazy when Finley moved into our house.

Regardless of my lack of enthusiasm for my looks, I do a fine job feigning confidence with my outspoken mouth and unapologetic sense of humor.

I genuinely smile as the pastor instructs them to exchange rings. Finley's trembling hands and glowing smile are warming my frosty heart. At least I don't have to say goodbye to Finley now that both of them have decided to stay in London and continue living with us. Thankfully, Brody is pretty badass and totally understands our crazy, eccentric friendship. He's never once appeared annoyed or judgmental of our crazy antics.

"...I'll do whatever it takes to continue making you...and *us*...happy in our marriage. And I promise to be honest and open with you for the rest of my life. I love you," Finley says, her voice cracking at the end. *Oh fuck me, now they've gone and done it.* I inhale a shaky breath and quickly swipe away my tears, sniffing loudly and silently praying I don't have to dig in my clutch for a tissue.

Brody wipes tears out of his eyes too, somehow managing to make it look manly and sexy. Bugger it all to hell, my best friend is really getting married. Finley getting married and joining the army of traditionalists is essentially just a big, fat nail in my fashionable coffin.

I shake my head slightly knowing full well that I'm never getting married. Even if I wanted to get married, it wouldn't matter. Guys don't date the funny, eccentric girls. They sure as hell don't marry them. I can't even get laid properly!

I shudder as my first sexual encounter in years invades my thoughts and distracts me from listening to Brody's beautiful vows. It was horrid and awkward—and in public for Christ's sake! Climaxing on a guy's leg in the middle of a nightclub is definitely one for the *Ripley's Believe It Or Not: Pervert Edition* record books.

Theo was his name. *Tiiiiits*. I couldn't forget that name if I wanted to. It happened six bloody months ago and is still burned into the mortification vortex of my brain that fires off any time I try to act like I have an ounce of cool factor. What a mess I am.

If only I had successfully dodged him for good that night. Only with my luck would the bastard, Theo, show up at a bloody house party Frank and I were throwing just a couple weeks after said incident!

CHAPTER TWO

5 Months Earlier
TARTS & VICARS PARTY:

I squat down in my tiny little outfit, not giving a shit who can see up my skirt at the moment. This is a Tarts and Vicars party for crying out loud. We're all dressed like hookers and clergymen. The point of it all is to look like a fool! At least I'm wearing underwear tonight.

"Here's to the wound that never heals, the more you rub it…the better it feels. All the soap this side of hell, won't wash away that fishy smell," my roommate, Mitch, toasts and takes a quick drink. We all stare wide-eyed and deathly silent at his girlfriend Julie, waiting for the definite rapture coming Mitch's way.

"Wait, what?" Julie says, cocking her head seriously. "I don't get it."

We all erupt into riotous laughter. Julie lives here too and is always so sweet and innocent. Mitch is always sulky and quiet, so to see him tease Julie in such a manner and she's not even getting it, is way too much. I could die at the hilarity of this scene right now. And then seeing Frank out-of-control laughing in his ridiculous pope costume is like comedy overload!

I stand up, wiping tears from my eyes, finally feeling like I've regained control of myself. My gaze follows Finley as she moves towards the dining room to greet our new guests that just walked in.

It is in that briefest of seconds that I see him. My heart plummets to the floor at the sight of who Finley is talking to. *Theo.*

Holy fucking fuckity-fuck. How in the hell...?

My eyes bug out of my head and refuse to blink as I mindlessly take a huge swallow of my boozy punch. When his gaze collides with mine, I know I'm fucked. I'm fucked right up the ass right now. I want to look away and run and hide but my stupid, insolent body won't listen.

Leg Boy is here. Not the most creative name I could give a man who somehow miraculously pleasured me on a public dance floor at a posh nightclub, but there it is.

Okay, okay, his name is Theo. I remember his bloody name but I'm doing my damnedest to forget. He is standing next to Liam, the sexy bloke Finley met at Shay Nightclub a couple weeks ago. Theo barely acknowledges the introduction Liam is attempting to give Finley. He suddenly moves them aside and comes storming over to me. His eyes look positively murderous, every muscle in his tight body is rigid and tense. *Good Lord, he looks pissed as hell!*

He reaches out and grabs my arm. Not roughly, but not sweetly either. It feels urgent. Desperate. He pulls me off to the side of the kitchen away from the pack of people. "Are you bloody kidding me right now?" He seethes with a huge huff of air.

"I have no clue what you're talking about," I reply and glance down at his hand gripping my elbow.

His eyes flutter downward and he looks taken aback at finding his hand on me. He quickly releases my arm and softly rubs the area he had been holding so urgently before. I nervously adjust my white filmy top that purposefully shows off my red lacey bra. It's a Tarts and Vicars theme party, why am I feeling self-conscious all of a sudden?

"Are you seriously here, standing in front of me right now?" His eyes flash across my face like he's still confirming that it's really me.

"I uhh, I don't even know your name," I say, because I'm a dick and have no clue what the hell else to say right now. God, I want him to say he must have the wrong girl and walk away so incredibly bad right now.

"I'm Theo. I told you that night. You don't even fucking remember? I'm going to…fuuuuck," he aggressively rubs the top of his short buzzed hair and lets out a loud huff of air.

I shake my head, nervously looking over at Finley eyeing our exchange cautiously. "Okay, I remember you, alright? I just…" Okay, I need to extinguish this guy's flames before he blows a gasket.

"You're Leslie," he adds, like he's trying to remind me.

"I know my damn name, okay?" I snap. Jesus, now what? What's he want from me? Is he expecting me to tip my head and say, *'Thanks for the leg hump kind sir. It was the first time I'd cum in years!'*

"Um, this is really uncomfortable. How are you here right now?" I ask, looking back into his light brown eyes. They suddenly look sad and desolate.

"I'm here with Liam."

"I see that, is he your friend or something?"

"Yeah, we're best mates." He shakes his head. "I can't believe you're bloody standing right in front of me. How are *you* here right now?" he asks, repeating my question back to me.

"I live here," I shrug, unable to tear my eyes away from his pale brown gaze.

He shakes off his stunned expression. "You live here." He pauses, regrouping. "What happened to you that night?"

A warmth creeps up my neck and I know I'm blushing like crazy. This can't be happening. I can't be facing the man I mortified myself on top of in public. I bite my lip, instantly tasting my lipstick. I quickly release it worrying over making a mess of my makeup. I open my mouth to answer, but nothing comes out.

"You didn't come back. You just…" he starts, but I interrupt before he can finish.

"What did you want? A fucking thank you card?" I bite at him quietly, feeling my inner redheaded temper flare. Why does he give a flying fuck?

"Oh sod off," he barks and I'm instantly knocked down a peg by the brooding storm flaring in his eyes. "Answer me. I need to know why you just left…" Theo stops as Finley approaches and puts her arm around me protectively.

"Hey!" she says, brightly, obviously trying to lighten the mood. "You guys know each other?" Liam is standing next to her looking just as confused.

Theo turns and scowls at me while nodding a silent answer to Finley. I turn and look at her with wide, urgent eyes. I'm trying to ESP-talk with her right now so she gets me out of this situation. After what feels like hours of Finley not getting my damn message, I gesture my head toward the dining room and beckon her to follow me. Her perplexed expression infuriates me as I finally grab her arm and yank her away from the guys.

Before we can get too far, Theo grabs my arm and hits me with another intense killer stare, like he's not going to let me pass. This just pisses me off so I pierce him with a don't-fuck-with-me look. Liam breaks the tension between us by placing a hand on Theo's chest.

"Let the ladies chat, Theo," Liam says, gently pushing Theo back. "C'mon mate, there's beer in the fridge."

I stumble hurriedly toward the dining room attached to the kitchen, pulling Finley haphazardly behind me. I bulldoze through the dining room, through the foyer and into the living room on the opposite side. I give her an exasperated look because the music is way too loud, so I lead us down the attached hallway and into the small bathroom.

After Finley pulls out the entire story of me having a dance-gasm on Theo's leg, she has a riotous laugh at my expense. I feel even more mortified than I did before. Typically I don't embarrass easily, but cumming on a bloke's leg in the middle of a club happens to be my one exception.

CHAPTER THREE

Present Day
FINLEY & BRODY'S WEDDING cont.

"Christ, her dress is fucking gorg. I'm so glad we helped Finley. She'd probably be up there in one of her nasty Uni-sweatshirts and denim shorts," Frank whispers into my ear and I giggle, taking in the sheer beauty of Finley's wedding dress. Angela elbows me coarsely.

"Don't make me separate you two." She smiles playfully, leaning forward to eyeball us both in our chairs. Mark stretches out and throws his arm lazily around Angela, sweetly massaging her shoulder.

Frank glances over at Mark's hand on Angela's shoulder. "You may not want to let him do that to you, Angela. We were both in the loo earlier and I know for a fact he didn't wash his hands. The knob."

I stifle a cackle as Angela's jaw drops in disgust. The hate/hate relationship that Frank and Mark have developed in the few days we've all been hanging out together in Mexico is ludicrous, but extremely entertaining.

For some odd reason, as soon as we landed in Mexico, they declared each other mortal enemies. It may have had something to do with the fact that Mark was convinced Frank was one of the Weasley twins from the Harry Potter movies and attempting to conceal his identity. Apparently being rich, redheaded, and British means there is no other possibility in Mark's eyes. For the first three days they bickered about it constantly, like an old married couple.

I've only met Mark once, briefly, back when I was visiting Finley in college. Angela was Finley's college roommate all four years so I saw her several times before I moved overseas my junior year. Mark was Brody's roommate and all of them lived in the same apartment complex senior year. It was quite cute actually. Two roommates, dating two roommates. Mark gave off a kind of bizarre first impression with these weird questions he throws out randomly. He never wanted you to answer them…he just wanted to ask them and answer them himself. He reminded me of Zack Galifianakis, but way cuter, and with less hair—and in no way chubby. Honestly, he and Angela are a freaking gorgeous couple. Makes me green with envy.

Apparently, Frank doesn't find Mark as funny as I do though. Mark leans forward and cuts Frank a nasty glare. "Question: is urine non-sterile but also non-toxic? Answer: Yes."

Frank and I both frown at Mark and Angela mirrors our disturbed expression. I have no clue what he just said, but either way, it didn't sound good. He shrugs his shoulders, "My dick was clean. I'd just showered." We all blanch at his blatant admission.

Angela turns and eyes him speculatively and I lean closer to hear her response. This should be good.

"Question: Will you wash your hands after you pee from now on? Answer: Freaking hell yes you will or you won't touch *any* part of me with those hands ever again." Angela raises her dark eyebrows up to the heavens and Mark's eyes widen in surprise. "And," she adds. "I won't touch any part of you ever again."

He recoils and leans into her, "Anything for you my raven-haired beauty."

I grin, noticing how she instantly relaxes. A smug smile plays on the corners of her mouth. They are so cute together. Polar opposites, but they fit together perfectly.

As a wealthy politician's daughter, Angela ruffled a lot of feathers when she and Mark eloped to Vegas immediately after graduation. But being married five years now, everyone's doubts seem to have been in vain. Mark is Brody's best friend from childhood. Angela met Mark around the same time Brody and Finley started hooking up in college. Mark appears to worship the ground Angela walks on. They are sickeningly sweet together, just like Brody and Finley.

Man, I'm only twenty-six, how is it that everyone around me is getting married already? I thought I'd have well into my thirties before I'd have to worry about being the third wheel!

I'm just grateful I don't have to stand up at the altar next to Finley. Granted, I'd do it in a heartbeat, she's my best friend in the whole world, but it's so much easier to not be on display with all these crazy wayward thoughts of mine.

Frank, Mark, Angela and I are technically part of Finley and Brody's bridal party. But it's more of an honorary roll. Finley and Brody just wanted it to be the two of them up there saying their vows. She said she didn't want all the pomp and circumstance of a whole bunch of people parading down the aisle. And I'd be lying if I didn't think it was cool as hell that they were doing their own thing.

One huge perk of not being a traditional bridesmaid was no matching dresses! I feel rather chuffed by my homemade little shift dress. The straps are thick and angle sharply in toward my neck. The print is a gorgeous black clingy fabric with tiny coral rosebuds scattered everywhere. It was a bitch to sew, but worth it in the end.

Finley said our only job as an honorary bridal party was to get drunk and weird. I can handle that. Especially if there's any thick legs around for me to ride.

For fuck's sake, Leslie.

When the pastor tells Brody to kiss his bride, Frank and I both instantly start hooting and hollering and catcalling like crazy. We look around to several bemused faces, but no one has the same eagerness for this moment as Frankie and I do. Screw it, my best friend only gets married once!

"Yeah, Brody!" I growl out in a yell as he deepens the kiss enough to make us all feel like we shouldn't be witnessing such a passionate encounter.

"Take your shirt off!" Frank hollers and everyone erupts into laughter, including myself.

Finley and Brody break the kiss, laughing. They look over at me and Frank and my face flames red with sudden embarrassment. Frank just stands up and claps and cheers more and the rest of the crowd follows suit. I see Finley wipe tears away from her eyes and my eyes well instantly at how perfectly happy she looks. I laugh and bat away my tears, but more just follow. I'm truly pleased for her. After all she's been through and all that she's had to learn to accept, she deserves this moment. This day. This happiness. It's just hard because I guess I still am getting used to the possibility of never having something like that.

I need to shake that remorse shit right off because this is my choice. I'm done with guys. They ought to be the furthest thing from my mind. Theo especially. I didn't move to London to find a man.

I have my reasons for moving far away from home. Reasons even Finley doesn't know about. Guilt momentarily slices through me as I think about how upset she'd be to find out that I've kept this from her all this time. We're supposed to tell each other everything…*even the cracks*. That was what we said to each other growing up, "Empty out your brain…even the cracks!" It seemed to help us get through whatever personal dramas we were faced with back then. The fact that I've held this in for years basically spits in the face of our honest friendship.

It's just not something I can share because it's not entirely my story to share. But it's forever affected my outlook on love. It's a big reason why I haven't been intimate with anyone since coming to London. Sure, I went on a couple of dull dates that my coworkers bossily set me up on. But I only agreed so they'd stop wondering if I was actually *Leslie the Lesbian*.

As much as being in a relationship with a woman sounds like an easier pill to swallow, I'm afraid I'm just not attracted to them. Men, especially men that look like Theo, still rev my engine and provide ample material for me and my vibrator. *Balls. Stop thinking of Theo, Lez!*

How I managed to avoid brooding Theo for most of the night at our Tarts and Vicars party is beyond me. After our initial scuttle, followed by sharing with Finley the truth about my dance-gasm, I avoided him like the black plague. Since he couldn't really get me alone long enough to talk, he eventually quit trying and sulked the rest of the evening. I did my best to drink and laugh, and most importantly—try not to notice him.

Too bad I could feel his hot stare on me all night long. And damn it all to hell, I liked it. I liked feeling his eyes burning into my back. It was like I could feel them undressing me and licking my spine.

Stop, Leslie. Stop the fantasies right now.

I didn't remember to pack my hotdog so I'm up a shit creek. Not to mention, I'm sharing a bloody room with Frank. And since I'm one-hundred-percent not Frank's type, he will definitely not be interested in helping me out of my semi-aroused state.

Frank still gives me shit about the nickname I gave my vibrator. Talk about a great first impression! I laugh to myself thinking back to the first day I met Frank.

CHAPTER FOUR

Five Years Earlier
FRANK & LESLIE FIRST MEET:

I'm a green-behind-the-gills twenty-one-year-old attempting to take London by storm. I've just dropped out of college and landed a freelance gig sewing costumes for a community theater in Hampshire. They aren't my designs but I'm in charge of hunting down fabrics for them. I'm lucky if I actually get to touch a sewing machine. Regardless, the pay is decent and I love shopping for fabric, so it's a good gig.

I found Fab Fabrics deep within an internet search one day. The original poster was raving about the intricate selection, so I had to see for myself if it really was a diamond in the rough. The Brixton area of London isn't *all* sketchy, but this street definitely is.

I stroll into the dark and musty smelling store that's no bigger than a dorm room. The bolts of fabric on display are strewn haphazardly on rickety folding tables and cheap shelves.

This is what I came to this dodgy part of town for?

"My name is Ameerah, what do you need, child?" a large Caribbean woman asks in a thick accent as she enters from behind the beaded doorway-cover. She's cloaked in a fuchsia muumuu and her short hair is dyed straw-yellow blonde.

I conceal a smirk, feeling like any minute she's going to ask me if I want my palms read. "Um, I'm looking for some crewelwork. Seventeenth-century stuff…for a period-play costume. Do you have anything like that?" I ask, looking at the meek display of fabrics and feeling hopeless.

"Crewel, eh? You sure you know what you're talking about?" She eyes me speculatively. "One moment." She disappears behind the beads for a bit and re-emerges holding a primitive jacket inside her chubby hands.

My jaw drops as I take in the beautiful piece. She nods slightly when I reach for it in question. My fingers rub over the top of the intricate embroidery, relishing in the tiny spider-knots. Looking closely at the distressed look of the thread, I can tell instantly this is a true period-piece, not a remake. "This is period silk taffeta," I say, touching the jacket lining to my cheek and feeling a fission of excitement. "From the 1600s." I am in awe. Stupefied awe. "Spider knots…stem stitch…chain stitch, and buttonhole stitches! I'm…how? How do you have this?"

Ameerah smirks at me. "I have many things. Come child, I'll show you the back room."

Most people would feel uncomfortable following a stranger into a back room. But I would follow this blessed woman anywhere after she showed me that incredible jacket. And boy am I glad I did. I may have peed myself a little as she reveals the back room to me. It's a night-and-day difference from the front room. I should clarify that the back room is more like an entire building. It's huge and sorted in orderly neat rows of bolts, accessories, and even a longarm sewing machine. *Fab indeed.* My new mothership. My lifeboat. My second home. Fab's was the proverbial fabric store jackpot. It has everything you could ever need from period fabrics, to bag straps, to webbing and fabric handles for camera bags. I spend more time at Fab's than I care to admit.

After sharing some tea and visiting with Ameerah for the better part of the afternoon, she informs me that her husband runs the shop next door. I find myself curious about what other treasures this power couple could be stashing away, so I gratefully accept her offer to take me over and show me.

"Ameerah, you saucy minx!" I state brazenly as she walks me into a sex toy shop. I'd be lying if I didn't say I'm a little more than shocked!

She chuckles good-naturedly. "Don't be so coy, child. Sex sells, everybody knows that. Something tells me you can handle this. This is my husband, Umar."

Umar pops up from behind the counter with a bright twinkle in his eye. "Amee, what are you up to?" he asks dubiously.

Ameerah begins telling her husband about my vast knowledge of fabrics and what a great afternoon we had together. I smile and take in the quaint little shop of toys. It's beautifully decorated with thick purple fabric draped over the walls and romantic track lighting dimmed.

Feels a lot like the back room next door but with strap-ons. I giggle immaturely. I'm not extremely sexually experienced, but I'm also no prude. Suddenly I hear the bell on the door jingle with a voice already hollering like he's been shouting his way up the whole block.

"It's been weeks since I've seen anything new. Umar...those bloody magazines better be in or there will punishment. Severe. And *not* sexual. Just bad. I have a feeling you *like* bad, you kinky bugger. But I'm not to be trifled with!" A tall, skinny redhead comes to a stop right in front of me and gives me a look like he's in the wrong shop.

He stands stock still, staring at me with his mouth dropped open.

"Forgive me, but…are those not dildos sitting right there?" He points to the left. My head, Ameerah's, and Umar's all swerve in the direction he's pointing. We simultaneously look back at him.

"I thought so. And pray tell…are those not butt plugs and anal beads…over there?" Again, we all glance to where he's pointing.

"Frank," Ameerah chastises.

"Amee, no, give me a tic." He turns pointedly at me.

"And it might seem obvious, but I do believe that behind you, there are kinky vintage porno magazines."

I scowl at him, completely unable to see what he's getting at right now. Suddenly I'm shocked by his hands clapping loudly in front of my face.

"Miss…hello!" He claps again in front of me like he's trying to get my attention.

Does he think I'm deaf?

"Do you speak English? Whaaat issss your native tongue?" he shouts loudly, enunciating every syllable slowly, standing mere inches from my face.

I scrunch my expression into shock and glance to Ameerah and Umar. They appear to be enjoying the show.

"Right, I'll show you to the door," he says. The skinny redheaded man then places his hand on my back and herds me forward. "If you're looking for fabric, it's next door. Ameerah will be over soon. This is a sex shop." He stops at the door as I stare incredulously at him. He actually makes a ring with his left hand and thrusts his right pointer and middle fingers in and out. It's everything I can do not to burst into laughter!

He sighs heavily and musses his frizzy orange hair. "What are you…Dutch? I was crap at languages in school. *Dueches spreaka*…ah, fuck it. Piss off, will ya? There's sex shite in here!"

Ameerah now looks more frustrated than amused and begins to approach us. Before she can say anything, I ask, "Is this your normal clientele? 'Cause I gotta say, I think you need to cast a wider net. Or just a better net that lets the assholes slip through, maybe?" I look pointedly at Frank while Ameerah and Umar erupt into laughter.

The redhead looks at me—his mouth hanging open. "You're American?" he croons.

"Yes, and I'm a little pissed that you spoke to me like I couldn't speak English and I was deaf! Also, the fact that you so pigheadedly assumed I'd never come to a place like this is insulting!" I'm in no way traditional. I resent his stereotyping of me.

Frank's shocked expression morphs into confrontational. "Alright, *American*. What's your name?"

"Leslie."

"Listen, *Lezbo*, aside from the decent looking kicks you have on, and the apparently mildly-passable fashion sense, I can spot a pervert from a mile. Right, Umar?"

"Yes, it's true." Umar shrugs his shoulders apologetically.

"See, Umar knows. I can appreciate someone with good fashion sense. But I appreciate pervs even more. Umar is a perv, I'm a perv.

Even Amee is a perv. Pervs belong here. You're not pervy darling, I'm sorry. I think you'd be much more comfortable next door at the fabric store. Or maybe at a *McDonald's* or something. Off you go."

Frank turns to rejoin Umar and Ameerah at the counter. Ameerah looks like she's about to let Frank have it, but my indignation reaches its own boiling point before she has a chance to say anything. I actually stomp my foot. Frank turns back in surprise.

"I won't be shooed out of a sex toy store," I state, balling my hands into fists. "It just so happens that my hotdog stopped working recently and I want to replace it while I'm here." A brief moment of embarrassment flutters across my face as I realize I just used my pet name for my vibrator.

Balls. Hold it together, Lez.

It usually takes a heck of a lot more than this to embarrass me. I just need to look strong and confident. This skinny ginger isn't going to tell me where I belong. Even if a large part of me does want to live in the magical back room of Fab Fabrics.

"Hot….dog?" The words sound so strange coming from Frank's mouth with his posh British accent.

"Yep. Hotdog." I shrug my shoulders. "Like you don't have a pet name for your sex toys?"

He raises his eyebrows as a silent answer. "Well, Lezbo, it appears I was wrong about you. Please, make your selection." He gestures around the store, boldly challenging me.

"Do you have the dolphin deluxe? The one with a g-spot twirler?" I ask expectantly to Umar who looks flustered. My expression is deadly serious. I will not smirk. I will not show this Frank guy any discomfort whatsoever. Not to mention, I'm totally bluffing. My hotdog is just a clit stimulator.

Ameerah looks even more impressed than she did when I recognized the detailing on the period jacket. She smacks Umar who's staring at me with his jaw dropped. "Oh, yes. Sorry. We do. Right this way."

I make my way past Frank and glance back. "If it ain't broke..."

His brow furrows momentarily.

"I thought you said yours was broke."

"Orgasms. I'm talking about orgasms...Frank, was it?" I cajole cockily.

He nods slowly and smiles at me like I've just aced a test I didn't even know I was taking. "I'm taking you to The Pub once you've replaced your precious hotdog."

"I'm not in the market for a human hotdog," I say, coolly.

He titters at my comment and I feel confused.

"Babe, trust me. You're not my type." He eyes me up and down like he sees nothing interesting, except maybe my shoes.

"And what if I refuse to go to The Pub with you?" I ask, walking backwards toward Umar trying to show some pep in my step.

"You can't fight me darling. Two pervy gingers in one shop at the same time...this is destiny."

His smile is infectious, so despite myself, I laugh.

It takes only a few lagers with Frank before he demands I move out of the hostels and in with him in his huge three-story Victorian house. His parents own it but live in Tuscany most of the year, so now it's his.

Normally I wouldn't jump to live with someone I'd just met, but Frank and I just click. I feel like I've known him for years. And truly, living in a big house with him can't be worse than the creeps that come in and out of the hostels all the time. I'm ready for a change, and to live somewhere that feels more permanent.

Frank's honesty and vulgarity are a blast to live with. Our friendship might appear superficial on the surface, but deep down, I know Frank is yearning for that sense of family that he doesn't get from his own. Frank's parents have been to the house a couple of times, but they always seem so distant and standoffish—even to their only son. I see an ache in Frank that could directly mirror my own. Maybe it truly is destiny that we found each other in that porn shop. We are kindred spirits.

CHAPTER FIVE

Present Day
FINLEY & BRODY'S WEDDING cont.

"Honestly, what is it with you, Lezbo? You've been sulky all day," Frank says, pulling me out of my reverie. We're seated at our reception table on a huge wraparound balcony attached to the resort. I tear my gaze away from the ocean view and smile sadly at the general splendor. Brody and Finley's reception is stunning. It's all white linens with pale pink peonies everywhere. Understated elegance—just like Finley.

"I don't know, Frank. I'm happy for Finny, I really am. But shit, I can't help but feel like everything's going to change." I screw my face into a pathetic pout as I watch Finley and Brody glide effortlessly across the dance floor for their first dance.

"What the bloody hell is going to change?" Frank twists in his chair to face me straight-on from across the table. "Brody and Finley are going to keep living with us, just like they have been! Nothing's changing except for Finny's last name! Honestly Lez, you're being a daft cow."

I grumble quietly, knowing he's right. I take another long drink of my frosty beverage. These strawberry daiquiris are good. I am feeling absolutely no pain.

After Finley and Brody's huge breakup last year, they patched things up and decided to move to London together. They considered looking for a place of their own, but Frank's three-story house has a master bed and bath on the main level that is completely vacant. Previously, it had always been locked…even I hadn't seen inside. Since real estate is crazy expensive in London, it was an easy decision for them to live with us. I'm thrilled they aren't moving away, but now—I don't know…something just feels different.

"I know I'm being dumb, but it's just weird. When they were living with us unmarried, it was like no big deal. It was normal, like Mitch and Julie. It was exactly like the kind of thing I'd expect Finley to do."

Frank frowns at me, clearly not understanding my drunken ramblings.

"It's like this," I start, hoping to make things clearer. "Fin and I were always just different together. Alternative or whatever. We didn't conform to what everyone else in our hometown did. I was proud of that. I loved that. She was my partner in crime, ye know? She helped me not feel so…so…" I sigh, deciding I've said too much.

"So *what*, Lez? Finish!" Frank snaps.

"Alone!" I screech, feeling surprised by my outburst. "Now she's all married, and…*normal*," I pout.

"What am I, chopped liver? Not to mention, I don't think it's considered normal to live with four other roommates as a married couple," Frank says, grabbing my daiquiri from my hand and downing nearly all of it.

I start to yell at him but his face screws into a look of pain. He clasps his head between his long, slender fingers.

"Bugger! Fuck! My head!"

"Serves you right for stealing my drink," I say, grabbing the glass and finishing the rest. I look around for another server. Instead, I see Angela and Mark come stumbling and giggling toward us. They sit down on my side of the rectangle table and look worriedly at Frank.

"What's with you?" Angela asks, looking confused by Frank's slumped position.

"Don't mind me…worry about the Lezbo. She's the one who desperately needs a good shag." Frank finally straightens and smoothly tweaks his bowtie. "By something a bit more substantial than a hotdog, I might add." He eyes me provocatively.

"Hotdog?" Angela asks, batting away Mark's hand as he trails his fingertips over her exposed collarbone.

"It's my vibrator," I answer. "I'm not embarrassed. I would never shame my hotdog in public. He's my knight in shining armor and deserves respect and validation," I add seriously.

"Question," Mark says, finally tearing his gaze away from Angela's chest. "True or false: Sex improves a female's bladder control?" I giggle at the ridiculous question and Angela swerves an incredulous look at him.

"Mark, I'm much more curious as to why you have all of this bottled up knowledge on urine. First the crack during Finny's ceremony and now this. It's a bit pervy! I venture to guess that you have a fetish for golden showers." Frank's face contorts into one of disgust as he takes a pull of the straw on the now empty daiquiri glass.

"Answer: It's true. A strong pelvic floor in the female anatomy is something that we would all do best in our lives to take note of. These women will be rearing our children someday. And if sex is what keeps them healthy and strong, I will surely do my civic duty," Mark replies, completely serious.

Angela and I both bark out a laugh and then laugh even harder at the ridiculously disgusted expression on Frank's face.

"I assure you that I can't help with that duty. Does this mean you *are* into golden showers?"

"Irrelevant," Mark replies flatly, not looking the least bit shaken by Frank's accusation.

A waitress appears and Frank orders three more daiquiris and a beer for Mark. I smile inwardly at Frank's courtesy of ordering Mark's preferred beverage. Maybe he doesn't totally hate him. Frank looks pointedly at me.

"What?" I whine, unable to ignore his stare any longer.

"When is the last time you've been with a man, Lezbo? How long since you've had a real, genuine dick?"

I scowl as he scrutinizes me further. Angela and Mark turn toward me, apparently interested in my reply. Refusing to feel embarrassed by being put on the spot, I glare at Frank. "It's been a while, Frank. I'm not embarrassed about it either. You're not having a laugh at my expense over this. This is by choice. I'm done with men." I adjust the bust of my dress, feeling uncomfortable beneath his pointed glare.

"Oh, pish posh. I'm not saying you have to jump into a

relationship. But a certain level of sexual interaction with the human species is…as Mark so eloquently said a moment ago…*healthy.*"

"I feel perfectly healthy," I murmur into my empty glass that I snatched back away from Frank. Finally the waitress shows up with our refills. I grab mine from her and take a deep, cooling drink.

"Yes, but you're a scowling wanker right now, Lezzie, and it's your best friend's wedding! Surely you can see an issue with that?" Frank screws his eyebrows at me and I take in fully what he's trying to say.

I suppose he has a point. It truly is shameful how much I've been sulking at Finley's wedding. I'd be mortified if she and Brody noticed. They've had a bitch of a year and they don't deserve my melancholy jealousy. Maybe Frank's right.

"I think you need a spruce, Lez," he states deadpan.

"A spruce? And what the hell does that entail?"

"Like a spa visit?" Angela asks excitedly.

"Not a spa exactly. More like…*a cleanse.*" Frank fixes a salacious grin on me as he appears excited for what he has in mind. I squirm, feeling nervous about where the hell this is going.

"I've done cleanses before, they are miserable," Angela says, dramatically raising her glass and taking a drink.

"This is a different kind of cleanse. It could be miserable for Leslie, but I know many mates who would bloody love it."

"What's involved?" I ask warily. Why the hell would I agree to something that might make me miserable?

"It's…what I would call…a seven-step program. You have to follow all of the steps in order to gain the maximum benefits and achieve full happiness. Do you agree to it?"

"Agree to what? To doing this crazy cleanse that I have no clue what's even involved? Absolutely not! I can't even drink black coffee, Frank. If this cleanse drink tastes disgusting, I can't do it."

"Nothing will taste disgusting on this cleanse, I assure you," he replies cryptically.

"I don't know."

Frank's expression softens. "You need this, Leslie. You've been in a funk ever since Finley got engaged to that sex monster, Brody."

I blanch. Frank has a huge man-crush on Brody. It all started when he got a full-frontal *Magic Mike* image of Brody and Finley one morning at the house. Brody's a good-looking guy, don't get me wrong. But I see him more like a brother.

"So, this cleanse you're suggesting will get me out of this funk?"

"Without question," Frank replies, and turns his wide brown eyes on me. He's sincere. I can see it in his demeanor. He genuinely wants me to do this.

"I'm not interested in a boyfriend, Frank. I don't want a relationship."

"That's not what this is about. I promise."

"Question," Mark says, suddenly cutting into my faceoff with Frank. "A quote by Walter Anderson: Our lives improve only when we take chances, and the first and most difficult risk we can take is to be honest with ourselves. True or not true?"

Frank, myself, and Angela all turn stunned expressions to Mark who appears totally calm, cool, and collected. "Mark, my dear boy, that's the first mildly interesting thing you've said all week," Frank replies, looking shocked and awed.

Mark's quote stuns me and I contemplate the meaning behind it. Angela reaches over and strokes my hand with a soft smile tugging on her lips. I need to be honest with myself and stop moping about like I'm oblivious to the opposite sex. Why shouldn't I do this cleanse? Why not go balls-to-the-wall and do whatever weird shit Frank has in store for me. Could be a bit of fun! I've never been one to back down from a challenge. I can do this!

I smirk sneakily and Frank jumps up thrusting his hands into the air in victory, knocking his chair down in the meantime. Several people gawk at his obnoxious display.

Holy balls. This is Frank. What have I gotten myself into?

CHAPTER SIX

Present Day
FRANKS SEVEN-DAY CLEANSE:

"When do Brody and Finley return then?" Julie asks, nestled into the booth situated in our large kitchen.

"Just a couple more days," I reply, dumping a load of milk into my morning coffee. I yawn briefly, leaning myself up against the wooden countertop. "Fin said she had a big pitch for Faith's Miracle Jewelry that she couldn't reschedule."

"Still, it'll be nice for them to have a little time to themselves," she muses. I nod and smile politely while taking a small sip of my coffee.

"I wish Mitch and I would have had the funds to come. Your tan looks bloody awful," she adds sadly.

"You should have taken Frank's offer to pay! We missed you guys."

"You know as well as I do that Frank would give away all of his money if we let him. It's bad enough he hardly ever cashes our rent checks," she scoffs sweetly, narrowing her dark eyes at me. Julie's Asian skin tone is a beautiful olive. She always has this glow about her. Probably because she's so damn nice—if not a bit ditzy at times. Her boyfriend, Mitch, is polar opposite with his rough skater-boy look.

Julie and Mitch moved into Frank's house about a year after I did. Frank and Julie were old friends from when she worked for the catering company that his mother hired for all their posh parties. They keep to themselves a lot but have been a bit more social now that Brody is living here. Mitch and Brody seem to have developed a bit of a bromance. I'm guessing Mitch was just missing some good ol' testosterone in the house. I'm afraid Frank doesn't really emit that masculine energy vibe.

"Hopefully Brody and Finley stay in their area of the house when they get back. I keep catching them sneaking up to the third floor to Finley's old room to shag. It's bloody awkward!"

I giggle at Julie's disturbed expression. Finley revealed to me a while ago that she and Brody created some fond memories in her old room and enjoy frequenting memory lane. They must have created some pretty fantastic ones to want to do it in that tiny room since they now live in the coolest part of the house. I was right pissed when I saw it had an attached spa bathroom for heaven's sake! Why the hell is Frank not living in there?

When Finley told us she and Brody were moving to London, I thought they'd be looking for a flat of their own. But Frank offered them the master bedroom located down the hall from the living room and it took all of three seconds for them to accept.

Frank's house is a beautiful Victorian three-story. Frank, myself, Mitch, and Julie occupy the three bedrooms on the second floor. The third floor consists of a small bedroom with cute little curved windows. Brody and Finley's original love nest. I've often thought about making it into my sewing room so I can move my machine and fabrics out, but I hesitate because I love having my stuff near me all the time so I can work on it whenever I please.

It took me all of three minutes to put the pieces together for why Frank never lived in that master bedroom. Frank craves people. He craves family, friendship, and love. His parents have been absentee most of his life, caring more about society and parties than they did about their own son. I think Frank truly felt like he was living the dream having roommates across the hall. We were the family he never had. Now, it would take a small army, or years of intense therapy, to get him to admit that little nugget of knowledge. But I know it's the truth.

"Anyway, I best get to work. I've got the lunch shift and Teddy will have a cow if I'm late again. Can you make sure Mitch wakes up before noon? He can't be late again either." I nod and smile. "Laters!" she sings, grabbing her handbag and scurrying through the dining room and out the front door.

I settle into the kitchen nook and sigh heavily. Damn, I am so glad I took an extra day off just to re-coop. Seven days in Mexico is exhausting!

"Lezzie, love, you're awake!" Frank bellows, waltzing into the kitchen with an extra pep in his step. Bollocks, why is he so perky this morning? "Are you ready to begin?" he asks, eyeing me brightly. I sip my milky coffee and scowl at him.

"Ready for what?"

"Ready for what? Ready for what, she says!" he howls out an obnoxious laugh and rushes over to me, yanking me out of the booth. I grumble and follow him into the dining room. Spread across the table are several white pieces of paper. How did I miss those when I came through earlier?

"What's this?" I ask warily.

"Lezbo," Frank tsks, apparently disappointed. He pulls one of the ten plush dining room chairs out and directs me to be seated. He flounces over to the other side of the table and grabs the first paper, flipping it over and showing me.

"Frank's," I read aloud and he sets it down and grabs the next sheet.

"Seven," I continue and he nods approvingly and grabs two pages at once this time.

"Day. Cleanse." He bounces over to the other side and grab's the last two.

"2. Happiness."

Frank's Seven-Day Cleanse 2 Happiness. Oh, fuck me sideways. He is taking this way too seriously.

"Did you steal this paper display idea from Brody?" I ask, feeling like I remember Finley telling me how sweet Brody is with his dumb little notes.

"That's rubbish, Leslie! Surely Brody isn't the first man on the planet to write words on paper." I roll my eyes. "Not to mention, he knows all about this cleanse I have planned for you and he fully approves! Now love, before you begin scoffing at me, calling a nutter, and telling me to piss off like you always do, I'd like to remind you how serious you were about this in Mexico. Nothing's changed. You haven't suddenly snapped out of your melancholy, correct?" he widens his eyes expectantly.

"No," I mumble, taking another drink of my nearly cold coffee.

London Bound

Damn, when you load it with so much creamer, it goes cold so fast.

"Brilliant! Let's get started then," he dashes over to me and jerks my seat sideways. I nearly slop coffee all over myself and glare as he drags another chair out to sit straight across from me. *Fuck me, he's dramatic!*

"We can do this one of two ways, Lez." I frown, waiting impatiently for him to get on with it. "You can either know all seven days' worth of duties straightaway, or you can wait and I can inform you of each task on a daily basis."

"I need to know them all. Now. Yesterday. Immediately." I peal out before I think about it another second. My stomach is in knots over agreeing to this ridiculousness that Frank has in store for me. Somehow I just know I'm going to painfully regret agreeing to this.

Mark's inspirational quote suddenly flashes in my memory bank: *Our lives improve only when we take chances and the first and most difficult risk we can take is to be honest with ourselves.* I exhale a deep breath, silently repeating the mantra over and over. I need something to get me over this hump. That's all. Maybe just a quick hump. Oh look! I made a pun!

"I thought as much. Lezzie, you're no bloody fun." Frank sticks his tongue out at me and grabs the blue leather-bound notebook on the table with an etched picture of the tower of the London Tower on it. "This is it, Lez. Frank's seven-day cleanse to happiness. Now, I wrote two out as a number because this is all about relationships, Lezzie. Romantic relationships."

"Oh, fuck me," I roll my eyes.

"You hold your tongue! I'm not saying we're trying to get you a boyfriend out of this. Christ no. But we do need to start getting you back in the land of the living. People fuck, Lez...they kiss, they dry-hump, they flirt! It's the excitement of the chase. It's that little chance—that small sliver of hope for love that keeps our hearts ticking, poppet. And Frank's seven-day cleanse will get you there!"

I try to interject but he dives in again before I can say a peep. "Now, I'm not saying you don't have a heart, love. 'Course not. You're bloody fantastic." His lips twitch in a scandalous way and I giggle at his wry expression. "Even your pajamas are fierce." He adds deadpan. I smile, glancing down at my purple, satin, button-down night shirt and cheetah slippers.

"But you've focused much too closely on friendships the past few years and now it's time to focus on your libido." Frank bites his lower lip. "*Hotdog* needs new material!" He winks at me—the cheeky bastard!

"So, here we go. Frank's seven-day cleanse shall commence! *May the odds be ever in your favor.*" He winks saucily and clears his throat while cracking open his notebook. "Day One...you know what? I'm going to request absolutely no interruptions until I've completed the entire list, alright?"

"Will you just get on with it?" I cry, growing eager.

"Brilliant. Here we go. Day One: Speed Date...it's about quantity, not quality." He eyes me warily, waiting for my reaction. I frown but give him a slight nod to continue.

"Day Two: Wing-woman...help a random bloke in a bar close the deal with another woman." I find myself wondering how that helps me with my own libido, but it sounds easy enough so I tilt my chin in acceptance. It could be quite fun!

"Day Three: The Tease...balance two guys at the same establishment, on the same night." My lips screw up in disgust. "No, Lez, not a bloody ménage, you perv." I exhale in relief. Still sounds tricky either way.

"Alright, Day Four," Frank pauses, eyeing me warily. "Girl kiss...self-explanatory."

"You want me to kiss a girl?" I ask incredulously.

"You promised to hear them all before you commented!" Frank blares loudly in my face, knocking our knees together as we sit in the middle of the dining room. He's clutching his notebook to his chest protectively like I'm going to rip it away from him at any second.

I go to speak again and then clamp my lips back together. "Let's just get this over with."

"Day Five: Make out...with a bloke." I sigh and roll my eyes. I figured this much. Frank continues before I attempt to speak again.

"Day Six: Display Night," he pauses, refusing to meet my eyes.

Display night? What on earth could that be?

"Like a Go-Go dancer in Las Vegas...front and center, at a nightclub, for all to see. No stripping, you perv! Just dancing in the designated go-go costume of the establishment. Though stripping would count for extra credit if you felt so inclined."

I feel my face go pale. "Are you fucking fucking with me?"

"Day Seven!" Frank shouts, blatantly refusing to make eye contact with me. "One-night stand. There, that's it. That's the last step! This is my magical seven-day cleanse to happiness. It's extreme and it really ramps up there at the last bit, but it's all life-experiences, you see. Things that people remember 'til the end of time. There's a method to my madness, I've put years of thought into this treatment plan. You shouldn't have agreed to it if you thought it was going to be easy! I never promised it'd be easy. I only promised it would snap you out of your droopy state. I never, ever..."

"FRANK!" I shout, snapping him out of his monologue. "Stop

being a pussy. I'll do it!"

Frank looks up in shock and awe. "You will?" I've obviously impressed him.

I shrug my shoulders. "The most difficult risk we can take is to be honest with ourselves, right?"

"Right!" Frank agrees eagerly, obviously excited by how easy this was.

The one-night-stand part sounds awful. But it's seven whole days away, so I'll cross that bridge when I get to it.

"I gotta do something," I murmur, feeling melancholy over how I've been behaving these past few years in London. I'm twenty-six years old. I need to get over this shit. Specifically, I need to stop thinking about Theo and everything he said to me in my bedroom. It was four months ago—why am I still obsessing over it?

CHAPTER SEVEN

4 Months Earlier
FAMILY FLICK NIGHT:

It's been two weeks since our Tarts and Vicars party and life is great. Finley is cheering up a bit over her recent breakup, and Frank and Finley are actually becoming good friends. Even Mitch and Julie want to hang out with us!

I zip-up my long one-piece cheetah-print pajama getup that Frank and I ordered online after sharing a bottle of vodka and no true tonic to speak of. Honestly, what Frank and I get up to some nights is truly terrifying. But hey, this ensemble is the perfect outfit for Family Flick Night with the roomies—so it isn't all for nothing!

I dash out of my room and foot-surf toward the staircase, feeling happier than I have in quite some time. Having Finley in

London with me in my new life here has improved my mood immensely. Who needs a man when I have the best of friends?

I come bounding down the stairs, singing obnoxiously at the top of my lungs, "Faaaamily fliiiick niiiiiight."

My eyes land happily on Finley coming out of the dining room as she's shooting warning daggers at me fiercely. I frown in confusion as I stop in the foyer and she rushes over to me. She jerks me roughly around so she's facing my back.

"Thank God," she mumbles.

Just as I turn to look back at her, my eyes lock onto Theo's staring at me from the living room. I tense immediately. Finley swerves me back around to face her wide aqua eyes. My green eyes have to be as big as plates right now! She silently shoves me back toward the stairs.

Yes. Retreat, Lez, retreat immediately! Abort mission! Abort mission!

I shoot up the steps and hear steps following closely behind. Assuming it's Finley, I reach my room. I quickly open it and am suddenly manhandled inside. The door slams shut behind me and I turn around, shocked to see an out-of-breath Theo, panting as he holds the door shut and locks it.

The loud click of the lock radiates inside the room. My jaw drops at the audacity of his actions. I hear Finley shouting something from behind the door.

I want to scream at him and ask him what the hell he thinks he's doing right now. But I can't find my voice. Theo and I stare at each other silently for what feels like ages, both of us catching our breaths from our mad dash up the steps. Neither of us say anything, yet it feels like we're communicating somehow.

"What are you doing, Theo?" I ask softly, feeling strangely emotional after our silent communication exchange.

"Please, Leslie," he sighs, licking his lips earnestly. His expression is nervous. Vulnerable. My eyes travel down taking in his taut muscles smashed inside a grey, long-sleeved thermal shirt. His expertly faded jeans are loose and ripped in all the right places. I instantly remember what he felt like under my body that night at the club and my betraying libido stirs.

"I…" I start, but am interrupted by Finley's shouts through the door.

"Leslie! Are you okay in there, hon?" she asks, knocking loudly at the same time.

I let out a huff of exasperated air, unsure how to answer that question. I have no fucking clue what's happening between Theo and I right now. Feeling strangely safe, despite how little I know about him, I attempt a reply. "Umm," I cock a questioning brow to Theo. He widens his eyes pleadingly but says nothing.

"Uhhhh," I say again, trying to make a decision. "Yes!" I shout dejectedly. "We'll be down in a minute." Theo sighs heavily and relaxes his defensive stance.

"What are you doing?" I ask again with more conviction this time.

"Leslie. I can't stop thinking about you," he says hastily, without a hint of hesitation.

I eye him incredulously. "Theo, you don't even know anything about me." I pull on the neck of my onesie pajamas self-consciously. Seriously. Seriously. Like I haven't been mortified enough in front of this hot man? Just put another shrimp on the barbie I guess! Maybe I'll get explosive diarrhea and we can call it *the trifecta turkey of humiliation for Leslie*: A dance-gasm, embarrassing PJs, and diarrhea, cha cha cha.

"I don't need to know anything about you, Leslie. I see everything that matters. It's a feeling. It's in my gut. My core. I can't…I can't…" he pauses, looking down. "I can't get you out of my mind." He looks back up at me earnestly.

I shake my head dismissively. "You are cuckoo for cocoa puffs, man! You couldn't possibly see anything interesting…" I start, but he cuts me off.

"Screw that, Leslie. Still," he growls, slightly. I look at him in confusion. He clears his throat and continues, "*Still*. You *still* light up a room. You sparkle. It wasn't the beer that night at the club, or the spinning lights, or your incredibly sexy outfit at that stupid, stupid party. It wasn't any of that shite. It was you! *You for me. No one else. Still.*"

"I don't even know what that means, Theo. Still what? Why do you keep saying still?"

"When I walked into your house two weeks ago and I saw you crouched on the floor, wiping tears out of your eyes from laughter, I felt it, Leslie. That feeling that you're supposed to listen to. It changed me. I've never felt that before. It was *you*. You are…enthralling! Stunning. Somehow, you inspire feelings in me, Leslie. Feelings I thought I had no chance at having since…" he frowns slightly and stops himself from finishing. "I can't walk away from it…it means something."

I stand completely still and silent for what feels like hours, my mind reeling through all of the words he just said. I feel frozen. Frozen in time…shock…whatever! Suddenly, he peels himself off my bedroom door and stalks toward me. Again, just like that night at the club. That serious look in his eyes that scares the bejesus out of me. I shake my head, attempting to clear out the stupor in it. When he's so close to me I have to look up to see his face, my breath hitches at his pale brown eyes inside those dark-rimmed glasses. It's like they are perfectly displaying his sincerity. *Is this guy for real?*

He reaches out and brushes my bangs off to the side of my forehead. I instinctively close my eyes at the sensation of his rough fingers on my smooth skin. I can feel his warm breath closing in on my face and I'm powerless to stop it.

When I feel the smooth softness of his full lips, my kneecaps tremble. Holy shit, I didn't know being weak in the knees was a real thing! His arms band around my waist and he holds me to him, kissing me ferociously. I am consumed by him in this moment. Entirely his. I feel like a snowflake, melting and absorbing into his hot touch. The only muscles in my body working in this moment are my lips as they meet his kiss with equal vigor.

I stumble sideways and he lifts me, easily perching me on the edge of my desktop. I feel the keyboard pressing on my bum as he fits himself perfectly between my thighs. When his growing arousal nudges my center, that stupid keyboard is immediately forgotten.

His hands rove hard up and down my back, sides, and arms. It's a firm pressure that feels urgent and desperate and further stokes the blazing fire inside me. Our kiss turns bruising and feverish. Finally, I break away from his mouth for an overdue breath.

"This is crazy," I pant and pucker my lip, attempting to get control of myself. Honestly, this shit doesn't happen in real life.

"I don't care, Leslie. I'm into you. I'm not holding anything back. I don't want to. You should know, I think I…" he stops himself suddenly and swallows, looking nervous and unsure.

The tension between us is crackling. There's no way he's actually into me. He doesn't even know me. He doesn't know anything about my life, where I grew up, or my family. *My family...*

"Theo," I say, placing my hand firmly on his muscled chest as he leans in for another kiss. "I need some air. I can't do this like this. I'm not...looking for a boyfriend. Or relationship. Everything you said was...major! And that's just not what I'm about."

"Not what you're about?" he asks, gawking at me in horror. His expression transforms from lustful to spiteful in a matter of seconds.

"I just... I have other things to focus on in my life. Boyfriends and relationships aren't one of them." He steps back from between my legs and I suddenly feel very stupid and vulnerable spread eagle on my desk in a fucking cheetah onesie.

Welcome to a day in the life of cheetah onesies and brooding alphas!

He scoffs hard and glares at me meanly. "Don't look at me like that," I say, feeling a bit less flustered now that there's some space between us. "And don't make me feel like you want more than just a good time!" I hop off the desk and straighten my hair, attempting to muster up a shred of confidence.

"You sure seem to know everything I'm thinking, don't you, Leslie?"

I eye him seriously, taking in his puffed-out chest. "Look, before we say anything we'll regret, let's get some air. This was supposed to be family flick night. Fun...not...whatever this is," I say, gesturing back toward the desk.

Theo's angry expression disappears and he stares at me now, clearly feeling wounded. A part of me wants to run to him instantly and comfort him. But I know that will only confuse things further.

He stands so still. I can't even tell if he's breathing. I wait patiently for him to say something or just turn around and leave.

When he continues not moving and not breathing, I feel nervous, his face turning redder and redder. Finally, he lets out a long puff of air and I find myself doing the same. *Was he holding his breath just then?* He transforms his wounded expression back to angry and brooding.

Good, I'm sure he's deduced that I'm not worth it. And I'm not the done deal that he thinks I am. If he wants someone to screw, he needs to look elsewhere. Despite how obviously attracted to him I am, I just don't want to open up like that to anyone right now or anytime soon.

I awkwardly walk to the door, open it, and stand back waiting for him to leave. He pauses next to me, shooting daggers. I can't even make eye contact with him. I feel ashamed and embarrassed about all the beautiful words he said to me. I simply cannot accept them. He probably regrets them now anyway.

He doesn't even know you, Leslie.

After what feels like ages of him staring at me in stony silence, he storms out the door and I let out a huge breath, following him down the stairs.

We all sit awkwardly in the living room for the rest of family flick night while Finley deals with Brody showing up on our doorstep out of the blue. Liam and Frank disappear into the kitchen for quite a while. Mitch, Julie, Theo, and I all sit silently watching the movie. There are a few excruciating moments where Mitch and Julie decide to make out.

Fucking kill me…please.

Theo glances at me broodingly but remains silent waiting for Liam so they can leave. Many times I think he's going to say something to me, but he somehow restrains himself, for which I'm grateful. I don't trust myself around this guy. He is way too tempting.

When the time finally comes for them to leave, Theo doesn't even look at me. I should feel relieved and happy to be rid of him, but I wasn't.

Frank ardently harasses me about what's going on but I don't reveal a word. I play it off like it's no big deal, because really, it isn't. What happened? Nothing. A kiss and some words. That's all. But I can't help but wonder how different things might be if I didn't have my own messed-up past causing me to box out any chance of a real romantic relationship.

CHAPTER EIGHT

Present Day

It's been nearly four months now since I last laid eyes on Theo. At least, in person. I'm ashamed to admit he's been a recurring act in my dreams. No matter how hard I try to think of David Beckham instead. But Theo is now categorized into a part of my past life. And he will remain exactly there—in my past. My present, is London. London is more than enough.

I fit into the lifestyle here instantly. Growing up in a small town in Missouri, I just never fully felt like I belonged. I never felt understood. I wore clothes no one could understand, and I styled my hair differently. I was the oddball. I was living my life in vibrant color and my hometown was in black and white.

Things were black and white even with my family. My younger brother and I were so different. When Tom was younger, we were close and played together, but as he grew older and became the epitome of a high school small town hero jock, we began talking less and less.

My dad was so damn proud of Tom when he managed to score a wrestling scholarship to Iowa. That was all anyone talked about when I'd call home from college. Sure, I was happy for my brother! But what I was doing was great too! I was in the middle of a semester abroad in London, assisting huge name designers for London Fashion Week! That's no small potatoes for our small town, yet nobody seemed to care.

Everything was about Tom. To friends, to family, and even to me, he was all my parents talked about. The timing of Tom's full ride was the push I needed to have the courage not to go back to Missouri. London started as a simple semester abroad program my junior year. But I made the decision to remain overseas permanently.

Honestly, as soon as I set foot in London, I knew. My whole world was rocked. There is a vibe here I had never felt before. It felt like it was designed just for me! It was like I finally felt like I was home. And it still does.

When I told my parents I was dropping out of college and staying in London for the foreseeable future, it did not go well. Even Tom called me, reprimanding me for being a fool for not finishing college. I tried explaining to them that in the design industry, experience is ten times more valuable than school. And London has tons of amazing opportunities for me.

Not to mention, I am a huge nerd when it comes to my craft. I studied, researched, and constantly kept my ear to the ground to learn all the new tricks and trends coming out. I don't need a degree to continue doing that. I don't even need a teacher. I just need life experiences.

I almost immediately started booking decent freelance gigs in the fashion industry. Not all of them were glamorous—or entirely legal, since I didn't quite have my work visa. Then a dream job popped up designing fashionable camera bags for *Nikon* and I fought tooth and nail to get it. I've been there nearly two years now and have had the most amazing experiences.

Best of all, my job made the move to London one-hundred-percent permanent. I have felt freer ever since.

Which is exactly why I don't want a man. I don't need one! I more than love my job. I lust it. I lust designing. When I sit behind my sewing machine in my bedroom and create something just for me, it feels sexy and exciting as hell! I'm not even ashamed to admit that I get turned on by the sound of my sewing machine. Watching that sharp needle plunge into a great fabric over and over again… Screw it. I'll say it… My sewing machine makes me horny!

That and apparently a good thigh.

London is a dream and I am truly happy here. I'm not sure when exactly I started getting so down on myself. That's why I'm throwing caution to the wind and partaking in Frank's seven-day cleanse. Anything to get me out of my damn slump.

CHAPTER NINE

"You best get showered, Lezbo! Speed dating starts in two hours and I imagine you have some sewing to do."

"Oooo! My skirt! I gotta finish it!" I squeal, taking off upstairs. That's one unexpected perk about this cleanse, I get to dress the part for seven whole days!

Two hours later, I look up from the concrete pavement, sighing wistfully at our house. This beautiful place has been a security blanket to me for many years. It feels more like home than my parents' house in Missouri ever felt. Maybe it's the wild purple door and green ivy wrapping up the side. God, it's a charming house.

"Stop thinking about running inside and slipping into your onesie, Lezbo. You have seven days under my tutelage and they will go much smoother if you just submit to my whims."

"I'm so getting drunk tonight," I mumble as I quicken my step to catch up to Frank's long strides.

"I expected this. I think it might help actually. Loosen you up." He wraps his slender arms around me as we walk. His fitted leather jacket is shoved up onto his forearms and his black Skinny Jeans look smart and yet still so uniquely Frank.

We arrive in front of Club 413. A local meat market nightclub near our house. God, I hate this place. It's just…too much. It really doesn't belong in our trendy little neighborhood of Brixton, but it does exceedingly well, so I don't see it shutting down anytime soon. Tonight, it will definitely serve its purpose.

Frank ushers me gallantly inside. The club is a transformed factory of some sort and has various steel beams and rods still in place from whatever used to be manufactured here. We sidle up on a couple of open spots at the huge square-shaped bar. I take in the elevated DJ booth and swirling lights. The dance floor is pretty empty—most of the patrons are probably still trying to get liquored up enough to get freaky on the dance floor.

I blanch as images of Theo and I romping at Shay Nightclub come screaming back into my brain. The memory of his firm muscles beneath my hands…and between my legs…

Balls, balls, balls! Get over him, Lez. That's why you're here, isn't it?

I pull down my scandalously short skirt as Frank orders us both vodka tonics. It's a warm, cream-colored skirt with white lace overlay. I have been trying to finish sewing this little number for months and this night out was just the motivation I needed. It ended up a bit shorter than I would have liked, but that's the risk you take when you try to fit clothes to yourself! I paired it with a slate-grey tailored top with an obscure skull embroidered across the front. I love to mix and match styles. Pretty with punky. Edgy with flowery. For a touch of vintage, I threw on my black suede platform pumps that have a big bow across the top. They are fun and flirty and most importantly, cheap! Fifteen pounds from a street vendor in Brighton. *Score!*

I take a few large gulps of my V&T, trying to tame my still lingering thoughts of Theo. This cocktail, along with the two I had before we left, should be just the ticket to some libation freedom.

"Alright, Lezbo, here's the rules: You can't tell them about the cleanse, you can't tell them you're a lesbian, you can't ask about their family, and you can't ask about their job."

"Why would I tell them I'm a lesbian?" I ask, incredulously. Frank arches a knowing brow at me. "I'm here Frank, I've agreed to this ridiculous cleanse that I'm convinced you made up just for me." He has the nerve to give me an 'I would never!' expression. I roll my eyes. "I mean it, Frank. I want out of my funk."

I need to stop thinking about Theo is more like it.

"So tell me then, what the hell am I to talk about?"

Frank swivels me outward and places his hands gently on my shoulders. He surveys the room from behind me, his soft breath puffing slightly in my hair.

"Flirt, Lez. You just have to flirt." His breath tickles my neck and I giggle, squirming away from him. "God you're a horny cow. Shape up! Just say come-hither comments, like 'Oi, your muscles look too large for that shirt!' Or…'Oh my, isn't it warm in here.' Think daft cow meets Barbie in a meat market full of Prince Charmings. Got it?"

"Got it," I nod courageously and quickly suck down the remainder of my drink. Fuck me, I drank that fast! That's fine, I need all the help I can get!

"Keep it moving, Lez. If you get stuck on a guy for too long, I will come relieve you. I'll be watching…every step of the way."

"How many do I need to talk to?" I ask, feeling nervous like I'm about to take a final exam.

"Seven, of course! Seven guys…seven minutes each! This cleanse is a science, Leslie," Frank states deadpan.

Seven! Jeez, that seems like a lot. I nod subtly. I already have my sights set on *teen wolf* across the bar. "Let's do this thing!"

Frank promptly pulls out a stopwatch. I eye him curiously. "I stole it from Brody. He's the only bugger in our house that works out. He fuckin' times himself when he runs! Can you believe that rubbish?" I giggle and straighten my face into all business again.

"Off you go!" I hear the beep of the stopwatch and Frank cracks my butt hard with his hand, sending me shooting down the bar and toward victim number one.

Hello there, Mr. Teen Wolf, my what bushy sideburns you have!

"Hi," I say brazenly, approaching the empty side of the bar next to him. He turns to face me and scowls at my hair. I might have hurt feelings if this guy didn't look like he was transforming into a wolf! "I'm Leslie," I offer, trying to get a different reaction out of him.

"Frederick," he replies.

Chatty fella, isn't he?

"Like the Von Trapp family singers!" I sing excitedly. He sneers at me, his eyes moving languidly down my body. "Not a Sound of Music fan?" I ask. No reply. Nothing. Balls, this is a terrible start. I glance back to Frank who appears to be chatting with some bloke I can't quite make out. Leave it to bloody Frank to throw me to the wolves as soon as a pretty thing scampers his way.

"Are you American?" Teen Wolf asks.

"I am. I'm from the Midwest. Missouri specifically. Ever heard of it?"

"No." He faces forward and tips his glass to his mouth, holding it there for an exorbitant amount of time until his beer is completely finished.

"Are you from here?" I ask, trying to remember if this question is against Frank's rules. Am I creeping up on my time limit yet?

"Glasgow," he grumbles, and looks urgently up and down the bar for the bartender.

"Nice! I went to Edinburgh once. Never been to Glasgow though."

"'Course you haven't. You Americans think all that matters in Scotland is Edinburgh."

That's not entirely true! Eh, who am I kidding, it's probably totally true. I should get my ass to Glasgow sometime. But surely not to see this fellow.

"I had to go there for…" my mouth stops midsentence because Frank told me I can't talk about work.

Shit! Think, Lez. Think!

"Pleeeeaaasure," I blurt.

Oh God Leslie, you idiot. Why did you say it like that?

Frederick sets his glass down and turns slowly, looking directly into my eyes. I feel my skin heat from embarrassment. I started this, so I may as well own it. "It was very pleasurable," I pull the word out slowly, thinking I'll score extra points with Frank's come-hither advice. I watch Frederick's Adam's apple dip and rise as he swallows, gauging me seriously.

"Right then. So, you *are* here for the meeting?" His eyes flash with heat and mine feel like they are about to bug out of my head.

What bloody meeting is he talking about? "Meeting? Um…"

"Sorry, I couldn't tell at first. I'm usually quite good at telling."

I pucker my lips and nod thoughtfully. What is this guy going on about?

"So, you're completely finished then, I take it?"

"Finished?" I ask, swallowing hard.

"Yeah, I mean…shite, topnotch job. I hope you plan to share your doctor's name at the meeting."

"My doctor…"

"I wonder if you'd give me a quick peak before everyone else arrives." Frederick smiles at me wolfishly and I squirm, still trying to decipher what the fucking hell he's talking about!

"Is this real?" he asks, reaching up and tugging my hair.

"Ow! Yes, it's bloody real! What are you going on and on about? What meeting? And what doctor? I feel like I've entered the Twilight Zone right now!"

"Your gender reassignment doctor of course!"

"My what?"

"You're not here for the transgender meeting?"

"You think I'm a dude?"

"I mean...not anymore. But at birth, yeah, 'course."

"Of course? Of course? Oh my God! This has been very enlightening Frederick, whatever your name is. I'm sorry to tell you, I am a woman. Not a man. Never been a man. Never had a dick. Never had balls, though it sounds like a blast—I'd helicopter all the time I think. But truly, *truly* thank you for assuming I once had them though...that's fun!"

"Time's up, Lez," Frank says, joining us with the stopwatch in hand.

"Oh, time's up! Sorry, Teen Wolf...I gotta dash. This has been super awesome though!" Frank gives me a startled expression and begins ushering me away. I swerve back around to finish my thought because now I'm really on a roll. "Maybe I should ask if you're a human transitioning to wolf? I'm pretty sure you need a trans-species group then, not transgender! Not exactly the same thing!" I say, gesturing to all the hair on his face. There are even sprouts crawling up his back from his shirt collar. He must take some amazingly powerful hormone treatments!

"Leslie!" Frank bellows at me, but I won't be distracted.

"I have to know! Who's your surgeon? Huh?" Maybe it's the drink I slammed just before heading over here, but I can't seem to let it go that this guy thought I was a man—and had the balls, I think, to ask me who my surgeon is!

"I'm not transitioning at all," Frederick states disconcertedly.

"So, what then? Why else would you be at a transgender meeting?" I ask. Frank looks embarrassed by my coarseness but I continue piercing Frederick with my hard green eyes. This guy is going to give me answers. No one calls me a dude and gets to go about their night like it's a normal Tuesday.

"I'm…" he pauses, glancing over to Frank, then to me again, "I'm what they call a transgender admirer, or a transfan. I'm attracted to transgender people," he concedes.

"Well, that's very nice for you. I didn't know that was a thing! I learned something tonight for sure. Maybe you can learn something tonight too, because your pecker picker is in serious need of sharpening! I have had a vagina my whole life and it's not going anywhere in the foreseeable future. But I truly thank you for the permanent complex you've gifted me in our short time together tonight and for calling me a man."

"A man with a really great surgeon," he says, faintly.

"Leslie, let's go." Frank drags me by the hand before I say something I'll really regret. I glance back and see Fredrick, the transgender admirer, looking me up and down skeptically. He still thinks I've had the surgery!

"What the bloody hell is going on?" Frank asks when we reach our stools, clearly exasperated by my fiery temper getting the best of me again.

"He thought—and very obviously still thinks—I am transgender, Frank! A dude transitioning into a woman! I mean…shit! I…I…" I want to finish my tirade but Frank's giggles erupt into a full-on belly laugh.

"It's not funny, Frank. You fuck!"

He laughs even harder now, holding his narrow waist in pure elation at my furious expression. I scowl at him for only three more seconds before smirking back and joining in on the cackles. Oh, fuck me…this is so my life!

"Why me, Frank?" I whine. "Seriously, do I need to wax my mustache or something?" I ask self-consciously as I wipe laughter-tears from my eyes.

"Blimey, Leslie. 'Why you' is right! How do these things always happen to you?"

"I don't know! I could have used a savior, you know! I think that was way over the seven-minute limit! Who the hell were you talking to?" I ask, crossing my arms but still smirking at the whole sorry scene.

"Liam actually," Frank replies, calming his cackles down considerably.

"Finley's Liam?" I ask and immediately wonder if anyone else was with him.

"Yeah, haven't run into him in a while. He seemed good. Says he's single. I'm really hoping he's not still hung up on Fin."

"Yeah, no kidding," I reply. "Anyone else, uhh…ye know…here with him?" I attempt to sound casual but fail miserably.

Frank's eyes squint briefly then straighten back to indifferent. "I think his mate, Ethan. But that's all."

I feel myself sag with relief…or is it disappointment? I can't tell. Shit! I can't tell! My mind starts reeling with that little nugget of information.

"Shall we get crackin' again? You still have six to go, Lezbo."

I shake away my thoughts and jump down off my barstool eagerly, like the good little student I've never been.

"Six more you say? Can only go up from here, right?"

CHAPTER TEN

Wrong.

Oh for the love of God. So, so wrong.

"Can only go up from here...HA!" I say and laugh out loud to myself while brushing my teeth vigorously. I groan and stifle my laughter quickly. Oh this crippling hangover sheathed tightly over my whole body is awful waffle. Dammit, how many V&Ts did I drink last night?

After Frederick, Mr. Teen-Wolf-Transgender-Lover, things definitely didn't improve. First there was Mr. Married Guy, whose wife showed up while we were chatting. Then there was Mr. Gay Man, who Frank tried to disqualify. Then I met Mr. Duck Face who kept puckering his lips at me and refused to look at my face. Mr. Nice Guy was okay, I guess, but he just did nothing for me. Seriously...crickets in the cooch. There were also a couple other completely forgettable blokes I can't even picture anymore.

I better not drink as much for day two of Frank's cleanse. I'll never make it. Fucking hell, thinking back to last night's daters was like a freaking shock to the system. They were just all bad. Bad, bad, bad.

I wipe the toothpaste off my mouth and eye myself closely in the mirror. There's no manly stubble anywhere on my face. Sure, my eyes aren't round and large like Finley's, but they don't look manish! Do they? And I'm even one of the lucky redheads with dark eyelashes! Most I know have blonde.

Well, my hair looks great! Thick and shiny auburn that falls just above my shoulders. How could he think this was a wig? I shove my wayward bangs off to the side, chastising myself briefly about needing to get them cut. If anything, pixie bangs would make my hair look even more like a wig!

I close the door to eye my body in the full-length mirror on the back of the bathroom door. Sure, it's nothing super curvy and hourglass, but it's not boxy and flat like a man. I have breasts! I guess they *could* be augmented, or stuffed with tissue. I give them a jiggle for good measure. They fit pretty easily in my hand. But still, they are there…and they do NOT look fake. I turn to inspect my rear. Hmm, that could be plumper I suppose.

I scowl and reach for the knob, swinging the door open while staring at my legs, and suddenly knock straight into something hard and boney. My balance shifts much too quickly and I try desperately to find something to catch myself. But it's in vein as I tumble backwards and land hard onto my flat boyish ass.

"Lezbo! Watch it!" Frank cries after his unsuccessful attempt to catch me.

"Jeez, Frank! I didn't see you! Why are you lurking outside the bathroom door?"

"Duh…I have to use the loo! What were you doing in here for so long?" He looks a bit hungover, like me, dressed in a rumpled matching satin PJ set.

"Nothing," I mumble and lower my head. I accept Frank's hand and he hauls me up off the floor. I attempt to shuffle past him to my bedroom, but his tone stops me in my tracks.

"Leslie," he scolds, like a father would to his errant teenager.

I pout, feeling exactly like a petulant child. "Frank, do I look manish?" I whirl back around, propping my small manish hands on my petite, boyish hips.

"For fuck's sake, Leslie…NO!"

"Are you sure my hips aren't boyish?" I ask, snapping the elastic on my flannel shorts. "I hoped this cleanse would pull me out of my funk, Frank! I just feel worse."

"Leslie, you are crackers! You look brilliant. Your body is tight and petite, and just curvy enough. Many men like wee women. They can toss ya around in the sack, ye see! Throw you up against the wall!" Frank winks adoringly at me and I smile. "Stop moping about, Lez. Tonight's challenge should be a bit more relaxed."

I nod, still feeling a bit gloomy. "Go get your sexy redheaded-self ready for work and stop feeling sorry for yourself. I'll see you at happy hour at that pub I told you about, yeah?"

I nod and head to my room to get myself ready to go.

CHAPTER ELEVEN

After dressing sharply in a pair of Houndstooth Bermuda shorts, a mustard shelf tank, and tan strappy sandals, I feel like I've concealed my hangover enough to face the powers that be at *Nikon*. And this seems like an outfit fit for happy hour later with Frank. Tonight's cleanse challenge is being a wing-woman and helping a bloke land another chick. Seems right up my alley. Quite honestly, easy as pie. After last night, I'm excited for this.

After a quick fifteen-minute Tube ride, I'm outside an old warehouse on the east central side of London. I love it over here. My office at *Nikon* is located in one of the oldest neighborhoods in London, near Shoreditch—a really groovy part of town. In this neighborhood, if there's a brick wall, there's a graffiti mural. I love it. The area is full of old warehouses turned into trendy art studios, cool cafes, or offices like ours.

"Leslie!" a voice calls from behind me. I turn around and see Vilma smiling brightly at me. "You're back! We've missed you like crazy!" She leans in and gives me a quick peck on the cheek, her round cheeks push back into a large smile. "You've got some sun!"

"Howdy Ho!" I sing as Vilma gives me an obvious onceover. "Didn't fry too bad, thank goodness. I'm a lucky ginger. How have things been here?"

"Pretty quiet. The models came back perfect and Roger pushed through all the orders to China. We've just been waiting on production since then!" She runs her hand through her long blonde locks and looks at me proudly.

"Good, yeah, Rog' emailed me while I was in Mexi'. Thank God it was all okay. I was so nervous there would be issues while I was away!"

"You did splendid! You always do over there."

Vilma is referring to my last trip to China. I frequently head over there to communicate our designs with the factory workers and get everything set up perfectly for them to produce mass quantities. It's not the most glamorous part of my job, as I'm usually staying by myself in some dank apartment in the bowels of a village in China, but I do enjoy the adventure of it all.

"You ready to go in?" she asks. I sigh heavily. Holiday was nice, but it's back to the real world now. "I know someone who will be very happy to see you!" she says, giggling, and climbs her lean, willowy body up the cast iron fire-exit steps.

Our office is located on the second floor. There is a more appropriate interior entrance, but it connects to a call center situated on the lower level. That call center feels like a funeral when you walk through to get upstairs, so we all opt to use the fire escape when weather permits.

We climb through the huge swing-out window and the familiar smell of canvas, leather, and furniture polish greets me. *Nikon* is located on the entire second floor of this building. It's a huge wide-open space with stark white support beams peppered throughout.

"Leslie!" Benji rushes over as soon as my feet hit the glossy wood flooring. "You look brill'! How was your holiday?"

"Fan-freaking-tastic, Benji. How are ya?" I smile politely.

"I'm well, I'm well! We missed you round here, that's for sure." Benji follows me as I walk over to my desk area. It feels like it's been ages since I've been here. I guess it has because prior to Mexico, I was in China—so, shit, it's been three weeks now I guess.

Benji perches up on one of the three tall barstools that sit perpendicular to my desk for when I design with my team. I smile tightly, listening to Benji talk about what's been going on around here. I really try not to encourage him too much. He's our office personal assistant, twenty-two years old, and fresh out of university. Everyone in the office laughs at how nervous he is around me, so I do my best to put a plug in it. I'd be heartbroken if poor Benji ever found out people gossiped about him. He's so sweet and cute in a dopey, puppy-dog sort of way. Just way too young. And way too not my type. I prefer the thicker, more muscular builds.

"Listen, Benji, I need to get settled and caught up on the gobs of emails I've missed. Maybe we can have a chat later?"

"Oh, sure thing Leslie. I'll go grab your coffee!"

I smile and fire up my huge *Mac* screen. I glance over at Vilma in her area next to mine. In our open office, one entire wall is set up with five large office bays. No cubicle partitions—thank God. Each area is separated simply by the designer's own decorations. I haven't done much with mine. It's just covered in fabrics from Fab's. But I think it's got that shabby-chic look about it. My large cast iron floor lamp with red tassels was something I'd found in China and paid a small fortune to have shipped back to London. It was cheap to buy though, so in the end it's still a squeal of a deal.

The other huge perk of this job is that *Nikon* pays for me to have a computer here and a computer at home. And the two mirror-image each other so I can work from either location. It's really nice because I tend to get my inspiration at the oddest of times.

"Roger said we're all meeting at ten," Vilma says, not even bothering to look up from her computer screen. She's already engrossed in what she's doing.

"Roger that!" I say, cheekily.

She peers at me from around my lamp. "You actually have been missed, Leslie. Let's not ruin that with terrible jokes." I pinch my lips together and chuckle quietly.

An hour and two coffees later, the entire staff is sitting around the huge wooden plank table we use for meetings. Our full London team consists of three designers—myself, Vilma, and Hector. Our production manager, Natalia, takes care of all of my travel needs whenever I go to China. She's nice enough, but she's all business and does not do well when we try to change plans last minute. Then there's Benji, and our boss, Roger.

"Good to have you back, Leslie," Roger's deep timbre voice cuts through the chatter. "You did an excellent job with the China factory. The models were perfect. We should have our first burst within the next month."

"Thanks, Rog'!" I reply, flushing slightly. Roger is great with praise. I'm just not great at receiving it. I've never had a job where I felt so appreciated. But Roger's definitely one to give credit where credit is due. He's tall and a solid thirty-years-older than me and Vilma. Hector and Natalia are both in their forties. Then there's baby Benji.

"I may need you to head back out there in the next month for a quality check. Nothing official yet, just wanted to give you a heads up."

"No problem," I say. I'm the only one that travels to China, as I have the most sewing experience. Communicating with the factory workers via an English translator is not the easiest thing to do. It helps if I just sit with them and work, having them look over my shoulder and mimic. The Chinese seamstresses I work with pick up new techniques fast, so it's a fun silent buzz of energy exchanging when I'm training them.

Roger continues the meeting and I feel myself becoming invigorated again. This is what I'm good at. This is what I was meant to do with my life—design, travel, experience, explore. I don't need a man in my life to do any of this. Maybe being on holiday for Finley's wedding just gave me too long to think.

Perhaps Frank's cleanse is a huge mistake. I know he's not trying to get me a boyfriend, just laid I suppose, but why *can't* celibacy be more appealing to me? I shudder at the thought of packing away my precious hotdog for good.

Maybe just giving hotdog a break for something a bit more lifelike is what I need. I just have to make sure that whoever I end up with in that final step of the cleanse is impervious to love and relationships—NO chance of them wanting more. I gotta trust in Frank's cleanse. He knows that a relationship and marriage ain't happening for me! No siree.

Leslie Lincoln is never getting married. For some reason, saying it in my head in the third person seems more serious.

Regardless, I just know I can never get married like Finley. Not after everything I witnessed. Everything I've been through. I swallow hard trying to bury that deep, dark memory into the back of my mind. Finley would kill me if she ever found out I kept something like this from her. Keeping the cracks from Finley will get my ass kicked. But this particular crack is for my own sanity. She doesn't need the darkness of my past tainting her new, bright future.

CHAPTER TWELVE

I meet Frank at the historic pub in the Mayfair side of town. This is a posh, financial district and nowhere near where Frank and I usually hang out in. I walk into a decidedly swanky cocktail bar inside the Millennium Hotel. It's all dark woods and rounded leather armchairs stationed around low glass tables. It's filled to the brim with young business professionals.

Frank waves me over to the corner of the bar where he's wedged tightly between two gentlemen seemingly ordering drinks.

"'Bout bloody time, Lez. I've been going mental trying to get a drink in this racket! Get up here and show 'em ye tits."

I roll my eyes. "What tits, Frank?" I surely won't fare any better than him. I'm not the get-drinks-easily type that hot bartenders usually go for.

"Finally!" Frank sighs heavily when a bartender makes his way over to our side. He orders us two red wines and gives the 'tender a sexy wink. Frank. Always on the hunt.

We get our drinks and find a spot near a window overlooking Hyde Park.

"Alright Lez, do you know why I picked this place?"

"No," I reply, sipping my wine and staring excitedly at Frank. I'm ready for the next challenge. This one sounds like fun.

"This is the business district. Men are plentiful and women are scarce. More competition, therefore, more opportunity for you to chum it up with a bloke." Frank's all business today in a smart white button-down and grey slacks. His orange hair is greased off dramatically to one side, so much that it looks wet to the touch.

I tug at my Houndstooth shorts, feeling like my outfit looks a bit outrageous around this crowd. "Stop fidgeting, Lezzie. You look fab. You have nothing to be self-conscious about. You aren't these blokes' type." I visibly deflate. "Don't give me that wounded puppy look, poppet! You know how I feel about you. You're the finest piece of arse in this pub, but these blokes are shallow tossers. You're best to be shot of them. We're using them for day two of Frank's cleanse. Nothing more."

I giggle at him using his name in the third person. "Duly noted, professor!" I salute him snarkily and he scowls.

"Alright, see those two girls sitting over there by themselves?" I glance behind me and nod. "All these tossers want to shag their knickers off. But none of them have the balls to talk to them. We're British, Leslie. We're not known for balls. That's where you come in."

I bite my lip excitedly. "Do I talk to the girls or do I talk to the guys?"

"Start with the girls. Befriend them, make them like you. Won't be hard," he winks at me and smiles. "Then we move on to the cavemen."

Twenty minutes later, Sally and Veronica think I'm the best thing since sliced bread. I've got them in stitches over stories of Frank and his vintage porn collection. They've even bought me another glass of wine. They are busy yammering about their jobs as I notice a couple of sharply dressed businessmen eyeing us curiously.

I glance at Frank and he nods his head over to the same two guys and mouths "Get on with it."

Okay Leslie, it's go time.

I clear my throat and make eye contact with Mr. Bleach Blonde. "Jesse?" I squeal, fakely. "Oh my Gawd, Jesse!" I jump up, interrupting Veronica's story about her boss' latest unreasonable demand and dash over to the men seated two tables over.

He looks at me quizzically as I lean down and air kiss both his cheeks. "Jesse, I haven't seen you in ages! You must come sit with us!" Before he can reply, I grab his arm and yank him out of his seat. "Bring your friend!" Mr. Dumb Face follows dutifully behind us.

"Sally! V! It's my dear friend Jesse from university!" I shove Jesse toward Veronica and she shakes his hand curiously.

"I'm afraid you…" he starts.

"Sit guys, join us! You've got the next round, Jesse! Are you still at the same firm being hugely successful, making loads of dosh?" I giggle and grab my wineglass to take a sip.

"I am at a firm, but I'm afraid you…"

"Who's your friend…what's your name?" I ask.

"Ryan," he offers, his face still looking as dumb as it did a second ago. Get your game face on man, I can't do this alone!

"I was just telling Sally and V what a pig of a day it's been for me! Playing catch up from holiday is the pits!"

"I'm afraid you've got the wrong guy," Mr. Bleach Blonde says, apologetically.

"Whatever do you mean?" I ask, batting my eyelashes accordingly.

"My name isn't Jesse. It's Will. You must have me mistaken." He looks hilariously disappointed at his misfortune of not being Jesse. Sally and Veronica's eyes bug out of their head, obviously feeling horribly mortified for me. I laugh loudly and long and just when they think I'm done laughing, I laugh some more and bat Will's arm.

"I'm such a fool! I must still be jetlagged!" I fan my face. "Well, you're here now. You guys work on this side of town? Veronica was just telling us about her job around the corner! You guys look very successful in your dapper suits. You should take these nice girls out for dinner, there's a great four star just two blocks down that I've heard serves the best pudding!" I glug my wine a bit sloppily and snort in laughter.

Will and Ryan look at each other in confusion and turn to the safest of the three women sitting at the table right now. The ones not rambling on and on and snorting when they laugh. They give the girls a sheepish smile and I sit up straighter, feeling like I am killing this cleanse step.

The four of them find some common ground to talk about and I look over to Frank excitedly. He silently applauds me with a quiet gesture. I then look at him quizzically and he returns my quizzical look. I shrug my shoulders waiting for further instruction and he shrugs his shoulders right back. Bloody hell.

"Oh, would you look at the time! I have to be going. I have an evening colonic scheduled." All four faces blanch as I rise from my chair. "I'm sure I'll see you all around!" I wave dumbly and toddle over to Frank.

"You suck at bailing me out of awkward situations," I hiss at him as I take my seat back.

"What d'ya mean? You did brilliant! Look at them!"

I glance back over and see Sally laughing at something Ryan must have said. I did do good!

"Well, great. Is that it then? Did I pass the wing-woman challenge?"

"Flying colors, Lezzie! Let's have one more drink to celebrate and then get home. Tomorrow night's challenge won't prove to be nearly as easy."

CHAPTER THIRTEEN

"We're home," a voice whispers in my ear. My eyes flutter for a second, squint shut, and then fly open. It's pitch black in my room.

"What time is it?" I squeal, sitting up. I'm suddenly feeling nervous that I'm late for work.

"Relax, lay back down, it's still early." I recognize it now as Finley's voice. "It's not quite six. Sorry, we just got back. I wanted to see you!" She pulls back the covers and slips into my daybed beside me. I sigh heavily and lie back down.

"Fin-Bin, I don't have to be up for another hour," I groan and roll so I'm facing away from her. I shove my butt out far, nearly pushing her off the bed. She laughs and wraps herself around me.

"I missed you, Lez!"

"You were just with me for a whole week!"

"I know, but you seemed...*off*," she says quietly.

"What do you mean?" I whisper, waking up a bit more now.

"At the wedding. You weren't yourself, Leslie. It's been bugging me since you left. Brody told me to leave it, but I can't. Are you okay? I'm worried." I roll over and we're now facing each other, lying on our sides with our hands tucked under our heads.

"Where's Brody?"

"He went to bed, it was a long flight."

"I'm sorry you were worrying," I frown and catch a glimpse of Finley's round aqua eyes as the early morning dusk begins seeping into my room. "I'm fine. Just thinking."

"I gathered that. Thinking about what? I want the cracks, Lez."

I sigh. "Finley, it's so bloody early."

"Hey!" she says. "You would do the same shit to me, so spill!"

I suppose there's no point in fighting it. "I'm fine. Really. Just thinking about my life and what I'm doing and how it's changing. My dumb head is all over the place, Finny."

"Changing 'cause of me?" she asks nervously.

"Yeah. But not in a bad way!" I rub her arm soothingly. "I'm happy for you and Brody! Really, I am. I love Brody. You guys fit perfectly here. It just makes me feel like I'm such a loser."

"You are not a loser!"

"I know, I know." I roll my eyes. "It's just…I'm not the pretty one. I'm the funny one. The crafty one. The odd one. I'm not beautiful or interesting. I'm definitely not the marrying type. Nor do I even want to be! It's not what I want in life…ever. But if all my friends up and marry, I'm gonna have to buy cats! I hate cats!"

I look at Finley who appears shocked into a very rare silence. Finally she replies, "Forgive me, but you just spewed a load of crap at me and it's taking a moment for it all to process."

I roll flat onto my stomach and bury my face into my pillow. Finley was smart to wake me up to chat. I'm in a vulnerable and honest drowsy state of mind. I'm saying way more than I should be.

"For starters, if you tell me you're not the pretty one ever again, I will slap you right across the face because that's just stupid. Secondly…funny, crafty, and odd all sound like the best possible characteristics! And lastly, why don't you ever want to get married?"

"Oh, you're one to talk! There was a time you never wanted to marry!" I bark incredulously at her.

"I was lying to myself Leslie, like I think you are right now."

"I'm not lying. I don't want what my parents have. Ever," I reply and flinch at how much I just revealed.

"What's wrong with your parents? They always seemed happy to me."

I nod. "I was just using them as an example." I can't tell Finley this crack. She's just too close to home and I don't want my family name tainted in Marshall. Despite everything, I still don't want that.

Finley scowls in the soft morning light. "So what's your life plan then, be a lonely spinster with cats?"

"Well, eventually I'm sure. But not immediately. For a bit of fun, Frank's got me on this new romantic cleanse."

"Romantic cleanse? What the heck is that?"

I relay all seven steps to her and tell her that tonight's challenge is to string along two guys at once.

"Oh, this I gotta see!"

"Oh yes, please do! Buy a ticket to my show of humiliation! It should be a great laugh!" I giggle.

"If Frank's planned this, I'm so in. I have a huge presentation this afternoon, but I'm meeting up with you guys later! Can I bring Brody?"

"Sure! Bring the whole family! Or better yet, a video recorder. Let's capture this wonderfully pathetic thing I'm doing so we can enjoy it for years to come."

"It's not pathetic!" Finley crows. "I think it's brave actually. I'm very proud of you, Lez."

I smile. "Get out. I got at least another thirty minutes before I have to be up." I roll away from her, nudging her out of my bed with my bum again.

"Love you, Lez," Finley whispers in my ear and exits quietly.

"Love you too," I sigh with a smile.

CHAPTER FOURTEEN

After a busy day of shooing Benji away from my desk so I could actually get some work done, I'm heading to yet another London bar. I asked Frank this morning during my pep talk if any of these challenges would take place anywhere other than a bar and he just looked at me like I had six tits. Okay then. Seven straight days of bars. If this doesn't get me out of my funk then I don't know what will.

Finley, Brody, Frank and I hop off the Tube and walk a couple blocks, arriving at a cute little cocktail bar in Soho. Frank knows all the hot spots in London and apparently this one will have a good stock of men for me to practice my ménage skills.

Tonight's challenge is juggling two guys in one night. I am to flirt, tease, and string along two perfectly innocent men throughout the night—basically leading them to think I might be easy, but then leave them high and dry. The leaving high and dry part sounds like a snap, it's the bits before that scare the bejesus out of me.

I selected a pair of plum-colored leather skinnies with flashy gold zippers at the ankles. My sky high black pumps have a sharply pointed toe and look like they mean business. I felt pretty ironic when I paired the skin tight pants with my billowy tank that says FLIRT across the chest in large, bold letters. Frank didn't seem as amused as I was over my selection.

Armed with drinks, the four of us survey the crowd and suck down some bottled beers.

"This one is going to suuuuuck," I groan, looking around and trying to decide who to start flirting with first.

"Don't be a defeatist, Lezbo! You can do it. Your arse looks sexy as sin in those buttery trousers of yours. Just feeeeel that leather and let it lead your pussy to peckers."

I snort out a laugh.

"But perhaps a bit less of that," Frank murmurs, gulping down more of his beer. "Just remember…flirt, get them on the hook, and then leave them for the other. You have to bounce between two blokes for two hours in order to be successful. Got it?" I cringe.

"You can do it, Lez! That guy's looked over here a few times—I think you should go for him," Finley says, glancing over at a standard tall, dark, and handsome bloke at the bar.

"I'm certain he's looking at you, Fin," I grumble, feeling frumpy standing next to tall bombshell Finley. Normally it doesn't bother me, but when my goal of the night is to pick up a guy, I can't help but compare.

"He better not be," Brody interrupts, draping a protective arm over Finley's tall frame. God, why did I let them come again? They are too bloody cute.

Finley shakes her head. "He's checking you out, Leslie. I'm certain! Just go!" She shoves me gently. I gulp down the remainder of my beer, straighten my shoulders and strut over his way.

"Hi cutie," he says, before I have a chance to say anything.

My posture sags. "Cutie?" I ask, feeling a bit put off by him already.

"Sorry, didn't mean it as a bad thing," he says. He looks embarrassed.

"It's just not the most ideal pickup line I've ever heard."

"You think I'm picking you up?" he asks, sardonically.

"Well, you did call me cute," I giggle, feeling silly over this entire exchange.

He smirks at me, revealing exorbitantly white teeth. "Are you open to being picked up?" I shrug my shoulders coyly. "See?" he says, brushing my wayward auburn bangs from my face. "Bloody cute." I laugh loudly at his cheekiness.

I glance behind me for encouragement from my friends and my blood runs cold when I see him. *Theo*. He's standing next to Frank, who looks decidedly guilty. Finley and Brody both appear nervous, attempting to chat with Theo—but he doesn't even look at them.

His eyes are clapped on mine. And he's not happy.

"Can I get you a drink?"

"Hmm?" I muse, turning back to the tall, dark, and handsome guy. I glance back nervously and see Theo walking straight toward me. "You know what? I'll be back. Just gotta..." I shoot out and head toward the loo, in the opposite direction of Frank, Fin, and Brody.

Bloody hell, why is Theo here?

I reach the hallway to the women's loo and am almost to the door when a warm hand clamps around my elbow, hauling me backwards so my back is flush with his front.

"Leslie." Theo says my name deliberately slow. I breathe heavily, unsure how to respond but already feeling a nervous excitement at his close proximity. "Funny seeing you here."

I bite my lip and muster up an ounce of courage and turn to face him. He releases my arm and cocks his head sideways, scrutinizing my face. I'm sure my green eyes look like saucers right now. "What are you doing here, Theo?"

"Little bird told me you might be here…on the prowl." His neck veins pulse angrily.

"*On the prowl?* Oh, whatever!" I balk.

His lips form a thin line as if it's taking everything in his power not to say exactly what's on his mind. "Liam ran into Frank a couple nights ago. Said you were on some sort of mission to get laid." My jaw drops and I'm stunned into silence.

Fucking Frank!

"Imagine my surprise to hear that, when not only two months ago I was on your doorstep asking for yet another shot with you, Leslie."

I wince back at the memory of Theo and Liam stopping by one Sunday. Finley and Brody had just moved in with us and it was about two months before their big wedding. Liam had something to talk to Frank about and Theo presumably came along to try and talk with me. He wanted me to let him take me on a proper date. I adamantly refused and said I wasn't interested in any type of relationship. A door was slammed, Theo was pissed—what else is new?

"That's not what this is about, Theo," I hiss, feeling frustrated at having to explain myself to him.

"Then enlighten me," he crosses his arms and pins me to the wall, eyes locked on mine. "Because you look like you're dressed for prowling, *Leslie*."

I glance down to survey my outfit through his eyes and then check his to compare. He's wearing a pair of sexily tailored brown tweed pants and a manly plaid shirt. The sleeves are rolled up, revealing his rippling forearms looking taut with tension. And *damn* those sexy black-rimmed glasses.

"Would you just stop saying my name like that?"

"Like what," he scowls.

"Like it's a stupid swear word or something!" He flinches and his expression softens. "Look, nothing's changed. I'm not looking for a relationship here. This is just a bit of fun! I've been in a bit of a funk." I regret saying the last part knowing that I'm over-sharing, but the beer I chugged when we got here, and the two we consumed at the house before that are apparently making me loose lipped.

"I'm sorry. I didn't mean for it to come off that way. I fancy your name." It surprises me that after everything I've just said, that's what he responds to. "So, what's tonight's challenge?" he asks.

I look at him surprised. "You don't really want to know." He shrugs his shoulders, waiting for my response. I sigh heavily, certain this will just set him off again. "Ménage—not in that way," I say, quickly, when his expression transforms into horror. "Just flirting. With two different guys." Jesus, this is mortifying to talk about. In the privacy of our own little house, this cleanse sounds perfectly normal.

"So, who are the two blokes?" he asks with an edge to his voice.

"I've only found one so far."

"Not true," he says deadpan. I scowl and then realization dawns on me that he's including himself in this little challenge. "I can count, right?"

"Theo, you've made it clear what you're interested in and that's not what I'm doing here."

"Don't you worry about what I'm interested in. I'm a big boy. I'll be your second." I attempt to argue, but he presses his hand over my mouth, halting my tirade. The touch of his hand on my skin sends shivers through my body. "In fact, you've probably been talking to me too long as it is. Off you go, but I'll be waiting for you to come back." And with that, he turns and walks back out toward the bar.

What the fucking tits was that all about? What am I supposed to do now? Feeling confused and a bit agitated, I make my way back out to the bar and tall, dark, and handsome greets me warmly upon my return.

"You're back! Lovely. Let's get you that drink." He waves over the bartender who pops the top off a fresh beer. I sit down on the barstool right next to him, still trying to work out in my head how to handle this whole sordid night.

I take a big swig.

"My name's Leslie," tall, dark, and handsome says, brightly, turning my attention from the air in front of me to his wide, eager eyes.

"You're kidding," I reply. "*My* name is Leslie."

"No! Is it really?" he laughs, heartily. "Two Leslies. Isn't that cute?" He winks briefly and I huff out a laugh because this whole night truly is ridiculous.

As I come down from my genuine laugh, I am bumped from the other side. I turn over to see Theo sidling up into the open barstool right next to me. I look at him in silent mock horror and he barely glances at me, ordering a beer from the bartender.

Seriously? Sandwiched between two men? I think that's taking this cleanse challenge a bit further than necessary, isn't it?

"Name's Theo," Theo bellows over toward Leslie and me, his eyes not breaking away from the soccer game on the TV.

Leslie looks briefly to me and smiles politely at Theo. "We're Leslie."

That gets Theo's attention and he swerves his pale brown eyes to the two of us. "One name?" His brow furrows playfully.

"Two Leslies…just a bizarre coincidence," Leslie laughs heartily.

"There's a lot of coincidences happening tonight," Theo says, pinning me with a serious look. "You share a name with a beautiful woman, that's to be sure." His eyes rove over my face briefly and then swerve back up to the TV behind the bar.

Beautiful? Ha!

Leslie mumbles something beside me that I don't hear over the racing thoughts in my head.

"Tell me about yourself, Theo." I hear the words being spoken aloud and am shocked to discover they are coming from my mouth.

Theo smirks, eyes still facing forward. He adjusts his glasses slightly and then turns his whole body so it's facing me, encasing me—surrounding me. "What would you like to know?" he asks, his voice low and husky.

I shrug my shoulders slightly. "What do you do?"

"I'm in design. I make furniture. Woodwork stuff mostly. End tables, some dining sets. My style is very….primitive. Masculine." His tone sends shivers down my spine.

"That sounds interesting! What do you do, Leslie?" Leslie asks, attempting to turn my attention back to him. Begrudgingly I turn away from Theo.

"I'm in design too. I design camera bags."

A small huff of laughter echoes in my ears. "Coincidence again," Theo murmurs quietly.

"Quite right!" Leslie peals. "Couple of arteeests in the room. Very interesting. I'm a dull taxman, I'm afraid. What a bore."

"Numbers can be fun," Theo says. "I once got shut down from a woman four times. Hoping fifth time's the charm." He winks straight at Leslie and then looks pointedly at me.

Leslie coughs awkwardly and gulps down his beer. "I suppose…"

"Not everything is a numbers game," I say, stopping Leslie midsentence and turning my neck to pin Theo with a death stare. "Sometimes life and choices are about *more* than just numbers."

"And sometimes, you have to go all in to know if something's worth it or not."

"Going all in can leave you flat broke and then no one's happy!"

"But at least they'd know. At least they'd have an answer and wouldn't just be pining away by themselves wondering and waiting for nothing."

"Not everything is worth pining over!"

"Some things are *incredibly* worth pining over."

His words stun me into silence as I realize how close our faces got during our heated exchange. His expression is serious and sincere. I glance briefly to his mouth, he mirrors my gaze. Finally I scoff and turn away from him.

I chug down the remainder of my beer. What does he know? Nothing. I'm nothing. He's an idiot. I slam my bottle down and shove my barstool back hard and fast. The loud scraping of the legs on the wood make both Leslie and Theo cringe. "It's been real boys, but I gotta dash. My number is up."

Theo looks pointedly at me and I avoid his eyes and storm away, leaving a gaping Frank, Finley, and Brody in my wake.

CHAPTER FIFTEEN

"What's the next cleanse challenge?" I ask the next morning when I happen upon Frank, Finley, and Mitch in the kitchen.

Frank frowns at me. "I thought…"

"What's the next challenge?" I ask again, feeling frustration rising. I pour myself a cup of coffee and dump a load of milk in. They all just stare at my actions without saying anything. I look up incredulously.

"Leslie," Fin says, finally breaking the awkward silence.

"Don't you start, Fin. I'm ready for the next challenge. Let's keep this moving. I have to finish, right? To receive maximum benefit." Frank looks down uncomfortably. "Out with it," I bark.

"Girl Kiss." He has the audacity to look shameful.

"Piece of cake." I say, striding back out of the kitchen with my mug in tow.

Vilma, Benji, and Hector insisted on coming out with me tonight. After my sullen mood at the office all day, they ended up dragging the whole sordid tale out of me. Having my coworkers present for my girl-kiss challenge isn't my idea of fun. But having seen these pervs drunk at the Christmas party every year, I know this is child's play to them.

Shay Nightclub. Frank had to choose this spot of all spots. I feel anxiety prickle all over my skin. Images of Theo and me dancing provocatively on this very dance floor bang around in my head. It's official. Shay Nightclub is ruined for me. I wonder if anyone here ever found my panties I ditched in the bathroom.

Screw it. I'm on a mission. I'm going to blast through this challenge and it's going to start with shots. Lots and lots of shots. I order everyone a round of lemon drops. A girl kiss draws a big crowd apparently because we've got my three coworkers, Frank, Finley, Brody—and even Mitch and Julie graced us with their presence tonight.

"Whoo!" I hoot after tossing back the sweet shot. It's stronger than usual. "One more!" I bellow and gesture to the bartender to bring another round.

"Leslie," Finley chastises.

"Finley," I croon. "Turn that frown upside down! It's girl-kiss night!" I sing merrily, propping my knees up on the high barstool to get a bird's-eye view of the crowd. "Now, who's going to be the lucky lady getting a nice smooch from me tonight?"

My view is pummeled by the sight of Theo strolling toward me with Liam and Ethan flanking either side of him. Oh fuck me up the ass. Is he for real? I mean, honest to Pete! Was tonight's challenge announced at the freaking changing of the guards today? Do all of these people have to be here tonight of all nights?

I shake my head and slip down off the stool. My skirt nearly catches and flashes my bare ass. Oh shit. Not good when you're not wearing any knickers! Finley likes to scold me for that but the things are uncomfortable and annoying as hell. I don't intend to ride any man's leg, so what difference does it make?

Tonight I skillfully selected a sweet floral-print dress with a short flowy skirt and sweetheart neckline. I think if I'm going to attract a woman for a kiss, she'll need to know I am the flowery kind.

"Can I get you a drink, Leslie? A regular one, not a shot," Benji asks, approaching me with caution.

I throw my arm around him. "That'd be grand, Benji! A V&T please, and keep 'em coming!" I snort out a laugh. He squirms uncomfortably but dutifully orders me my drink.

Finley comes to steady me on the other side and I smile saccharinely at her. Benji hands me my drink with my arm still awkwardly tossed over his shoulders. I swerve around to take a sip and see that Theo and his crew have arrived.

Oh joy.

Looking at these three guys, you'd think they just stepped off of a London runway. Liam has a posh blonde quiff hairstyle—sexy messy volume on top. Ethan is broad, tall, and chocolate skinned. And Theo…

Oh, Theo. He is just my bloody type. Dammit.

"Leslie," Theo says, cautiously glancing over to Benji with a frown.

"Theo, my dear boy. Fancy seeing you here!" I say, loudly, in my nearly perfect classy British accent. I then drop my jaw open for dramatic effect.

He squints slightly, adjusting his thick-framed glasses. God, I want to rip those damn things off his face right now. Why are they so sexy?

Liam looks down, uncomfortable, then suddenly says, "Congratulations, mate." He offers his hand to Brody who's standing by Mitch and Julie. Brody eyes Liam sternly for a second and then smiles politely.

"Thanks. Good to see you again," Brody offers coolly.

Oooo, it's chilly over here. Finley's British fling and her hubby facing off! I drag my arm off of Benji and break away from the pack to join my other coworkers who are huddled up at the bar.

"What are you guys talking about?" I slur, suddenly feeling no pain.

"We're placing bets on whether or not you'll actually follow through with it!" Vilma snickers and Hector smiles smugly.

"Screw you guys. I'm gonna make out with a girl *so hard*," I say, whirling around to survey my prospects and turn smack into Theo.

"Theo, dammit. What?" I whine, wiping the spilt drink off the back of my hand. Benji is standing right next to Theo, looking so young and innocent in comparison.

"Leslie, you're drunk," Theo scolds.

"An astute observation, fine sir," I curtsey dramatically. "Must be those stunning glasses that make everything so crystal clear for you!"

He lets out a frustrated sigh. "Please, Leslie. I don't like this."

I shake my head haphazardly. "It has nothing to do with you!"

"It has to do with anyone who bloody well cares about you!" he booms loudly, getting closer to my face.

I stumble slightly. "And you think that's you, do ya?" I say it softly but with malice. "You don't know me well enough to care, Theo. If you did, you'd change your mind in a flash! I'm not the one to care about. I'm not the one to fall for. I'm *certainly* not the one who wants what you want."

"Stop this, Leslie," he barks thunderously. "Pleeeease?" his voice rises in question, his face looking pained and desperate. His hands are clenched firmly by his sides like he's doing everything he can to contain his fury.

That. That is exactly why this will never work between Theo and me. I won't be controlled. Even if he asks nicely. I won't live under a man's thumb that controls all situations. I've grown up around that shit and it's so far from anything I'll ever accept in life.

"Give her some space man," Brody says, placing a calming hand on Theo's puffed out chest. Liam and Frank come over and grab Theo's arms, gently pulling him away from my bubble of space. The space around us feels tense with unspoken foreboding.

Ethan cuts the tension by sauntering right between us and starts blatantly flirting with Vilma. Figures. She's blonde, willowy, and beautiful. Fuck my life.

"Let's dance, Fin-Bin!" I sing merrily, grabbing her hand and yanking her out onto the dance floor. "No boys!" I say, swerving around and halting Brody and Frank in their tracks. "I'm sorry Frank.

And you know I love ya Brodster, but sometimes a girl just needs her girlfriends." They both nod and smile sadly at me.

I grab Julie and pull her out with us too. We make our way down the few steps to the sunken dance floor. In seconds we're all three losing ourselves to the beat of the music. I adamantly attempt to ignore the audience of brooding men staring down at us from their tables on the upper level near us. Just being away from Theo makes me feel lighter, more carefree.

When Finley throws out an imaginary fishing pole to reel me in, I laugh heartily. Dammit, I wish I would have worn underwear—the lack thereof is preventing me from busting out some of my favorite moves.

I risk a glance up at the guys again and their expressions are almost heartbreaking! Frank and Brody both look sad and concerned. Liam looks uncomfortable. Mitch looks sulky. And Theo—Oh God, what is Theo's face right now? Angry? Nervous? Desperate? I can't tell. It's a hodgepodge of worry I think. And fuck me! Why are they all looking at me like I'm suicidal?

Enough of this shit!

I stop dancing and Finley halts her moves too, looking at me like she thinks I'm going to be sick. She approaches, touching my back all nervous and worried like I'm a damn child.

This just irritates me even further, so before I can think better of it I grab her face in my hands and plant my lips on hers, hard and fast. I don't move my lips at first, simply allowing the shock and sting of our teeth clinking to register fully in our minds. When her tense face relaxes beneath my hands, I open my mouth ever so slightly and start really kissing her. If I'm gonna do a girl kiss, I'm going to make it the best girl kiss of all time!

She squeals a little and brings her hands up to rest on my wrists. I think she might be laughing but she doesn't shove me away. She relaxes and begins moving her lips against mine as well.

Hell, my bestie is a good kisser!

I crack up laughing at that thought and our moment is broken. We pull apart both in hysterics with tears welling in our eyes.

"You fucking kissed me!" Finley cries.

"You're damn skippy!" I say, smacking my lips on hers for yet another chaste kiss. She laughs again and shakes her head incredulously.

"You've got some nerve! I'm a married woman!" She flashes her ring at me like I need to see the proof.

"Like you haven't been wanting to kiss me for years," I state smugly.

"That was seriously hot guys!" Julie says, breaking into our little Finley-n-Leslie bubble.

"It wasn't hot when she clinked my teeth," Finley rubs her lips goofily. We both continue laughing and glance up to see all the guys gawking at us in admiration. Frank is positively beaming as he gives me two very enthusiastic thumbs up. I chance a glance at Theo and his expression is a little harder to read. Is he jealous?

Brody makes his way down to us and smoothes his hands down Finley's hips. "I'm glad you got that out of your system, Lez. But let's not make it a habit, eh?" I frown quizzically at him. "I don't really need my wife and her best friend being the objects of desire to a club full of dudes. I'll kick anyone's ass who touches you girls, and doing that shit just opens the door for assholes."

"Sorry Brod-ster," I offer meekly.

He shakes me off and ruffles my hair playfully. "It *was* entertaining," he adds sheepishly. Finley smacks him against his chest and turns in his arms as they tangle together in a dance.

"You can kiss Julie anytime," Mitch says, walking past me and pulling Julie into his arms. I snort and look up to see only Frank sitting up above now, so I make my way up.

"Well done, you! A right proper girl kiss if I ever saw one!" Frank rewards me with a smacking kiss on the cheek. "Couldn't have done it better myself, love. Truly. Impossible."

"Thanks, Frank," I half-smile and look back toward the bar searching for a familiar face. "So…?"

"So, what?" Frank asks, knowingly.

"Where'd Theo go?" I inquire, feeling silly for caring.

Frank shrugs his shoulders. "He left, Lez. Sorry love."

"Oh! Nothing to be sorry for. I was just curious." I shake my head dismissively and take a drink of my V&T on the table.

"You don't have to keep doing this if you don't want to," Frank whispers softly in my ear.

"What d'ya mean? 'Course I want to! This is fun!" My happy tone is forced and my smile is fake as hell.

Frank nods and smiles sadly. "Tomorrow is make out with a bloke."

I feel stunned. Make out with a dude? Already?

I can do this. I can. I think I can. I'm pretty sure I can.

CHAPTER SIXTEEN

I so cannot do this.

Thank the Lord it's Saturday. After last night's booze-fest, there's no way in bloody hell I'd be able to get up and go to work today. I toss myself out of my creaky daybed and make my way over to my window to check the weather. It's raining, like it always does in London. The weather here is rather dreary, always making everything so gray. But the pulse of the city is what drives me. That and the fact that it's so incredibly different from where I grew up.

Checking the weather was something we did regularly on the farm growing up. The rain gauge and temperature gauge were regular talking points at the breakfast table. Our dairy farm was located on the outskirts of Marshall. We had a lot of livestock, so my father employed a pretty sizeable staff to keep it all operating. Growing up, I wasn't required to do very much work outside, but I remember as a little girl always begging my dad to take me down to see the cows getting milked by the big machines.

I can still picture my mother, barefoot and pregnant with my brother, asking my father timidly to take me outside for just a bit. He'd growl about having too much work to do and say he didn't want me slowing him down. I hate that memory being forever etched in my mind.

I think I hated him even then.

A knock at the door snaps me out of my reverie.

"Lezbo?" Frank croons softly through the door. "Are you up?"

"I'm up!" He opens the door and stands before me, looking like a child in his plaid two-piece pajama set. I genuinely smile.

"Thank heavens you are! Brody and Finley went out to Cambridge for the day and Mitch and Julie are still sleeping. I'm bored as fuck, Lez. Will you play with me?"

I chuckle at his sweet little sad face.

"Let's go to Fab's and then grab lunch," I suggest. His eyes instantly light up.

"Only if we can pop next door!" he says, exiting the room—to go get dressed, I'm sure. "I gotta see what latest magazines are in!" he shouts.

My Frankie…ever the pervert.

LB

A couple hours later, we waltz into Fab's and Ameerah is busying herself with a large box of new bolts.

"Ooo, new stuff?" I ask, hurrying over to check out the goods.

"Leslie, child! Where you been?" She stands up straight from her hunched-over position, giving me an eyeful of her ample bosom and curvaceous body. Ameerah is cloaked in a mustard-yellow maxi dress that matches her yellow hair.

After informing her that Frank and I were in Mexico for Finley's wedding, Ameerah seems resolved to forgive me of my absence. I stop into Fab's at least once a week after work to shoot the shit. She's super up-to-date on the industry trends. We usually chat over a bottle of her native country's wine that tastes like plain cranberry juice.

"What is this?" I ask, grabbing a bolt of a nude fabric that glimmers dreamily in the light.

"I haven't had a chance to look myself, child. Let's lay it out."

"I'm bored," Frank crows loudly. Ameerah and I barely look up as she quickly unravels several yards worth across her large worktop table. "You guys are dull, I'm going next door to hang with Umar."

I stroke my fingers across the beautiful nude chiffon, relishing in the intricately designed rosette texture. This is a fabric that screams bridal or high class evening gown. This is red carpet shit right here! My fingers are itching to make something with it, but I have no events to wear such a gown to.

"You think you could do something with it?" Ameerah murmurs in her thick Caribbean accent.

"Shyeah! Too bad I'd never have anywhere to wear it!"

"I want something for a display piece here. Something to dress up the window a bit."

My eyes bug out of my head. "You'd really want me to do that? This fabric has to be expensive, Ame!"

"You don't worry about that. I got this!" She rewraps the fabric and places it inside a large fabric bag and hands it over to me.

"You're not kidding!" She shakes her head, smiling. "I'll do my very best, I swear."

She pats me encouragingly and ushers me to the back room for some wine. "It's not even a question."

CHAPTER SEVENTEEN

The whole time I get ready for my big night out, I stare dreamily at the bolt of fabric Ameerah sent home with me. Bodice ideas are flowing in my head and I can't wait to be done with this cleanse so I can throw myself into that project.

"Lez?" Finley's voice says, outside my door. "I'm coming in," she says, as she opens the door. "Shiiiit!" she exclaims. "You look—" she stops, unable to finish her sentence.

"This work? I mean, I'm sure you'd look way hotter in it, but if I have to make out with a guy tonight, I need to try the whole sexy thing. Not the designer thing I usually do." I glance at myself in the floor-length mirror by my mannequin and cringe. "Did my hair get redder?"

"Leslie, shut the fuck up. You look hot!"

I exhale heavily. Okay, it must be halfway decent if Finley is so adamant right now. My dress is a simple deep-red mini tube dress, but the sheer lace overlay is what gives it that wow factor. The lace covers my arms and shoulders completely, giving me that nearly naked yet fully covered look. It's that impossibly perfect balance of sex and class. I add a touch of a smoky-eye effect and feel like I've mustered my inner siren for tonight.

Finley flops herself onto my bed. "So, you think Theo will show up tonight?"

My chest rises fractionally at the mention of his name. The thought has obviously occurred to me. Only 9,323 times. Part of me wants him to be the guy I make out with, but a larger part of me, the more practical part, screams and slaps me across the face for being such a douche canoe.

You can't kiss Theo tonight, Leslie. You can't!

"Even if he does, it won't stop me."

Finley shakes her head disapprovingly at me. "You're hiding something, Leslie. And that pisses me off. We're supposed to tell each other everything, remember? Even the cracks." She scowls at me, refusing to break her death stare.

"There's nothing to tell, Fin! Theo wants more. I don't. End of."

"Bullshit. I'll give you time, but not much." She stands up and strides past me. "Frank says hurry up," she says over her shoulder. She closes the door behind her as she leaves.

The gauntlet has been dropped. Finley is pissed. Well, as pissed as she ever gets at me. I know her enough to know that it won't get any worse than this. But still, if I don't come clean—the idea of losing her as a friend makes my stomach roil. I've never told anyone this shit and I don't want that to change now! I can barely admit it to myself!

I totter closer to my mirror in my nude platform wedges and eye my face closely.

"You're in the weeds now, Leslie," I say to my reflection. "Nothing's changed though. You're still the same girl from the same town you want to forget. A wolf in sheep's clothing." I huff out a laugh and smear my matte red lipstick across my lips.

"Game time."

CHAPTER EIGHTEEN

This is swank, west London nightlife at its finest. Colorful cocktails, women in dresses, men wearing expensive watches. I'm supposed to make out with a guy here? Surely one of the meat market clubs would have been a better option than this posh spot.

"Frank, why are we here?" I ask, huddled around a glass high-top cocktail table.

"You can make out with any ol' bloke in those danceclubs, Lez. This cleanse is about progression. I want high quality kissing to be the name of the game here. Toe curling, all-consuming snogging. This is day five after all!" he adds seriously.

"Okay, okay. Where do I start then?"

"Well, first off, kudos on the matte red lips. That's going to make them positively starved to kiss you!"

I chuckle dumbly and take a tentative sip of my cosmo. After last night, alcohol doesn't sound the greatest. But I need something to take the edge off for this challenge.

London Bound

"Just set your sights on someone. Start flirting and nibbling on your lip a lot. If they are half a man, they'll take it from there. Just be open to it, alright, Leslie? Leslie?"

I jump when Frank shakes my shoulder. I tear my gaze away from the door.

"What's your deal? What are you gawking at?"

"Nothing. I'm ready!" I squeal. I'm sure as shit not admitting to Frank that I was looking for Theo. But gosh, I feel disappointed he's not here. Not because I want to be with him. Not at all. But part of me wasn't feeling that nervous for tonight because I thought my make-out guy was going to be Theo. My mind clamors back to the time in my bedroom when he lifted me up onto my desk. He kisses like such a…a….*a man*. I never thought I could feel sexy in my cheetah-print onesie pajamas but shittin-A, I did that night!

"Just munch on your lip like you're doing right now and I'm certain you'll be all set." My lip plops out from between my teeth. I didn't even realize I was chewing on it. "Off you go," Frank says, taking my drink from my hands and motioning me up toward the other cocktail tables beside us.

Time to put your big girl knickers on, Lez. Too bad you're still not wearing any. I find the guy I had my sights set on as soon as I entered—and I'm glad to see he's still alone. He's a cute strawberry-blonde fella with kind eyes. He's definitely got something going for him.

"Mind if I sit here?" I ask coyly. "My girlfriend was supposed to meet me here tonight, but she bailed last minute." I pout my lips sexily, knowing I'm a big fat liar.

"Yes, please. Sit! It'd be my pleasure! I'm Jarrod." He offers his hand to me, helping me perch up on the stool, my tight dress hugging my thighs together.

"Leslie," I pull my lower lip into my mouth, wasting no time. I love this smudge-less matte lipstick. It stays on forever.

He watches my lip plop out of my mouth and returns his gaze to mine, his eyes twinkling ever so slightly. "So, you're all on your own then? Me too, actually. I'm here on business, staying at the hotel just across the street. It's good we ran into each other."

He's congenial, kind, and attentive. We talk about America and his hometown in Cornwall. He says all the right things and laughs at all my girlie jokes. I'm definitely dumbing it down for this bloke, though. I'm certain he couldn't handle the storm that is the cheetah-onesie-wearing-Leslie. Every time he glances at my lips, I feel myself getting closer and closer to the chance of a kiss.

"Would you like to go for a walk?" he asks, finally. "Get some fresh air? Soho Square is just over there. I'd quite fancy a toodle."

I nod and follow him out the door. I feel nothing when he touches the small of my back, guiding me down the busy sidewalk. I feel nothing when he compliments me and finds reasons to touch me. He's not pinging any sort of sexy radar on my speedometer and that disappoints me greatly. Maybe if I just kiss him. Maybe then I'll feel something!

"Jarrod," I say, stopping us near a small park area. He turns and looks at me curiously, his light hair illuminated softly in the golden streetlight. "I was just wondering if we could maybe…" Reaching deep into my redheaded bravado, I lean in and press my lips to his. I feel his shock at first, but within seconds his hands rise and clasp around the back of my head and neck. He begins reciprocating my kiss eagerly. A few seconds later, he pulls back and murmurs against my lips.

"Do you want to come up to my room? It's very close."

"No," I reply, honestly. "Can we just make out on this street corner for a minute?" I should feel embarrassed, but I don't. These challenges are getting to me. I'm growing tired of the pretenses of everything.

"Anything," he says, and leans in again to kiss me. It's a nice kiss. Full and warm, enticing and swirling. But I feel my mind drifting to other things. Other people. One person in particular. Growing frustrated with my thoughts, I kiss Jarrod harder, willing away my thoughts of a brown-eyed, dark-framed-glasses-wearing alpha. *Jarrod, Jarrod, I'm kissing Jarrod—a nice boy from Cornwall who works in financing and has three brothers and a cat.*

His hands drift down my back and he flushes himself against me. Feeling suddenly uncomfortable, I press my hands firmly against his chest and push him back. He relents easily and offers me a lopsided smile, looking sweetly dazed. I'm feeling dazed too, but I'm afraid it's not because of Jarrod.

"Sorry, I might've gotten carried away there. You sure you don't want to come up to my room? I've got coffee and tea," he says, running his hand through his hair. I shake my head politely, looking downward, unable to make eye contact. "Can I get your number at least? I come back here occasionally. I'd love to call you when I'm in town."

Not wanting to make things awkward, I give Jarrod my mobile number and indicate that I'd welcome a call next time he's in town. I know there's no future here. I just need to get away. The longer I stand here wishing he were someone else, the guiltier and more melancholy I feel.

We part ways and I shoot Frank a quick text telling him I'm taking the Tube back on my own and he shouldn't hurry back. He seems concerned but I mollify him by telling him I'm just hungover from last night but that I was successful in my mission.

If only that were it.

I can't believe I've let Theo get under my skin so damn much that I can't even make out with another guy without thinking about him. I picked Jarrod tonight because I could just tell he'd be easy. *Safe.* He looked like one of those guys that are too nice to even breakup with a woman. He'd just be congenial and compliant throughout an entire relationship. Why can't I date someone like him? It'd be safe and secure. Nothing like what I grew up with. Surely nothing like the brooding Theo.

I need to stop thinking of Theo. He's obviously given up on me since he was a no-show tonight. That's a depressing thought! I roll my eyes knowing I'm never the girl guys care about—not long term anyway. I'm a passing fancy. I'm intriguing because I'm bold and wild and make a splash with my fashion choices. Beyond that, I'm not the girl they really want.

So this is a wakeup call for me. I need to stop pining over Theo. He's obviously over me. This is not a new concept. Once again, I was just a plaything. Nothing more. Playing hard to get made me interesting for about two seconds, and now he's well and moved on.

I hop off the Tube and round the corner to our house. I nearly fall on my face when I see Theo sitting on our concrete steps. His posture is hunched and tense and he's punching away on his phone. He looks up when he hears my clacking heels approaching.

"Theo?" I ask, wondering if I'm happy or sad to see him right now.

"I don't even have your bloody number," he holds his phone up mockingly and tosses it down onto the pavement step next to him. I cringe at the sound, knowing he must have scraped it.

"What are you doing here?" I ask, climbing the steps toward

him, worried his loud voice is going to elicit our gawking neighbors—or even worse, the group of slackers that constantly congregate at the skate park kiddy corner from our house.

I gesture for him to follow me into the patio area by our front door. It's a dreamy little alcove that we barbecue in occasionally. It's got old, wrought iron fencing, completely covered in ivy, making a private little area from the street.

Theo stops at the entrance, bracing his hands on either side of the fence like he can't possibly break the threshold. The golden rope lights cast a warm, lamplight glow on him and I instantly think of sex. He sucks in large, deep breaths, obviously angry about something! He rips a leaf of ivy off the doorway.

"You look fucking stunning." He eyes me dolefully like he might be sick at any second.

"Theo. I..."

"Do you know that your eyes change color with your outfits?" I frown in confusion. "I'm quite certain they are green, but every time I've seen you, you have different eyes. Tonight they look..." He squints and leans forward to get a closer look. "Sage. That dress makes them look like the wallpaper in my mum's house." He stalks inside and I instinctively back up, my rear hitting the patio table behind me.

"That night...in your room..." he stops, playing with the ivy on the wall, his eyes flashing with heat. "They looked almost hunter green, with like, little flecks of amber here and there. Reminded me of this blanket I used growing up." I wrap my fingers tightly around the edge of the table behind me to stabilize myself. Physically? Emotionally? I'm not sure.

"And you have this black freckle on the right one. Right in the iris. I've never seen that before," he shrugs. "Your eyes are *impossible* to keep up with! It's frustrating as hell!"

"So stop trying!"

"Don't you think I am?"

"I don't know what you're doing, Theo!" I cry out, putting more distance between us by extricating myself from the table toward the wall.

"I know what you've been doing. Your stupid cleanse shite. I know about all of it," he says, sardonically, covering his black-rimmed glasses with both hands and releasing a loud groan. I shrink, feeling suddenly awkward and nervous.

"How do you know everything?" I ask, quietly.

"Frank told Liam," he grates the words out vindictively. "I'm going mental, Leslie." He sighs heavily and jams his hands into the pouch on the front of his thin, grey hoodie. "I thought I was done with you. I thought you were out of my mind. I thought, *she's made her choice. Stuff her.* But fuck!" he roars, making me flinch at the volume. "Thinking of your lips on another man's makes me feel positively gutted!"

"So stop thinking about it!" I reply snottily. His head jerks up and his pained expression turns murderous.

"You kissed someone tonight, didn't you?" he barks and I remain silent. "Didn't you?" he roars once more.

"Yes, I did. And it was nice." I don't know why I added the last part. Maybe in retaliation to his shouting. I've never seen him this angry before and I don't really enjoy it.

"Nice," he nods slowly and looks up at me seriously, his eyes hooded. "What if I told you I want to erase every trace of whatever wanker you've been with tonight, Leslie?" He stalks toward me purposefully, a man clearly on a mission.

Shit, I'm trapped.

"I don't even know—" I start, but he closes the last remaining distance between us in a flash and his lips slam into mine, ramming me up against the ivy-covered wall of the house.

I flinch at the harsh contact of the rustling leaves behind me. His hands grip my hips bruisingly, punishingly. I reply back even harsher in my own way. A battle of the mouths has ensued and we're both desperate to make each other pay for the pain we've inflicted on ourselves these past few months.

I grip his cheeks roughly, coaxing his mouth to submit to my own. Both of us kissing hard and fierce, fighting for the power, the upper hand, the dominance. Neither of us giving in to the other.

His tongue plunges deep and severe into my mouth and I meet it with my own. Moving and massaging his. A low rumble escapes his throat and his hands drop down from my hips to my thighs. He pulls my legs up to wrap around his waist, propping me up against the wall. When I've secured my legs tightly, his hands drift up the outer sides of my thighs, higher and higher until I'm fully exposed to him. He pulls my lower lip into his mouth and bites down on it, dragging his teeth along until it springs free.

"Are you not wearing any fucking underwear?" his guttural tone winds me. I pant loudly against his grim expression and shake my head silently. "Why?"

Seriously? He wants me to answer this question *now*? What the fuck! Let's get back to the kissing bit. I crane forward to find his lips again and he pulls back, repeating his question silently.

"I never do!" I bellow, feeling feverishly frustrated.

"Leslie." He says my name in a growl and kisses me savagely, not only erasing any memory of Jarrod's kiss tonight, but every man I've ever kissed. That phrase: ruin you for other men—was just that, a phrase. I'd read it in my romance novels and rolled my eyes at the ridiculousness of it. I'm eating my words now.

"I need to come inside," he says, earnestly running his lips along my jaw and neck, sending all of my lady parts woozing for England.

His words are a sudden wakeup call snapping me out of my aroused state of mind. Letting him inside my house and my heart is not something I want. At all. I shake my head, immediately feeling my protective shield slamming back into place. Whatever's happening right now needs to stop. It's as if my protective autopilot just kicked on—finally. My mind knows without my body listening that it does *not* want to let Theo in.

"Stop shaking your head, Leslie." I try to lower my legs and he grips them tightly and scowls.

"You're not coming inside, Theo," I say, finally digging my voice out of my vagina enough to speak some sense.

"I *need* to come inside, Leslie." He lets my legs drop this time and I blanch at the feel of his arousal as I slide down off of him. He's looking at me in utter shock.

I clear my throat tentatively. "Nothing's changed, except for the fact that I think my lips will be bruised tomorrow." I rub them softly, feeling irrationally turned on by the passionate exchange we just had.

"You've got to be bloody joking," he says and straightens his already straight glasses.

"I can't do this, Theo. I told you. That kiss was…nice. But I'm still not looking for what you want. I'm not wanting a relationship."

"*It was nice.*" He cocks his jaw out, seemingly outraged by my meager description of what just happened. He leans into me, fast and furious…my body hits the ivy wall again. His lips hover millimeters from mine. "I'll show you fucking nice." He shoves himself away from the wall and storms off, down the steps and away from the house.

My breath comes fast and short for what feels like a straight minute. I squat down in the dark alcove, raking my hands through my hair, tears springing to my eyes. Holy fuck. What's happening?

CHAPTER NINETEEN

I wake the next morning feeling crusty and overrun. It's Sunday. The day of rest, right? I wonder if Frank will let me take a break from the cleanse today. I only have two more challenges left though. Maybe it's better to just get them over with.

I thought doing this cleanse would get me out of my funk and interested in life again. So far, all it's doing is getting me interested in Theo. *More.* Exactly what I don't want. Theo so obviously wants something bigger from me, and that makes him dangerous. My heart is not in the position to let someone like him in and I need to remember that next time I'm around him. This cleanse isn't about finding a man, it's about having fun and living life to the fullest. But crying myself to sleep last night sure as shit wasn't fun.

Frank had to go and muck everything up by telling Liam every damn detail. Theo and Liam are best friends, surely Frank knew what he was doing. Sabotage is nigh and I will certainly make Frank pay.

I toss off my quilt, determined to fuck up Frank's morning. It's only eight o'clock, so he's probably still out cold. I heard him clamor in late last night. Obviously he found some fun after I left him high and dry at the bar. Frank is nothing if not resourceful.

I tiptoe out into the quiet hallway, mindful of the creaky spots on the wood flooring. I run downstairs and am happy to see no one else awake. I don't want to be distracted from my plan of payback. I quickly grab a wooden spoon out of the crock on the counter and one of the biggest soup pots I can find.

I dash back up the stairs, out of breath and giggly just thinking about waking Frank up. I pause outside his door, listening for any noises. When I hear nothing, I clasp the knob and swing the door open widely, barging into his room banging the spoon against the metal pan repeatedly. I squint my eyes shut in response to the deafening volume. I smile broadly and open my eyes and feel immediately horrified when I realize I'm gazing at a naked stranger in Frank's bed! The pan and spoon clatter to the ground and I back up quickly, running straight into someone. I swerve around to find Frank wearing nothing but a cowboy hat, a vest, and *oh my god! Chaps! He's wearing chaps and he doesn't have pants on under them!*

"Fuck me, Lezzie! What the bloody hell!"

"Oh my God Frank, cover yourself!" I shield fast, but not fast enough. I got a glimpse of Frank's package and I don't think it was happy to see me. He quickly pulls his hat off his head and covers his crotch, looking decidedly sheepish.

"What are you doing barging in here?" he asks incredulously. His skinny limbs and chest are bare beneath an extravagantly jeweled vest.

I drop my hand to look more closely, then swerve my eyes over to his large dresser.

"That's my bedazzler!" I squeal. "You said you wouldn't use it anymore without asking, Frank! Last time you used up all my jewels!" I stomp over to his dresser, looking inside the tackle box I keep everything in. He's greatly diminished my jewels again, just as I suspected. I glare at him and do my best to stifle a laugh as I watch him shift nervously in his ridiculous getup.

"Why does you playing make-believe with Billy the Kid here have to involve my bedazzler, Frank?" I bite my lip, doing my best to look mad and not laugh.

"Who the fuck is Billy the Kid? This is Lionel and he's almost thirty!" he barks out incredulously.

"Bill the Kid is a famous cowboy from the West, Frank!" A hyenic giggle escapes my lips as Frank just looks at me like a confused and slightly wounded puppy dog.

"I don't understand your American references, Leslie! Why do you do that to me?" he whines out so seriously that I laugh even harder, feeling completely out of control. My legs give out and I drop to my knees howling as I become eye level with the hat covering his crotch.

Frank's face turns homicidal. "Are you quite done, Leslie? Because I'm going to fucking kill you. A slow and painful death." His voice is low and menacing but I'm not the least bit intimidated with him standing there like that.

I peel myself off the floor and turn back to the man in his bed who is the picture of mortified. "I'm Leslie by the way. Frank's best mate." He shakes my hand uncomfortably with a blanket clenched tightly to his chest.

"You fuck with my friend, you fuck with me," I state flatly, eyeing him seriously for a second. When he appears to have heard me, I glance back at Frank who looks embarrassed and blundering.

"It's been real boys!" I shout loudly, stretching casually. "As you were," I curtsey cutely and exit Frank's room with a loud *yeehaw*. I laugh all the through the day as the visual memory of Frank in that hat refuses to leave my psyche anytime soon.

Damn, it feels good to laugh.

CHAPTER TWENTY

"It has to be tonight I'm afraid, Lezzie. No breaks. This is the only night they allow amateurs on the platforms." *Platforms. Oh my God.*

"And I have to dance on these platforms you're saying."

"Correct. Tonight's cleanse is about putting yourself out there, physically. You need to feel confident in your body and your movement, Lezzie. You act like you're an ugly hag and it's positively mental. You're fucking spot on gorge' and tonight will help you embrace that."

I nod and chew my lip thoughtfully as I push through the clothes in my closet.

"There's no need to get ready. They do full hair and makeup there." I screw my face up nervously. Frank winks at me cheekily.

"I'm still mad at you for throwing Theo into this whole sordid affair," I grumble.

"And I'm still mad at you for poking fun at my curlies! There is a population of traditionalist men that don't like to go bare down south. Get over it." I giggle-snort uncontrollably and Frank stares at me deadpan. "Payback is a bitch best served cold, Lezzie. And you'll be plenty cold tonight in the costume they have in store for you."

That sobers me right up.

We walk down the back alley attached to a place called Club Taint in north London.

"This your girl, Frank?"

A large black man inquires, stepping out of the shadows. The word *Security* is stretched tightly across his muscled chest.

"The one and only."

The guard motions with his head for us to enter. I follow Frank down a dark hallway and can hear Skrillex club music thumping through the walls. Frank comes to a sudden stop at a bright red door.

"Now, the only way they'd let you do this tonight is if I told them you were seriously auditioning, so just go along with whatever they say."

"What?" I exclaim nervously as the red door swings open. Standing before us is a tall man dressed in Liza Minnelli drag.

"You're late." His voice is deep and booming. "Get to hair and makeup now, your audition is in fifty minutes."

"Going, going," Frank says, casually. How does he know all

these people without me? I thought I knew everyone Frank knew! It's like he's got this whole secret life I know nothing about!

Frank clasps my hand and pulls me down the hall further into a small greenroom with a row of vanity mirrors and salon chairs. There are two other girls, way sexier than me, getting the final touches of their makeup applied. A crabby looking blonde with a giant hog style nose ring grabs my arm and shoves me into a chair, eyeing me seriously.

"Short hair. That should be interesting," she says, flatly. My hair's not short! It's medium at the very least. I glance at the other girls and notice they all have stringy, fake extensions bringing their locks all the way down to their butts.

Thirty minutes later, I barely recognize myself. I love dramatic makeup just as much as the next girl, but this is a step above. The blonde applied thick, fake lashes and black eye shadow over my entire lid. My eyes look large and dramatic making my green eyes appear almost neon. The contour foundation and blush she applied makes every angle of my face pop. I feel like I'm looking at a different person.

The deep purple lipstick is something I've never tried before, but it looks kind of cool with my auburn locks that she's teased and mussed into a messy rocker vibe. Suddenly, she thrusts a ball of fabric into my chest.

"Change."

"Here?" I ask, looking around for Frank who's suddenly MIA.

Fucking Frank!

"Yes here, come now, no need to act shy. You're on in ten, hurry up." She walks out of the room leaving me with the offensive outfit. I hold up the scrap of fabric and my heart drops. This is so not enough fabric. Shaking my head and mustering up my courage, I quickly shed my clothes—desperate to see if this outfit is as bad as I think it is.

Once dressed, I stare at myself in the vanity mirror having an out-of-body experience. The top is a black halter bikini with thick satin straps that crisscross over my torso and clasp onto the back of the booty short bottoms. I turn to see my ass and feel grateful that not too much of my butt cheeks seem to be hanging out.

Good night, what would my family say if they saw me now?

I tug up the sheer black thigh highs and jiggle slightly to see if they are going to fall down. They seem secure enough. The furry black knee-high leg covers are the real kicker of this smashing ensemble. Go-go dancer through and through. I pray to God no one recognizes me tonight. *Fucking Frank.*

I exit the greenroom and see three other girls dressed in the same outfit as mine. They eye me snottily, drinking in my entire body. I squirm, feeling like the ugly stepsister. All of them have way bigger breasts and way bigger asses than I do. They look like women. I look like a small boy dressed in drag. *Fucking Frank!*

"Oi, listen up!" A man with a clipboard and an attached headset hollers over the loud music. "You have thirty minutes. You're podium one, you're two, you're three, and you're..." he pauses, eyeing me up and down briefly then looks back to his clipboard, "...four. Get out there, give it all you got, and we'll let you know at the end of the night if we want you back for second auditions."

He pauses and presses his headset to his ear, listening closely. A short, Italian-looking man comes by with a tray of tall double shots and I watch each girl grab it and down it without a second thought. I follow suit, wishing I could have four more. Headset guy nods and swirls his hand and we all shuffle closely after him. These platform boots make me feel tall for a change, which is quite nice. That's about the only thing I like about any of this right now. Thank God Frank didn't let any of our roommates come along to tonight's challenge. If he had, I might have to well off and junk punch him. I can't believe I'm about to do this. *Fucking Frank!*

My eyes adjust to the swirly club lights and loud music. I follow in line, snaking through the swarm of Londoners grinding on each other, oblivious to me. Men on men, women on women, men on women, ménages. This club is full of all types.

Headset guy stops at a large glowing platform where another big black security guard is stationed. He holds his hand out to me. I accept it gratefully and step up onto the large, square pedestal. The entire thing is glowing blue and then changes, casting a red glow all over my skin.

The DJ's voice cuts into the music.

"Oi, oi, oi, you sexy Londoners. Round three of auditions are up next, let's give them a rap-tap-tap round of applause and get this party bumping!" The crowd erupts into cheers and I squint when the spotlights swirl around me. A hypnotic beat starts and headset guy gawks at me in annoyance.

Oh, shit, dancing! Right! That's what I'm here for! I begin swirling my hips to the beat and the color of my pedestal shifts to a blazing green. The bright lights of the spotlight make it easy for me to pretend there isn't a crowd of people clustered in all around me. I avoid eye contact with them for as long as I can, knowing that if I look at any of them I'll realize what the fuck I'm doing and piss myself. The music ramps into a great beat I've always loved. As the spots swirl away, my platform changes to an electric blue color. I jump up and down, actually enjoying myself—the double shot warming my veins some. Feeling brazen, I chance a glance down at the crowd around me. About half are watching, the other half are grinding with people on their own.

I continue shaking my ass and feel a sharp zap of shock when my I see my Theo. I mean, Theo, grinding on a tall blonde bombshell. My dancing falters as I squint to make sure it's him. It's definitely him. I'd know that thick muscular build anywhere. He has a certain gate to his movement that's unmistakable. And those fucking sexy glasses!

He looks up as if he can feel my eyes on him. Knowingly, he quips his eyebrows ever so slightly, right in my direction. He then looks down briefly adjusting his leg so it's between the skank's thighs. He smirks cockily. *Fucking Theo!*

Refusing to let him affect me, I drop down low and rise slowly, shimmying my ass the whole way. The crowd apparently digs my sexy move because I hear a rush of cheers and hoots. Theo looks up and eyes me warily. His smirk turns menacing and he pulls the girl close to his chest, his lips dragging along her bare shoulder.

Feeling anxiety rise deep within me, I attempt to look away and continue mindlessly dancing, trying not to watch him—or care. What is he playing at? Why do I even care? Out of the corner of my eye, I look over just as he grabs her face and kisses her like his life depends on it. I stop dancing—my jaw slack in shock. I feel like I've just been slapped, watching painfully as his face eats away at that woman. A shaky gasp quivers in my chest.

"You alright?" the security guard asks me, looking concerned as I stand there completely immobile. Tears prick the back of my eyes as Theo continues molesting the blonde's lips. I shake my head and cover my mouth, unable to stand another second of it.

"I think I'm going to be sick," I say, loudly, desperate to get out of this situation. The security guard turns and grabs me at the waist, hauling me down off the pedestal in one fell swoop. He drapes his arm over me protectively and shoves me through the swarms of people. My eyes boil over with tears as the image of Theo and that girl plays on repeat in my mind.

I gasp for air as the security guard pushes open the door to the greenroom. I clutch my stomach tightly and stumble into the first chair I find.

"I'll get you some water," he says, disappearing out the door.

What the hell is happening to me right now? I can't be this upset over Theo kissing someone! I wanted him to leave me alone. Why is this bothering me so much? I wipe my tearstained face and hear a commotion of arguing coming from the other side of the wall. I stand up on shaky legs and wrench open the door to find Theo, Frank, and the security guard arguing loudly.

"Leslie," Frank says, looking guilty as sin. Theo turns to look at me for the first time, his sexy face marred with worry.

"This guy says he knows you," the security guy says.

"I told you he knows her," Frank says, rolling his eyes. The guard doesn't seem to care what Frank says, he's only looking to me for approval. I nod slightly, turning my sad eyes to Theo.

"You want to see him right now?" The guard sounds territorial and protective. It's sweet really.

I nod again and step back, holding the door open. Theo grabs the bottle of water roughly out of the guard's hand and makes his way over to me.

"I'll be right out here, Leslie," Frank says, as Theo slams the door rudely in their faces. I shake my head and turn toward the wall, feeling physically unable to face Theo. All I can picture is his lips on that blonde bimbo, and it's nauseating. Not to mention, I'm certain I look like a hot mess of runny makeup and tears.

"Leslie." He says my name softly. I brace my fingertips on the wall for support, just to give me something to focus on besides Theo's face. "Leslie," he utters again, reverently.

I laugh pathetically. "You showed me," I croak in a high-pitched tight sound. "You said you'd show me 'nice' and boy did you." I sniff loudly and try to clear my gravelly voice.

"I didn't want to show you anything!" He presses his front to my back, mirroring my braced hands on the wall, encasing me. I can feel the intense rise and fall of his chest and I shiver at his close proximity.

"I just wanted to wake you the fuck up!" His breath tickles the hair on my head.

"I'm awake," I giggle sadly, biting my lip. "Who is that girl?"

"No one."

"You like kissing no ones, do you?" I roll my eyes even though he can't see them.

"I like kissing you," he says, slowly. "I *more* than like kissing you, Leslie." He removes his hand from the wall and grabs my waist softly, turning me to face him. His rough hands on my exposed torso send intimate shooters through my core. I look sideways, unable to make eye contact.

"Can't you see this, Leslie?" he pushes my bangs away from my eyes. "Can't you see this as something more? Don't you feel it?" I shake my head, willing my chin not to wobble. I'm scared shitless right now. Scared of what this could be. Scared of what it could turn into. Scared of letting myself have hope.

"You're all I'm wanting, Leslie. I've been this way since I first clapped eyes on you. I never thought I'd find anyone that could make me truly care again." He strokes his thumb along my cheek, making me feel like putty in his hands.

I finally find the courage to look into his eyes. His glasses frame his glossy brown eyes perfectly. I believe him. I believe every word he's saying, but I still don't understand it.

"Why me?" I ask quietly, looking away quickly, feeling embarrassed and raw.

He scoffs and looks incredulous for a moment. When I refuse to meet his gaze, he rubs his buzzed hair roughly, throwing his hand out. "You shine, Leslie! Christ, you're so bloody blind it's infuriating!"

My eyes snap up to meet his, needing to see into his soul to know for certain if he's full of shit or not. I don't think he can be serious but his veracious expression begs to differ. His face blurs as my eyes fill with tears. I blink quickly, trying to clear my vision. Before I can argue he repeats again, "You *shine* and you *sparkle* and you make me *feel* again."

Speechless. He's rendered me completely speechless.

"I want you...only you." He looks nervous and worried and starts to ramble. "I'm here. I've been looking for you, trying to make you see. I'm sorry I kissed her. I'm sorry I—" I grab his face and pull his mouth to mine, silencing his words.

No more words. No more talking. I have no idea what I'm doing anymore. Wanting Theo, not wanting Theo. I'm completely beside myself trying to figure out how to live this life without any type of love. And then this bruiser of a man pummels in so quickly, I can hardly breathe.

Feeling everything all at once, I break the kiss suddenly and gasp—the sound reverberating loudly in the room. I'm overwhelmed by the emotions behind this kiss. It's too much. He presses his forehead against mine, stroking his thumbs along each of my cheeks as we both breathe heavily, frazzled.

"Please let me in, Leslie." Tears slide quickly down my cheeks at his raw and honest request.

Why? Why does he want me?

"Just say yes," he pants heavily against my lips. I can't think anymore. I can't worry anymore. This is it.

"Please, just say yes," he adds again, softly brushing my lips with his.

"Yes," I whisper.

He exhales a long, ragged breath and crashes down on my mouth.

CHAPTER TWENTY-ONE

"Leslie," he says against my lips, breaking our passionate encounter and my internal warring. "As much as I want you so incredibly bad right now. We need to leave."

My eyes flutter open and I'm reminded of my whereabouts. Yes, I suppose getting acquainted inside the greenroom of Club Taint isn't exactly the most ladylike spot to reconnect. He pulls away from me, adjusting himself slightly and eyes my attire. I place my hands on my hips and smile dumbly.

"Not exactly my style," I snort and he smiles sweetly at me.

"I agree," he adds thoughtfully.

"I'll just change."

"I'll just wait," he says, folding his arms across his broad chest and eyeing me carefully.

"You're going to stand there and wait?" He nods and I roll my eyes. I quickly grab my long cotton maxi dress and throw it on over the top of the black stringy getup. I retract my arms inside the dress and begin undoing the knots and clasps.

"Shy suddenly?" he asks, sliding his hands into the tight pockets of jeans. "You weren't too shy up on that platform."

"That was kind of fun actually!"

"Not for me," he adds, looking grumpy.

"Not all of it was fun for me, I guess. Speaking of which, you probably want to go out and say goodbye to your little friend," I say, tossing my stringy get up right at him. He catches it and holds it to his chest laughing.

"You need to stop."

"Stop what?"

"You know what. She was a means to an end."

"An end to what?" I ask, sliding my feet into my ballet flats and looking around for my purse.

"You running from me." That halts me in my tracks. I shake my head, trying to stop my brain from tossing around all the reasons this is a bad idea.

"What I wouldn't do to get inside that head of yours," he says, reaching out and brushing my bangs back from my eyes.

"It's nothing special, I assure you."

"You have to stop doing that too."

"Doing what?"

"Putting yourself down like you're less than whatever warped idea of perfection you have in your mind. You're fucking perfect, Leslie. Every man in the room wanted you up on that stage tonight. Even some of the gay ones, I think."

I roll my eyes.

"STOP!" he thunders, grabbing my face between his firm hands. "Stop brushing away my compliments like I'm a liar. I'm not a liar, Leslie. You're stunning." He strokes my cheeks tenderly. "Though I do prefer you in your own style." I blush and throw my purse over my shoulder.

"I'm ready."

"No underwear?" he asks, adjusting his glasses. I smirk and bite my lip sheepishly. How did he notice I didn't put any underwear on?

"I have a bit of an aversion to underwear." I screw my lips off to the side, snarkily.

"You're going to be the death of me." He opens the door and we head out to find Frank around the corner chatting with Liza.

"Righto! Everything grand?" Frank asks, looking between Theo and me. I nod a yes. "You wanting to go?"

"I can take her home," Theo says, looking at me seriously like he's expecting me to fight him—or run.

"Are you good, Frank?" I ask.

"You two go ahead. Me and Larry, I mean, Liza have some partying to do." Frank winks at me playfully.

I give Frank a quick peck on the cheek and head toward the back entrance with Theo. We step out into the alley and he gives a tight nod to the security guard that was there when we arrived. He ushers me over to a black BMW and opens the passenger side.

"You have a car?" I ask incredulously. I slide into the tan leather seat and he shuts the door behind me. "I don't know anyone with a car over here," I say out loud to myself.

He hops into the driver's seat and takes off down the dark alley.

"How did you get them to let you park in the alley?" I ask, glancing at him behind the wheel and noticing how sexy he looks. A thin, script tattoo scrawls up the back of his arm from elbow to shoulder. I never noticed that before.

"A hefty tip," he answers, shrugging his shoulders.

"Are you rich?" I blurt out. People with cars in London have to be rich, right? Although Frank is rich and he doesn't have a car. Theo scowls at me and turns his eyes back to the road, remaining silent.

"What's your tattoo say?" I ask, realizing that I seriously know jack shit about this guy.

"It's a Gaelic word," he mumbles half-heartedly. I pause, waiting for him to elaborate, but his lips form a tight line and he doesn't seem to want to say anything more.

"I feel like I don't know you at all, Theo," I say quietly, looking out the window.

"You know all you need to know. The rest is just insignificant." I contemplate that thought for a couple miles.

"Where are we going?" I ask.

"Where do you want to go?"

"Not home."

I'm so not ready to face the Finley firing squad. She'll be relentless about emptying the cracks, and I still don't know what the heck we're doing here. Avoiding the house until things become clearer seems like a great idea to me.

"How about my place?" he asks, the timbre of his voice thick and husky. My tummy has butterflies instantly.

"Yeah, okay. I'm genuinely intrigued, Theo—oh my God!" I still, feeling shocked for a second. "I don't know your last name!" My eyes grow wide.

"It's Clarke," he answers simply.

I giggle and reply, "Like Clark Kent!" He scowls at me in confusion. "Superman's alter ego? Your glasses…ringing any bells?"

His confused expression turns sardonic. "And what's *your* dazzling last name?" he asks, arching his eyebrows at me in anticipation.

I purse my lips and sigh, "It's Lincoln. I know…Leslie Lincoln sounds like a cool celebrity name or something. I'm afraid it's wasted on me."

He grumbles and reaches over and grabs my hand. He pulls it up to his lips and nips the tip of my index finger.

"Ouch! What was that for?"

"For putting yourself down, Leslie Lincoln. It's really getting on my nerves."

I scowl, feeling uneasy at the idea that I'm annoying him already.

"Get over it, Superman," I murmur and he bites down on my finger again, then soothes the area with a warm kiss.

I recognize the neighborhood we're venturing into as it's near my office. I love east London. If I wasn't living with Frank, this is the area of town I'd house hunt in.

He pulls up in front of a decently sized warehouse. It's white-painted brick and looks really similar to my own office. He hits a button on his visor and a hidden garage door opens. He parks in the single-stall garage and ushers me through the attached entry. He turns sharply and begins climbing a steep set of stairs.

"What's in there?" I ask, gesturing to the doorway we just breezed by.

"It's just my workshop," he shrugs his shoulders.

"What do you mean?"

"Where I make my stuff." He looks at me like I should know this.

"I want to see!" I peal, feeling excited to see his furniture. I thought he was just a designer, but now that I realize he actually makes it with his own hands, it's sexy as fuck!

"Let's get a drink first."

I gaze longingly at the door but follow him upstairs. Walking into his flat, it's almost like seeing Theo dressed as an apartment, if that makes any sense. I've never seen a flat that so closely resembles the style of its resident.

It's a wide open studio-style where the kitchen, dining room, and living room all run together. Huge, by London standards. The living room is sunken and framed by two, grid-style industrial windows.

As soon as my eyes land on the dining room set, I can see why the rest of the walls are bare and stark white. This table is a show piece in and of itself. Nestled perfectly alongside a naturally exposed brick wall, I instantly walk toward it to run my hands on it.

"Yours?" I ask, feeling the bumpy, rustic grey wood. It's stunning.

He nods, watching me nervously. The entry table is a similar grey type of wood with lots of really cool, natural ridges. Rustic and primitive. Sexy and manly as fuck.

"These are beautiful, Theo." He shrugs his shoulders. Everything in the flat is so beautiful. All very rustic modern, letting the wood pieces have all the attention.

"I redid the floors last year." They too are a sort of a flawed knotty wood with wide planks. "Wine?" he asks, strolling over to his kitchen and rummaging in the glossy black kitchen cabinets.

"I love your place," I say, accepting a glass of red and appreciating the view from his living room. The expansive windows overlook a concealed little sun terrace with fake grass and potted plants everywhere.

"My room is up there," he gestures behind him and I catch a glimpse of a huge bed in the open loft style area upstairs.

Holy shit. Am I ready for this?

Kissing Theo after saying that small three-letter word changed things between us. As soon as I said yes, he seemed more relaxed, less brooding and pensive. It's nice. I feel lighter too. But I'm starting to doubt whether this is what he will really want in the end. I feel like we've lost that sexual tension and pull that we had before. What if he's starting to regret things now?

"What are you thinking about?"

"You don't want to know," I say flatly, touching the tip of my fake lashes. These will be a bitch to get off.

"Try me," he drawls boldly as I cross my arms and gaze out the windows, the soft blue security light illuminating our faces in his dark apartment.

I sigh heavily. "I'm thinking you'll regret asking me to say yes and chasing after me. Now that you've got me, the excitement is gone and you're realizing I'm dull and painfully ordinary." I form a thin line with my lips, looking at him glumly.

Blinking slowly three times, he seems completely dazed. Collecting himself, he grabs my wineglass from my hand and sets it down on the coffee table. He stands back up, drops his chin, and stalks toward me slowly.

"What are you doing?" I ask, suddenly really aware of my hands and having no clue what to do with them. I cross and uncross them feeling awkward and skittish.

"I'm going to fuck those thoughts out of your head, Leslie."

My heart grows inside my chest and I'm instantly flushed with arousal. Holy tits. I've never had one little sentence elicit such a carnal reaction from me before! He licks his lips slowly and pulls his lower lip in his mouth, shaking his head disapprovingly.

"And now I'm feeling frustrated because I want to undress you slowly right now but I know you're not wearing a scrap of clothing under that dress."

Oh.

"No underwear," he murmurs to himself bending over and grabbing the hem of my dress and dragging it up over my head.

"No bra." His eyes hood as he leans in and drops feather-light kisses across my collarbone. "Fucking stunning." His fingertips trail lightly across my lower back, dangling close to my rear.

"I meant what I said, Leslie. You shine. Your skin is luminous. Like it's just *begging* to be licked, sucked, and…" He captures my nipple in his mouth and I cry out in shock. "Treasured." Holy shit, is this guy for real? He kisses delicately between the mounds of my breasts and then pays just as careful attention to the other nipple.

"Theo," I say in a groan, desperate to see him as he's seeing me right now. I reach up with shaky hands and begin slowly unbuttoning his shirt. I start chewing my lip worriedly, trying to do everything right.

"What is it, Leslie?" he asks, tilting my chin up and dropping a soft kiss on my lips.

"Nothing, nothing. It's just…" I pause, feeling embarrassed. "It's been a while." I say, shrugging nonchalantly, but feeling anything but.

"How long?" he asks.

"Since America." He looks at me confused. "Five years."

He sucks in a harsh puff of air. "You haven't been with anyone in five years?"

I shake my head, feeling foolish. Jesus, he's so gorgeous and I'm an inexperienced loser. I'm not a virgin, but my track record with intimate relationships is very small. This moment feels like losing my virginity to someone super experienced all over again. I turn away and cross my arms over myself. Jesus. I'm butt naked and he's fully clothed still. This is mortifying.

"Hey," he says, turning my face to his. "It's been three for me." He shrugs his shoulders apologetically, the outside light casting mysterious shadows on his beautifully scruffy face.

"For real?" I ask eagerly and then wonder how on earth a man like him could go three years without sex and then choose me of all people to be with. "How is that possible?" I ask, trying to gauge if he is telling me the truth.

"Life…it doesn't matter," he kisses my shoulder tenderly and turns me to face him again.

He looks deeply in my eyes like he's just revealed more to me than I even know. I feel my heart surge with anxiety at the intensity of it. He looks briefly at my mouth and then shrugs out of his shirt.

My eyes feast on his large muscled chest. It's smooth and rigid in all the right places. I bring my hands up and lightly scrape my nails down him. His eyes close tightly and he shudders. When his eyes reopen, he looks nervous and unsure. It's a torturous expression—I can't take it. I pull his face to mine and kiss him ferociously. My leg crawls up his hip, half opening myself to him. The cold of his belt buckle smarts and I retract back, giggling.

"Christ, you're beautiful," he groans. "That laugh." He makes quick work of his jeans and boxers and I'm now staring at his gloriously naked body in a really attractive agog expression.

We both collide into each other, a mess of limbs, lips, hips, and groins. He walks me backwards onto the arm of his grey upholstered couch, laying me back so my hips are propped up on the armrest.

"Jesus, I can't believe this is actually happening," he says, reverently, watching me as I stroke myself in anticipation. I'd rather have him be stroking me, but I'm nothing if not resourceful and this ache I have inside of me is so intense, I've lost all my inhibitions.

He trails his fingers up my calf and inside my thigh. I feel myself clenching tightly when his thumb rubs firmly over my tight nub.

"Oh my God!" I cry. It's been way too long. I forgot how much hotter sex is when it's not with my fucking vibrator!

Sorry hotdog!

He plunges his fingers deep inside me, moving at a feverish rhythm, building me up toward the biggest climax I've had in years. I grab his wrist firmly wanting to stop him but wanting him to keep going at the same time.

"You're going to forget all about running from me, Leslie," he says, as I groan out in blissed-out agony. "You're going to feel *intensely*...my affections for you. And you're not going to run again."

"Yes!" I cry, unable to fully consider his demand but focused so entirely on the building pressure inside of me. His warm breath tickles my inner thighs and I swear it's two quick swipes with his tongue and I'm coming all over his hand and face. "Jesus, Theo!"

He leaves my center for another few seconds and then drags himself up my body, covering me head to toe with his firm rigid build. He kisses me coarsely as I blink dazedly coming down from the intense rush of spasms shooting out all around me.

"Holy shit, that was hot," he says in a shocked tone. My eyes flutter open and he's looking down at me in pure adoration. I smile sheepishly.

"I said it's been a while," I groan obnoxiously and giggle.

"You and me both, Leslie." I take note that he likes to call me by my name. And I like that he does. My name has never sounded more beautiful from anyone's mouth.

"Are you on anything? Birth control or whatever? I have condoms if you're not."

"I thought you said it's been three years?" I frown at him, blinking away my orgasm as much as possible. Why does he have condoms if it's been three years?

"I had high hopes for tonight," he grins wickedly at me.

I whack him on the back and he roars with proud laughter. I've never heard him laugh like that before. I quite like it!

"I'm on the pill—we're safe, if you're sure you're clean?" Gosh, I haven't had to think about this stuff for a while. It feels awkward.

"I'm sure." He kisses me softly, shutting down my awkwardness. He stands up, admiring me draped naked over his couch.

"I'm sure about us, Leslie. This feels so right."

I tilt my head, admiring the hard panes on his chest and the serious expression on his face. Theo wants more from me, but am I prepared to give him that? I've convinced myself since coming to London that I won't be anything like what I left behind in Missouri. I won't get into a relationship that shadows me in a man's wake. And here I am, opening myself up, *literally*, to a man that demands to be heard, no matter what.

"Come here," he holds his hand out to me and I stare at it nervously. "Please?"

That one little word. That one little word makes him pushing to get into my heart a request and not a demand. That one little word is his saving grace.

CHAPTER TWENTY-TWO

He threads his fingers in my hands and pulls me through his dark apartment toward the expansive iron spindle staircase. A long railing extends the length of his bedroom, overlooking his living area downstairs. Another industrial window casts that blue night lighting over the top of his white down comforter. His bed suddenly looks big and scary.

"You okay?" he asks, pulling me into his naked body. We both stand there gloriously naked in his dark room.

"I feel nervous," I say, exhaling heavily into his chest.

"Me too. We don't have to, if…"

"I want to!" I screech and cringe at the desperate tone of my voice. His chest rumbles with laughter. I love hearing him laugh.

"Me too," he kisses me, sweetly at first and then deepens his kiss, sousing his tongue deep into my mouth. So deep, I lose all inhibitions and my nerves evaporate. I'm transformed into a wanton hussie.

He walks us back to the bed and sits down at the base, pulling me on top of him so I'm straddling his lap. He nuzzles his face into my chest and appears to be relishing the feel of my skin on his face.

"So beautiful, so stupidly beautiful and you don't even know it."

I tilt his face up and cover his mouth with my lips. Our kiss turns passionate and frenzied as his erection presses tightly between my thighs. He reaches between us and adjusts himself so he's positioned at my apex. Without breaking our kiss, I slide myself onto him, cringing at the intense tightness.

"Does it hurt?" he looks nervously at my screwed up expression.

"Give me a minute," I groan, feeling the tightness shift slightly. Damn, it's been so long. I shift slightly and the painful bite begins to morph into pleasure. I grind into him, testing out the new sensation. When it starts feeling good, I nod my head in approval.

Theo kisses me sweetly, holding my hip with one hand and bracing his other behind him. He leans back and I gaze longingly at his body, my hands rubbing all over him in appreciation. He begins thrusting himself up and down, his chiseled abs tightening and lengthening with each upshot. I meet his movements and we grind together in perfect rhythm.

Feeling overwhelmed by the build, I drape myself over his shoulder, dragging my open mouth over his exposed skin. *Why did I avoid this for so long?*

"Come for me Leslie. You're close, I can feel it." His voice is harsh and guttural.

"Yeah, okay…" I say stupidly answering his sexy words and dropping a kiss to his shoulder.

"Theo," I gasp, when he bucks into me hard and fast. I come. Oh lord, do I ever come. He wraps both of his arms tightly around my waist, resting his head on my chest and suddenly stills, pulsing his own climax inside of me.

We hold each other silently for a few minutes. The only sounds in the apartment are our ragged breaths slowing.

"I can't believe I met you," he says, pulling back and looking deeply into my eyes.

"What do you mean?" I ask, closing my eyes as he pushes my bangs off to the side.

Oh, it feels so good when he does that.

"You're incredible, Leslie. You have to know that. You have to know how special you are."

I swallow around a hard knot forming in my throat.

"I've *never* felt that before," I whisper softly, my voice catching at my very raw and vulnerable admission. No hiding anymore.

"You'll never feel anything less with me. I *promise* you." He shakes his head disbelievingly. "You shine straight through me. You've brought me back." He kisses me softly on the lips and murmurs against my mouth, "You're impossibly special."

In all my life, I've never felt what Theo's managed to make me feel in a matter of seconds. Knowing my words will only pale in comparison to his, I return his kiss passionately, whispering a simple 'thank you'.

CHAPTER TWENTY-THREE

A constant vibrating sound wakes me from my deep sleep. I crack open my eyes and find myself in Theo's big bed. His arm is draped lazily over my naked waist. His breathing is heavy and long, so I know he's still out cold.

I glance at the clock and see it's almost two in the morning. Holy shit! I don't even remember falling asleep! I push back the white down comforter and pull myself slowly to the edge of the bed, attempting awkwardly to slip out from under his hand without waking him. Man, I bet I look super sexy right now, butt naked and falling gracefully out of this sexy bed!

I right myself and walk my naked butt over to the cast iron railing, peering down to see my glowing phone buzzing away on the dining table. I squint around Theo's bedroom for my dress, but remember I ditched that downstairs last night. *Thanks for that, Theo!*

I wrap myself in a tan cashmere throw blanket that was draped over a leather armchair by the window, and make my way quietly down the steps. I grab my phone and scroll through several missed calls and texts from Finley and Frank, both wondering if I'm okay. I quickly type a reply saying I'm good, not to worry, and I'll talk to them in the morning. I press my phone to my chest feeling an excited bubble deep in my belly. I'm more than okay. I could stay here for days in this happy, sexually sated fog, and not think about anything else.

Oh shit! It's Monday!

I quickly open my work email and send a message telling Vilma I'll be working from home tomorrow—or today, depending how you look at it. Roger's out of the office this week anyway and I know Vilma will cover for me. There's no way in hell I can make it to work bright and early tomorrow. I wonder if Theo has to work.

"Hey," his voice makes me jump and I glance up and see him standing gloriously naked at the railing, looking down on me. How is he so damn comfortable up there on display like that?

"Hey," I reply, feeling slightly foolish standing here gaping at my phone in nothing but a blanket.

"What are you doing?" he looks brooding and nervous.

"Finley and Frank," I answer. He nods slightly, his posture relaxing. "Hey, do you have to work tomorrow? Do you need me to go?" I ask, wondering nervously if he's waiting for me to leave or something.

"No! Why would you say that?" he asks, clearly agitated.

"I don't know…"

"I thought I fucked some sense into you," he interrupts, his tone clipped and annoyed.

"Maybe I need another lesson!" I giggle, attempting to turn his frown upside down. I'm rewarded with a sexy smirk.

"So, you don't have to work tomorrow?" I ask one more time.

"Not really, you?"

"Not really..." I'm totally lying right now. I desperately need to work but I know I can catch up on whatever I let slide for one day. The life of designers. "I want to see your workshop."

He nods and smiles, disappearing briefly and reemerging in a pair of low slung lounger pants and leather flip flops. I'm decidedly pleased he opted not to put a shirt on.

"Hang on. I'll just throw my dress on."

"No way," he says, grabbing my phone-clasped hand and pulling me to the door.

"What do you mean, no way?"

"I like you like this. Then I know you're not going to run." He smirks, but there's a sadness pulling at his eyes that makes my heart hurt. I decide not to argue and follow him down the narrow staircase.

He flicks the light on and the fluorescents flash once and then cast a cool, greenish glow over everything. It's a large room with particle board flooring covered in sawdust.

"Slip those on," he points to a pair of leather slip-on loafers. I oblige and giggle at my tiny feet in his huge shoes. He smirks at me. "Well, this is it."

There's a long wooden workshop table right down the middle of the room. It's covered with several pieces of rough, untouched wood and electrical tools and machinery. The far wall features several wooden pieces similar to ones in Theo's apartment at various stages of development.

"That's the showroom over there," he says, gesturing to another door.

"You sell it here too?"

"Well, it's not like a retail store. It's appointment-only kind of sales. My brother Hayden does all that."

"So, it's a family business?"

"Sort of. This is a separate entity. My dad has a large furniture distribution center in Essex. He runs that with my Granddad. They sell more commercial items, mass market stuff to hotels and chain restaurants. This is just a custom branch we started about five years ago."

"How old are you, Theo?" I ask, once again reminded of how little I know about a man who's just been so intimate with me.

"Thirty. How old are you, Leslie?"

"I'm twenty-six, going on sixteen," I state snarkily. "I didn't know I was dating old balls though!" He laughs heartily and I lose my faux serious expression, instantly enjoying the sound of his laugh as he props his arms on the long workshop table. The muscles in his back glisten in the light at his hunched stance. I catch a glimpse of that tattoo up the back of his arm again.

"You like working with your brother? Do you have any other siblings?" I ask casually, trying to dig deeper. I awkwardly crawl up onto the metal stool next to him, attempting to keep the blanket tight around my chest.

He looks down nervously clearing his throat. "My sister Daphney just finished her A-Levels—she's working with my dad. My mom is home fulltime now."

I nod and smile.

"What about your family?" he asks, turning and hoisting himself up onto the high table.

"What about them?" I ask, feeling uncomfortable now that I'm under the spotlight. My family is not the picture perfect family to chat about.

"Siblings?"

"A brother. We're not very close," I say simply.

"What about your parents? They must miss you now that you're living so far from home."

I think about that statement for a moment. Do my parents miss me? They sure don't act like it. I really only ever speak with my mom, and even then, she doesn't mention anything about me coming back. Things have changed so much between us.

I shrug my shoulders, giving him a non-answer. He eyes me curiously. Deciding a change of subject is in order, I slide off the stool and position myself between his legs. He smiles softly at me brushing my bangs back once again. I was planning to get them trimmed again but the feel of him doing that all the time is so wonderful I'm reconsidering.

"What's going on in that head of yours?"

I shrug again and bite my lip. Mustering up all the courage I can, I release the blanket to the floor. He sucks in a harsh breath and eyes me gravely.

"Leslie."

"Theo."

"There's dangerous machinery in here."

"I know." I wag my eyebrows at him and glance down to his

growing groin area.

"You are…" he pauses, looking curiously at me for a moment. "Are you sure you're real?"

"One way to find out," I whisper, grabbing his neck and pulling him to my mouth, losing myself in his drugging kiss.

CHAPTER TWENTY-FOUR

"Hey," I whisper-answer my phone when Finley's number comes up on my caller ID.

"You okay?" she asks with an edge to her voice.

"Yeah, I'm cool. You?"

"I'm fine, Lez. I'm not the one who's not at home right now! Mind telling me where you are?"

"I think you already know that answer, Finny." I drop my voice to a quiet whisper, attempting to conceal myself in Theo's kitchen so my voice doesn't carry up to his loft. It's only eight o'clock and the blazing sunlight and my dumb phone vibrating woke me up again, forcing me out of our cozy love nest upstairs.

"I do know the answer," she snickers. "Was it good? Did it happen after midnight?"

"What? And yes. I mean…wait, midnight? Why midnight?"

"The final step in the cleanse! Today is day seven. If you did it after midnight last night, then you completed the one-night stand in Frank's cleanse! That was the last one!"

I scowl and turn to glance upstairs, feeling nervous. I nearly choke when I see a half-naked Theo standing right next to me. Holy shit, how did he sneak up on me like that?

"Fin, I gotta go," I say, quickly taking in the thunderous expression on his face.

"One-night stand," he barks, before I can even manage to end the call.

"Why are you sneaking up on me?" I cringe away from the anger radiating off his sexy body.

"Answer me, Leslie!"

"I didn't hear a question!" I grip the blanket around me tightly, feeling uncomfortable being so naked when he's acting like this.

"Was I a fucking one-night stand?" he roars and I flinch at the deafening volume.

His tone and his question infuriate me. After everything we shared last night and everything he said to me when we were having sex, this takes the fucking cake. Gaping at him for just a second, I storm past him—purposefully smacking his shoulder with mine. I grab my dress up off the floor and fling it over my head.

"What are you doing?" he asks, grabbing my arm and whirling me around to look at him. His stubble is even longer this morning and his serious eyes look tense and wary behind his glasses.

"I'm calling a cab," I say flatly. It's taking everything I have to maintain a level head right now, but my red-headed temper is rearing her ugly head—and she's pissed as fuck.

"You're not leaving," he cries dramatically. "You just got here!" He scrubs his hands over his hair and looks around panicky.

Feeling dejected and overwhelmed by him thinking so little of me, I shove my arms into my sleeves. My eyes prickle with tears and I feel pissed for feeling emotional. I toss the blanket on the couch and glance around for my shoes.

I look up and Theo's eyeing me nervously, trying to gauge what's happening right now. My shield is slammed securely in place. He is not getting to me. I refuse to let him bulldoze me into feeling like a bad person right now. If he wants to think so little of me—that shit's on him. Not. Me. I sniff hard, mentally pulling my tears back inside of me.

I attempt to not ogle his rippling muscles as he starts pacing angrily across the living room floor. He rubs his hands over his buzzed hair anxiously and looks at me with a raw, desperate expression.

"This took so much for me, Leslie. So much! You don't even know!" he stops and looks anxious as I slide my feet into my shoes and throw my purse on my shoulder. Now frantic, he takes a huge gulp of air and holds it tight and high in his chest. I stare at him, waiting for a loud exhale because it seems strange to talk to someone when they aren't breathing. After nearly a whole minute, his face starts blotching with red because he still hasn't exhaled. Holy fuck, why isn't he breathing?

"Theo, breathe!" I cry, feeling scared to death and dropping my purse to the ground. I run over and shove my hands into his chest and the momentum forces him to whoosh out a huge swarm of air. My heartrate thunders beneath my chest as he gasps for breath and grips my arms pleadingly.

"Why did you do that?" I ask, flashing my eyes between his

quickly, unsure which eye will tell me more.

"You can't leave, Leslie. Please," he croaks.

That word again.

"I'm not leaving, Theo," I reply, knowing there's no way I can possibly walk away from him in this moment. "But you can fuck off if you think that what we did last night was a one-time thing for me." He purses his lips and nods acquiescingly.

"I'm sorry," he rushes out and kisses me chastely on the lips. It feels uncomfortable and forced. I hate it. I grab his cheeks in my hands, my eyes roving over his entire face.

"What's going on?" I ask again and he shakes his head pleadingly at me, like he's begging me not to ask.

"I don't want to tell you, Leslie," he groans and hugs me. My cheek hits his bare chest and his heart is hammering rapidly. What is going on?

"Theo, I need to know why you're freaking out. You're scaring me!" Why did he do that to himself?

"I'm sorry. I'm not crazy, I swear. I thought I was better," he says, and his voice cracks at the end. I pull away from him and see tears slip down his face.

"Better from what?"

He sighs, clearly warring with himself on what to say next.

"Not now, Leslie. Please. Not yet. I just got you here. I can't get into it all. I promise you, it's okay. I'm okay. I'm not scary. Do you truly feel afraid of me?"

His eyes bear into mine, raw and vulnerable, telling me so much more than words can say. Despite myself, I believe him. I'm not scared of him or what he's not telling me.

"You'll tell me someday?" I ask quietly.

His nod is almost imperceptible. "Can we just go back to bed…please?"

That damn word. I pull him into me, hugging away his pain and he leads me under his arm, back upstairs. We reach the bed and he pulls my dress off over my head and tucks me in. He slides his pants off and sets his glasses on the nightstand, then crawls in behind me, spooning me skin-to-skin. I pull his hand up to my mouth and kiss it, feeling his breathing begin to regulate again. Mine slows with his 'til eventually, sleep takes me.

CHAPTER TWENTY-FIVE

I wake a short while later, glancing at the clock. It's after ten. Shit. I really need to get home. I roll over and am greeted by a smiling Theo.

"Hey, you're awake. Did you not sleep?"

"Yeah, I did. I just woke up a bit ago."

"And you're watching me sleep. You creepy bastard." I giggle and nuzzle into his chest. Damn this feels so right.

"I was just thinking about that night at Shay…when you blew me off." He snickers, dropping a soft kiss into my mess of wild auburn hair.

"Oh God, don't remind me of that night ever again."

"Um, that's not going to be possible because that night was unforgettable."

I groan and cover my face.

"You were so fucking beautiful, Leslie."

"Oh yeah," I reply sardonically. "A beautiful orgasming-hussie climaxing on a stranger's leg."

"I resent that."

"Resent it all you want. That was the single most embarrassing moment of my life."

His chest vibrates with mirth. "I'm glad I got to be a part of it." He bites his lower lip playfully. "You have no idea what that did to me," he starts, and I frown, wondering where he's going with this.

He rolls over onto his back, staring at a spot on the ceiling. I prop my head on my hand, listening intently. "I'd been in such a fog for three whole years—a state of numbness. And then I saw you…" he says, smirking as if remembering a private joke. "You were dancing like nobody was watching. You weren't trying to look cool or sexy, you were just laughing. You were laughing so bloody hard I found myself laughing with you! I was drawn to you." He looks at me seriously. "I was desperate to know you. To know what kind of person can be that incredibly happy."

I gape at him. Is he fucking with me right now?

He ignores my stunned expression and continues, "And then when I touched you, it was like your body was hardwired to mine. Every movement, every flick…every adjustment…you were so…" he pauses, grinning mischievously, "*Responsive.*"

I smack his chest and he laughs buoyantly. It's a great deep resonance that stirs the warm fuzzies inside of me. "I knew then I had to have you." He pulls me down onto his chest, kissing the top of my head.

"Sorry I made you work so hard," I whisper, feeling slightly ashamed of my behavior. God, how many times did I run from him?

"You're worth it," he says, seriously, trailing his fingers languidly up and down my spine. I feel a familiar stirring in my core and know that if I don't get out of this bed soon I'll be here for another couple of hours. Plus, I don't know how many more compliments I can take. It all gets to be a bit much for me to accept.

"As much as I love this walk down memory lane, I really have to be going."

"No," he groans and squeezes me into him.

"I'm afraid so. I just got back from vacation and have so much work to catch up on."

"Can I see you tonight?" he asks nervously. I look up at him to stroke my hand along his whiskered jawline.

"Yeah! You want to come over to mine maybe?"

"Definitely," he kisses my fingertips, tracing his lips. "You have time for a shower? Please?"

Well, only because he asked nicely.

CHAPTER TWENTY-SIX

I feel like I'm about to do the walk of shame as I pull my dress from yesterday on over my freshly-showered body.

"I said you could have some of my clothes," Theo says, strolling into the bathroom while tugging his shirt down over himself. I feel a brief moment of sadness at his covered body, but shit, he looks just as hot in jeans and a t-shirt, so I guess I'll deal.

"That's an even worse walk of shame…to flounce home in another man's baggy clothes."

"Not *another* man. *Your* man." I look up quickly at the label he's just slapped on us so brazenly. My knee-jerk reaction is to resist the title and get the hell out of here. I'm battling against all my old insecurities about being under a man's thumb because I think Theo could be the exception for me. *At least I hope so.*

"My man?"

He looks at me incredulously. "I'd prefer it!"

I shrug my shoulders. "Okay, okay…my man. Keep your shirt on." He flashes a dazzling smile and grabs me roughly on the sides, pulling me into him. I squeal at the assault on my ribs and he laughs down happily at me.

"I thought you liked me with my shirt off."

"Mmm, I do. This is quite a pickle we're in." I bite my lip and stroke my hands over his pecks appreciatively. Needing something, anything, to distract me, I look around his bathroom taking in the all-white tile on the walls. "There's a lot of white in your place. Not much color. Are you opposed to color?"

"I like red," he says, nuzzling his mouth into my neck.

"You like red…" I repeat sarcastically. "Let's get moving you cheeky bastard."

We head down the stairs to his garage, laughing obnoxiously at a redhead joke I shared. Just as we reach the bottom, a taller, more slender version of Theo strolls in casually.

"Theo—" The man pauses, and stops mid-greeting, looking at me in obvious surprise.

"Hayden," Theo responds in a clipped tone, all his humor and lightness evaporated in seconds. He looks up at me uncomfortably and I blanch at his expression. "Uh, this…this is Leslie." He introduces us but doesn't move to let me down the stairs to shake his hand or anything.

Hayden continues to stare at me with his jaw dropped. Jesus, what the hell? Do I have fangs or something?

"Sorry, right. Hi Leslie," he says, shaking off his stupor and reaching awkwardly past a stiffened Theo to offer his hand to me. I give him a quick onceover and smile brightly. "I'm the brother."

"Oh! You're Theo's brother. Of course! Nice to meet you!" I say, looking more closely at him now. They look a lot alike. Hayden's clothes are quite a bit sloppier though, and his demeanor makes him appear younger. He doesn't really exude that air of mystery and confidence that Theo does. Although, looking closely at Hayden's face, it seems like it looks aged beyond his years. Long and haggard somewhat—like he's hungover.

"We have to go," Theo says, broodingly, and turns his back on his brother. He motions for me to go through the door first. He looks at me expectantly and I glance back at Hayden apologetically while I head into the garage.

Theo and Hayden exchange a few words while I stand awkwardly by his car. He then comes out and opens the door for me. I get in, wondering what's up with him right now. As he navigates through the busy streets of London, I start feeling offended about how that introduction went. I can't figure out why he was so reluctant to let me meet his brother! He goes from calling himself 'my man' in the bathroom to acting ashamed to introduce me to his family. I know we're still new in whatever relationship we have going on right now, but that's just bloody rude!

"How old is your brother?" I ask, tearing Theo's pensive attention away from his thoughts and back to me.

"Twenty-four."

"That's quite young to be running the business side of things all on his own."

"He's not all on his own. My parents help him a lot."

"What about you?"

"What about me?"

"Do you help Hayden?"

"No. I just make the orders. I have zero interest or time to manage the business side of things. Besides, Hayden needs to learn how to help himself."

What the hell does that mean?

"You know, I'd rather not talk about my brother. You don't need to worry about him."

"Did you not want to introduce me to him?" I ask boldly.

"No! 'Course not! Why would you even say that?" He looks affronted.

"You were a Grumpy Gus back there! Shooing me out the door like you're ashamed of me, barely letting me shake his hand."

"That's bloody preposterous. Why would I ever…"

"Then what was that?" I ask.

He's silent for a moment, the veins on his neck pulsing viciously beneath the skin.

"My brother and I have a strained relationship." His tone is clipped and short.

"Like how?"

"Like, *strained*. I'd rather not get into it all."

I want to ask more, but he's pulled up alongside the curb in front of my place and the tension in the car is palpable.

Feeling frustrated at his cryptic answers, I wrench the door open and fly out of the car. I glance back and see Theo roll his eyes and jump out after me. He catches me just as I hit the bottom step.

"Leslie, please." He wraps his arms around me from behind, clasping me in a tight hug with my back to his front. "I'm sorry," he utters softly into my hair.

"I don't know what the fuck your issue is right now, Theo. But if you don't want me to run from you, you shouldn't act like you're ashamed to introduce me to your family."

He laughs slightly and that just infuriates me more. I attempt to break out of his iron-tight grasp and he turns me around to face him.

"I'm sorry, Leslie. It's just crazy that you think I'd ever be ashamed of you. Christ, you're bloody perfect." He pushes his arms under mine, holding me intimately around my waist so our hips are flush against each other. "My brother is a sensitive subject for me. I'm sorry. I'm not used to this stuff."

"What stuff?"

"Having someone I care about in my life." He shrugs his shoulders. I relax my tense stance at that admission. I can relate, I guess.

"Okay."

"Okay?"

"Yeah, yeah. I get it. Sorry. Old insecurities and all that."

He kisses me sweetly, stroking his thumbs along my cheeks. "You're so beautiful. I'm not going to get shite done thinking about you being naked in my workshop."

"Well, that's too bad you're so obsessed with me. I have lots to preoccupy my thoughts today—none of which include you!" I turn my nose up at him playfully, trying to conceal my smirk.

"Get your ass inside before I come upstairs and remind you," he growls, nipping at my ear.

"Going, going." I turn to make my way up the stairs. "Catch ya later, Superman," I throw over my shoulder.

He shakes his head at me and I jog inside feeling giddy again, our previous misunderstanding completely forgotten.

CHAPTER TWENTY-SEVEN

I waltz into our house and Mitch gazes at me curiously from the dining room table. Frank comes bouncing down the stairs and his eyes bug out of his head as I approach.

"The dancing tart returns," Frank sings loudly, descending the stairs. I roll my eyes, climbing up to meet him halfway. "Lezbo, Lezbo, Lezbo." He tsks his teeth together in an admonishing tone. "I'm shocked by you. I thought I'd never see the day where you do the walk of shame."

"I'm not ashamed," I bark back confidently.

"No? So does that mean Theo old boy broke through your ice-cold heart?"

I scowl at him. "I couldn't possibly know what you mean." I look around briefly. "Where is everybody?"

"Finny and Jules are at work. Brody is at a job interview. And Mitch is being a lazy bastard."

"I can hear everything you guys are saying," Mitch's voice cuts into Frank's and my little stairwell rendezvous.

Frank and I both ignore Mitch. "And what are you doing, exactly?" I ask, knowing that I wonder most days what the hell Frank does with all his time.

"I've been tallying your score of course!"

"My score?"

"Yes, you didn't quite finish Frank's seven-day cleanse, so I'm not sure you're going to get your reward."

"What reward?"

"Oh, I don't know." He looks up coyly, kicking his feet.

"What's the reward? I have to know! And I did too complete the cleanse! The last day was to have sex, right? I did that…three times! So that's gotta be extra credit."

"Can still hear you," Mitch states flatly.

"Stop listening, perv!" Frank bellows.

"Kind of hard when you guys are literally shouting everything you're saying."

"Are we shouting?" I whisper-giggle and Frank's eyes twinkle with excitement. He shakes his head at me and swirls his finger by his temple like Mitch is crazy.

"The only way you'll complete the cleanse, Lezbo, is if it's just a one-night deal with Theo. I'm quite certain we haven't seen the last of him though."

"No…I don't suppose we have." I smile meekly.

"But shite, three times? That might just give you the extra credit you'll need to tip you over the edge!"

I smile, realizing Frank's crazy cleanse may have actually worked!

My killer reward is a shopping spree at a pop-up vintage store that Frank's known about for weeks and not told me. It's located just off Brick Lane and is chock-full of chaotic secondhand craziness—accessories, shoes, and hidden diamonds in the rough. I lose the rest of the day digging through everything. My huge find was this gorgeous 1950s vintage Chanel cocktail dress. I get into a near-screaming match with Frank when I discover he's purchased it for me while I was changing back into my street clothes.

"That dress isn't even your real prize! I was going to take you over to Umar's and get you a new hotdog for your real reward."

I full-on belly laugh as we walk back to the house and he chuckles with me knowingly. My old hotdog might be going into retirement for a bit.

Finley gets home and bombards me in my room for all the dirty details and we lose two hours giggling about the craziness of it all. Theo and I definitely didn't have a traditional start to our relationship, but I'm finally wrapping my brain around the fact that that's what this is turning in to—a proper relationship. I'd be lying if I said the idea of it doesn't give me pangs of anxiety, but the giddiness outweighs the anxiety, so I'm soldiering on for now.

By the time Theo shows up, I haven't even looked at a scrap of work all day. I'm going to be paying for that tomorrow, for sure. I feel nervous and giddy opening the door to him. It's great how excited I feel to see him again already.

He grabs my hand and yanks me out on the front step and into the enclosed patio area, smashing me up against the ivy wall. He covers my mouth and kisses me completely senseless.

"What was that for?" I ask, breathless—and, I'm not gonna lie, pretty aroused.

"I wanted to make a better memory out here." He kisses my nose and then drags me back inside like he's completely unaffected by our little exchange.

We join my roommates in the living room. Everyone chats casually and I'm stunned at the normalness of it all. Me and Theo. Finley and Brody. Mitch and Julie. Frank never seems to mind being the fifth wheel but I make a mental note to ask him about his friend from the other morning. We order Indian takeout and watch *Outlander* well into the night.

When ten o'clock rolls around, I've had enough togetherness with my roommates. I silently drag Theo out of the living room. Finley smirks up at me knowingly. I glare at her before pulling Theo upstairs to my bedroom.

He looks huge in my room for some strange reason as he walks around eyeing everything curiously. I perch myself on my daybed, drinking in his sexy swagger.

"I never got a proper snoop the last time I was in here." He wags his eyebrows at me.

I flush at the memory of the passionate exchange we had and the fact that I was in my onesie cheetah PJs.

"Why do all of our first memories together involve me making an ass out of myself? Seriously, why wasn't I cool and put-together in just one of those instances?"

He smirks lazily at me. "If that's you making an ass of yourself, I don't want to see you when you're on your A-game. I wouldn't have a shot in hell."

I giggle at the notion of Theo thinking I'm too good for him. God, he's delusional as hell.

"That night…before," he starts, looking serious all of a sudden at the memory of our PJ encounter. "That was the first time that I actually knew without a doubt that I had true feelings for you. Before then, I thought you might just be a passing fancy. But when I was here that night and I saw you singing crazily in your pajamas, I…" he falters on his words momentarily. "It was still there for me." He shrugs his shoulders. "All those feelings I thought might be gone. I just knew you were more."

"I was terrible to you, wasn't I?" I ask quietly

"You definitely wounded me." He crosses his thick arms and leans back on my desk. "I went home and tried to forget about you. I tried to tell myself you were a horrid bitch and that I was better off without you. And I was doing a right good job of it until Liam came over and told me he ran into Frank. Frank told Liam his entire schedule, you know. That's how I knew where you were every night."

"Liam," I huff softly.

"I wouldn't just blame Liam in this scenario." I look at him quizzically. "Frank had you on a romantic cleanse but he seemed very keen on giving Liam every stop on his list. Surely that wasn't for Liam's benefit."

Fucking Frank!

"But you didn't show up on the make out challenge night?" I ask, remembering how disappointed I was when he didn't show.

"I couldn't. I knew if I showed up and saw you kissing another bloke—I'd go nuclear." I cringe at his honesty.

"But I couldn't stay away completely. Then you walked up looking fifty shades of gorgeous and I felt like my whole world was being pulled out from beneath me." He looks at me, heat flaring in his eyes.

"You made me crazy, Leslie." He strolls over to me and stands above me by my bed.

"I'm the worst," I reply glumly.

He tilts my head up to meet his. "Like I said before…worth it." I roll my eyes and he growls at me. "Do you need another reminder-fuck, Leslie?"

I nod my head eagerly like a panting dog and he chuckles, catching my mouth with his. Feeling his laugh on my lips sends my heart into an emotional tailspin as he slowly leans me back onto my bed, pressing deep, drugging kisses on me.

He perches himself over the top of me and drags his shirt off over his head. I remove my own and he eyes my chest with appreciation.

"No bra again, Leslie? You're so bad," he kisses me, undoing the zipper on my skinnies and sliding his hand down into my pants. His fingers rub firm and brisk over the top of my clit. I break our kiss and cry out loudly at the pleasantly harsh sensation.

"Shhh…roommates, Leslie." His eyes are smiling with mirth. "What am I going to do with you?"

"Embrace it, Superman," I say saucily, pecking his lips.

"Superman." He shakes his head and sends me flying into a state of sexed-out, rocked-out, blissed-out satisfaction.

CHAPTER TWENTY-EIGHT

I kiss Theo goodbye on our front stoop. It's early. Too early. Our normally busy street is way too quiet as the sun slowly creeps up, waiting for the Londoners to join in the day. The loud clack of a skater crashing across the street is the only noise on the block.

"I want to take you on a proper date tonight. Somewhere nice. Would you be up for that?" Theo asks, standing one step below me so our faces are eye level. It's a nice vantage point for me to stare into those pale brown eyes ensconced in his Clark Kent glasses.

I place my arms cockily on his shoulders. "You know what? I have just the dress!"

He chuckles and drops a soft kiss on my lips. "Pick you up at eight?"

"I'll see you then, Clarke." I giggle, testing out his last name for the first time. He smirks knowingly at me.

It's insane how much you can miss someone you've only just met. Well, met properly. And by *met* I mean had sex with five times in two days. I chew on my pen at my desk, slowly closing my eyes and recalling Theo's lips on every surface of my body. God, how have I been avoiding sex for this long?

"Earth to Leslie!" Vilma's voice shatters my sexy daydream. "Christ love, I've been calling you for ages."

"Sorry Vilma. What'd you need?" I ask, shaking my thoughts away and squinting at the design I've been working on for the better part of the day.

"Are you going to tell me about him?" she wheels her big leather chair over to my area and props her head on her fist, obviously waiting for a big story.

I smile secretly and give her an admonished look. "I don't know who you're talking about."

"Oh come off it, Leslie! You look properly fucked!" she whispers the word just as Benji walks by and gives us a horrified expression and awkwardly scampers away.

"Nice one!" I admonish

She screws her face into an apologetic look. "Poor bugga', he's probably going to cry himself to sleep tonight. He's got it so bad for you."

"Would you stop with that?"

"It's true. Aww, poor little Benji needs a good snogging. We should try to set him up."

"I don't know anyone his age."

"Me neither," she states sadly. "So come on, tell me a little bit. Pretty please?"

I laugh as she gives me a pouty lip and I know I'm fighting a losing battle by trying to keep this from her.

Vilma is decidedly depressed after I recount the major highlights of my Theo love life. She promises to make 2016 her year and find a proper bloke to moan over at the office, just like me. I'm sure that won't be hard for her. She's got that willowy runway body and golden blonde hair after all.

"I saw you talking to Ethan the other night. What did you think of him?"

"I didn't think much! Talk about a player! No way. I may be blonde, but I'm not dumb."

"Probably a good call there." She nods and rolls back over to her area so we can both get back to work.

"Oh my God, Leslie! You look so beautiful!" Julie peals as she strolls by the bathroom, catching Finley and I putting the final touches on my outfit.

"Doesn't she?" Finley agrees, curling a wayward piece of hair in the back.

"Thanks, Julie. Thanks, Finley," I add as she sets the curling iron back down on the vanity. "I think I'm ready!"

"That's good because your bloke is downstairs," Mitch says, sullenly walking past us in the hallway.

"He is?" I ask, feeling panicky. "Shit! Thanks Mitch!" I scurry into my room and throw on the vintage merlot wedges I found with Frank.

"Relax, Lez. He'll wait."

"Is everything where it should be?" I ask, nervously smoothing the bodice of my dress.

"It's perfect," Julie sings dreamily, leaning on the doorframe and gazing at me longingly.

I check myself over one last time in my floor length mirror. God, this dress is stunning. Nothing tops vintage Chanel. It's got a boned, strapless satin bodice striped in burgundy and ivory. The knee-length skirt is full and wide in a spotted organdy. My top looks petite, but the full skirt makes me feel curvy and womanly. The fifties knew what they were doing with clothes.

Finley hands me my black clutch and smacks my ass playfully. "Go get 'em tiger!" she winks. I giggle-snort my way down the hall.

I falter on the first step when I take in Theo's back as he stands talking to Frank in the foyer. His ass looks hot as hell in a pair of fitted, grey, tweed slacks. They are slim, all the way down to his expensive black dress shoes. On the top he's wearing a tight, thin, black sweater that shows all the muscles in his back.

He turns, hearing Finley and I begin our decent. He adjusts his glasses as his eyes turn wide and appreciative.

"Leslie." He says my name reverently as I hit the bottom. He grabs me and instantly pulls me into his arms. "You weren't kidding when you said you had a dress," he whispers into my ear. "You look radiant." He kisses me sweetly on the cheek, his whiskers grazing my cheek ever so slightly.

"She does, doesn't she?" Finley smiles, sitting on the steps with her head propped in her hands. Brody comes strolling out of the dining room eating a bowl of cereal. He pauses, taking in my dress.

"Lez! You look great!" he says, good-naturedly.

"Okay guys, you have seen me dressed up before," I say, feeling awkward from all the attention.

"Not like this," Finley says with a dramatic sigh.

Brody rolls his eyes. "Don't mind her. Stop scaring Leslie's date, Fin." She scowls briefly and then looks back at me, resuming her dreamy smile.

"Ready?" Theo asks. I nod eagerly as he opens the door.

"Oh, Lez, you got a tic?" Frank asks right before I follow Theo out the door. Theo frowns briefly in question when I hold one finger up to him.

"What's up?" I ask curiously.

"I just had an accessory that would go perfectly with your new dress. I know how much you love it, so I thought I'd give it to you tonight."

I'm completely unaware what he's referring to but I feel touched! He scurries over to the closet by the entry and I glance at Theo waiting patiently on the front step. I turn back just as Frank pulls his cowboy hat out of the closet.

He turns and smiles wickedly at me. "I think this would go perfectly with your outfit…curls and all." He smirks victoriously at me, clearly pleased with his little attempt at a joke. He holds it out for me to take and I see Theo out of the corner of my eye, watching us curiously.

I grab the hat from Frank and hold it up to my nose, inhaling deeply.

"Yep," I say, seriously. "It's just as I suspected."

"What?" Frank asks, clearly confused.

"It smells like your junk." His jaw drops in horror. "Sorry, Frankie, I'll have to pass tonight. Maybe tomorrow though!" He falters, searching for a witty retort but comes up empty-handed. "Your friend the other morning seemed to like it. You should give him a call. He was cute!" I wink at him and kiss his cheek affectionately.

"I'll bloody well call him when I good and feel like it," Frank grumbles dejectedly as I stroll out the door.

"You don't want to know," I say to a confused Theo as he waffles his hand with mine.

"Wasn't even gonna ask," he says, chuckling softly.

CHAPTER TWENTY-NINE

Dinner out is beautiful. Theo takes us to Skyline Lounge which has a stunning vantage point of the London skyline. It's places like this that remind me what an exciting city I live in. God, I love London.

We split a bottle of red and I feel warm, fuzzy, and sexy. Theo continues glancing down at my chest throughout dinner.

"I'm feeling rather objectified, Superman," I coax saucily.

"There's a bow on your chest. It's like asking me to unwrap you. You can't blame a bloke for struggling." I giggle at his deadpan expression. "Honestly, as soon as you walked down those stairs, the only thing I wanted to do was turn you around and march you right back up so I could fuck you senseless."

"What stopped you?"

"Might have been the welcoming committee," he winks, clearly amused by my loving roommates.

"They are sweet."

"I don't disagree." He tweaks his eyebrows playfully.

"They're my pseudo family here in London. I don't know what I'd do without them."

"Why aren't you close with your real family? I mean, I know you're separated by thousands of miles, but still…what's the story there?" he asks.

I feel myself recoil, pulling out all my armor and tossing it haphazardly out to the line of fire, preparing for battle. This is not a conversation I want to have. Not now. Not ever.

"Just not close," my smile is saccharinely sweet but I can tell Theo's not buying it.

"Want to chat about *your* family?" I ask, pretty certain I know the answer to that question.

He squints skeptically but lets it go, seemingly wanting to protect his own secrets just as ardently as he wants to know mine. Both of us obviously have family issues and neither of us seem too keen on sharing. I feel anxious for how long we'll be able to get away with not opening up.

"Did you want to stay at your place or mine?" he asks, pouring the last bit of wine into my glass.

"Are we spending the night together, Superman?"

He looks up at me in confusion. "Why wouldn't we?"

I shrug my shoulders. "We've been together the last two nights. I thought maybe you'd want a break from me."

"I don't want a break, Leslie. In fact, I was going to ask you if you wanted to leave some clothes at my flat since your office is so close to mine."

Is he fucking kidding me?

"Are you asking me to move in, Theo?"

"No! God. Not yet at least. I mean, eventually, yeah, of course. But it's a bit soon, don't you think?" he looks genuinely curious about my thoughts on this matter.

I'm too busy feeling stunned at his blatant admission of planning a future with me.

"Yeah," I drawl out slowly. "I think it's even a bit soon for me to be keeping stuff at your place. It's been three days, Theo."

"Stuff that, Leslie," he chastises. "Don't put an antiquated label on us just because we've only been official for a couple of days. I think we can both admit to being something more long before you ever came over to my flat."

I shrink at his honesty. He's right. I've been consumed with Theo for months now. He floated into and out of my life, mucking things up every time. My feelings have been seriously involved since that first night at the club.

"Fair enough." I smile coyly. "I'll pack a bag," I shrug my shoulders nonchalantly.

"You do that." His eyes glitter with amusement.

"Let's get out of here. I need to get you to my flat right now."

I fidget with excitement. Yeah, his place is probably best. No need to stay quiet.

L8

Theo strokes his hands up my bare legs as I climb the steps into his apartment.

"Would you stop? I'm going to fall on my ass!" I berate half-heartedly, swatting his hands out from beneath my skirt.

"Leslie, you make me crazy," he says when we reach the top. I turn, waiting for him to unlock his door. He brushes my bangs away from my eyes and smoothes his thumb tenderly on my lips. He licks his own and leans in to kiss me, bracing his hands on either side of me.

I hear him messing with the lock as he covers feather-soft kisses all over my bare shoulders. The door swings open and I go flying backwards, coming so close to landing on my ass. Theo catches me just in time.

"You're so lucky right now, you dick," I admonish. He chortles like a teenager and rights me vertical again.

"Are you alright? I better check you out for damages. I don't have insurance, I'm afraid." He kisses my shoulders again and his hands find the zipper on the back of my dress. He pulls it down painfully slow, letting it drop to the floor. "It was a great dress, babe."

"Still is," I say, stepping out of it and draping it reverently over the dining room chair. I can feel Theo's warmth behind me and then his hands stroke slowly around my hips and down to my front.

"No underwear again," he growls into my ear.

"Not if I can help it," I whisper and giggle.

"You know what that does to me," he says, turning me around to face him. I'm gloriously naked except for my merlot wedges. He backs me up onto his beautiful dining room table. I sit and he spreads my legs, fixing himself between me.

"I've always wanted to fuck someone here."

"Does that mean I'm the first?" I ask, feeling uncomfortable thinking about someone else in his arms right now.

"There would have been no one else, Leslie," he says seriously, pausing for a second before assaulting me with his lips. I make quick work of his pants as he licks and sucks every part of my mouth.

He steps back, pulling his shirt off as he goes and I eagerly grab him, pulling him back to stand between my legs. I love him there—right there between my legs—feels like nothing else. It's like he's completely mine and I can wrap him up and keep him forever. Never in my life has sex been like this for me. The thought scares me as I instantly wonder how I'll be able to handle it when he moves on. Surely this can't last forever.

LB

I startle awake as Theo lifts me up off his dining room table.

"What are you doing?" I croak, feeling startled.

"Shhh, sleep Leslie. I got you."

"Are you seriously carrying me right now?"

His chest vibrates with laughter as he ascends the steps heading to his bed.

"Don't blame me tomorrow when your back's all fucked up," I

groan sleepily, nuzzling into his naked chest.

"You have to stop this, Theo," I sigh sleepily as he tucks me into his bed, dropping feather-light kisses on my arm.

"Stop what?"

"Being so good to me. It's just going to hurt more."

"What's going to hurt more?"

"When you leave me," I say, yawning, feeling exhausted.

"I'm not going anywhere, Lez," he whispers and slides in behind me. "I'm not going anywhere." He says it again, sounding sad and distant—I think. It's hard to tell as the fogginess of sleep returns, swiftly taking me hostage.

LB

I jolt awake suddenly, looking around trying to figure out where I am. Oh shit, duh. I'm in Theo's bed. Did he seriously carry me upstairs—did I dream that? I hope I dreamt that because I'm going to be mortified tomorrow when his back is all jacked up.

I look over my shoulder at a deeply-slumbering Theo. He looks so peaceful and young without his glasses. I kiss him softly on the lips and he doesn't even stir. He's exhausted. Probably from carrying my fat ass up here. My eyes fly wide as I hold my hand in front of his mouth to make sure he's breathing. I feel the faint puff of air and sigh with relief.

I slide out of bed to use the restroom and hear a faint clanking sound. I strain to hear and it happens again. It sounds like it's coming from the garage. I pad downstairs and throw on Theo's shirt that we left on the floor earlier. It falls nearly to my knees and smells distinctly like Theo.

The clanking echoes again in the flat and I go to peer out the fogged glass by his doorway. I can just barely make out someone at the bottom of the steps. Recognizing the mussed hair, I crack open the door to be sure.

"Hayden?" I whisper. He groans and waves dumbly, letting his hand smack down to the floor again. He's crumpled in a heap at the bottom of the steps.

"Hayden!" I say, a little louder this time. "What are you doing?" I ask.

"Nofin'. I'm right as rain. Don't you worry," he slurs. "Just headin' to the office for some sleepy time. I was 'round the corner at the pub and got a bit carried away, I'm afraid. Just gotta get myself up!" he groans as he tries to stand. He stumbles to his knees, knocking over the photo stuck to the wall.

Without thinking, I pad down barefoot to help him up.

"Oh, aren't you sweet!" Hayden slurs, with a half-dopey smile on his face. He tosses his arm over my shoulder and uses me as balance-support to stand. "Just gotta pop through the shop to the couch in my office and I'll be fresh as a daisy."

"I'll help you," I say, opening the door to the shop and quickly sliding my feet into Theo's leather loafers to protect my feet from nails and random bits of wood. We stumble awkwardly to the door on the other side of the shop and it opens up to a small office with a loveseat.

Hayden flops onto it and smiles politely at me through droopy eyes.

"So, you're the one, eh?"

"The one what?" I ask before leaving him to it.

"The one to bring our Theo out of the darkness," he mocks, his eyes flashing wide dramatically and then drooping back to slits.

"I'm afraid I don't know what you mean, Hayden."

"Don't you?" he tilts his head curiously at me. "Is our Theo keeping secrets?" I shrug my shoulders, unsure what to say. "Ask him about Marisa," he says, his eyes closing briefly and then opening back up to see if I'm still there.

"Who's Marisa?" I'm feeling a nervous anxiety tingle up my spine.

"People in glass houses." He huffs briefly and tsks his lips in annoyance. "You guys act all happy and in love," he slurs. "But life is a bitch. And that bitch is fast. You can't ever get away from her because she always catches up." He stops and looks at me seriously. "Do you have any lager?" He hiccups and giggles drunkenly.

"I don't think so," I reply.

He lays down, curling his long legs up tightly to fit on the small loveseat. I flip the light off and close the door, leaning on it for a moment to collect my thoughts.

Who the hell is Marisa?

I manage to slip back into bed without Theo even knowing I was gone. I'm certain that he'd be furious if he knew I went downstairs to help his brother without him knowing it, but I feel thankful as hell I did.

Hearing the things his brother said, drunk or not, was extremely eye-opening. I have a feeling there's a lot to still learn about Theo.

Before Theo, if something like this were to happen, I'd be running for the hills. But after everything we've shared, I can't just cut and run. We've only been official for a few days, surely he'll tell me in his own time. I can't pressure him into sharing when I don't want to open up about my own family dramas, can I?

Surely Marisa is from his past—right? He wouldn't make it so clear he wants a future with me if there was someone else in the picture. I can't think so little of Theo quite yet. I can't imagine him to be playing me for a fool. Not yet anyhow.

I need to give him time—time to open up to me on his own. He's earned that much.

CHAPTER THIRTY

Time flies for the next few weeks as I adjust to life with an official boyfriend. I'm feeling constantly tired and overrun because I work all day and am up way too late with Theo. But things are good between us. Great actually. I'm able to act utterly mental and he only seems to like me more for it.

We split our time between each other's places. We obviously prefer the privacy of his flat, but it's important for me to maintain close relationships with Frank and Finley. I've lived my entire life caring more about my friends than I have even my own parents, and that doesn't just go away for me because I find myself in a relationship.

Theo seems to enjoy the dynamic at our house too, even getting sucked into *Breaking Bad* marathons with Brody and Mitch. Brody pulled me aside after the first week and told me that he was really happy I ended up with someone that isn't a tool. I took that as a glowing recommendation coming from him.

We've spent only three nights apart since starting our little romantic affair. One night, Liam and Ethan demanded Theo go out with them for a guys' night. I did my best not to act like an insecure girlfriend, but I'd be lying if I didn't admit to worrying about other women flirting with him. Theo is attractive—it's not subjective, it's objective. It's a fact probably published in a book somewhere. And his friend Ethan is a womanizing man-whore who probably has no problem calling girls to meet up with them.

He texted me when he got home that night and told me he wanted to see me, but I put my foot down and said no. I don't want to become an interdependent couple who can't stand a night apart. It was hard because sleeping with him is so much cozier, but it made seeing him the next night even hotter. I guess it really is true that absence makes the heart grow fonder.

My favorite days with him are lazy Sundays. We veg out in comfy clothes, watch bad TV, and chat about everyday things.

"My mum wants me to ask you to the benefit we sponsor every year," Theo says, looking up from his phone with a small frown. He's looking decidedly sexy sprawled across my girlie daybed in a pair of sweats and a weekend's worth of scruff.

"Oh my God, you're so sweet! I'd love to," I reply flatly, swerving back to the dress I'm making for Ameerah's shop. I've been working on it diligently for the past two weeks and have only tried it on eighteen times.

"Look, I'm sorry. I just never go to this benefit, but my mum is laying on the guilt trip like crazy and I thought…maybe with you there, it wouldn't be so bad."

"Again, I repeat. You are the most romantic boyfriend ever." My face is stone serious as I bite off a loose thread from the hem.

"Leslie, I'm sorry. It's not you, it's this charity. I just…it's not my thing. But I want to make my mum happy. She's desperate to meet you and I don't know how much longer I can put her off."

"Try asking me nicely." I squint my eyes at him in challenge.

He tosses his sketchpad and phone to the side and rises swiftly off my bed. He stalks slowly toward me in that way that makes all my lady parts stand. I feel like a desperate tart. He throws a leg over mine, straddling me but not sitting down. My face is even with his belly and I look up at him, smiling.

He strokes his hands down my face reverently, languidly—passionately. "Leslie…you gorgeous, beautiful, funny, quirky, radiant woman. Would you please go to this charity ball with me?"

"A ball? Like, evening gowns?"

He nods half-heartedly.

"Duhhh—lead with that shit next time!" He smirks affectionately and leans down, kissing me speechless.

LB

After clearing it with Ameerah, I know exactly what I'm wearing to this benefit and I can't freaking wait. I purposefully made this dress my size with the very minuscule hope that I might someday have somewhere fabulous to wear it to.

A suicide prevention benefit isn't exactly something I would call fabulous, but it is Black Tie, so the dress will be more than appropriate. The ball is in only two days. I've been working late nights to finish the dress in time.

I pressed Theo about why his parents were involved with this charity and he mumbled something about them being the corporate sponsors. I shrugged it off and hoped it wouldn't be too heavy of an evening with such a sensitive subject matter. Surely it wouldn't be a ball if it's going to be a sad affair, right?

CHAPTER THIRTY-ONE

The day of the ball, Finley accompanies me to a full girlie spa day. I even make an appointment to get my hair styled, which is grossly unusual for me. Typically my hair is so thick and heavy, I don't have to do much to it. But this dress deserves something special, so I figure splurging for some quality time with my best friend is perfectly fine.

"I love this, Lez," Finley says during our morning pedicure appointment. We're both sipping lattes and feeling euphoric with a day full of pampering ahead of us.

"Me too. I haven't done a spa day in ages."

"No, I mean…seeing you so happy. It's nice. You have Theo, I have Brody. It's just all working out for us it feels like."

I nod silently, feeling nervous at her grand statement. The idea of things being perfect with Theo feels great in theory, but he still hasn't uttered Marisa's name in my presence, so I keep waiting for the other shoe to drop.

"What's your deal?" Finley asks, obviously noticing my reaction is less than congenial.

"Has Brody ever kept something from you? Are there some things you guys just don't talk about?"

She frowns, pondering that question for a moment. "No, I mean…we had a rough start in college, as you already know. And then the whole baby making mess." She rolls her eyes. "I handled that all so, so wrong. And I know everyone tried to tell me otherwise, but it just wasn't something I could handle I guess. I was weak!"

"But you guys came out happier because of it, right?" I ask, feeling hopeful.

"One-hundred percent. I'm lucky, really. I was horribly selfish leaving him in the dark for so long. But it felt like such a personal struggle. Even though it takes two to tango," she smirks at her double entendre. "I don't know, just…for me, I had to come to grips with it all myself before I could be mature about it all."

I ponder her insight silently, staring down at my feet soaking in the spa.

"Who's keeping secrets, Lez…you or Theo?" she asks, eyeing me cautiously.

I shrug her off quickly. "It's nothing major really. But there is something he's not told me yet."

"Sometimes it takes guys longer to open up."

"Yeah, I'm sure that's it." I smile, feeling a pit in my stomach. Theo is the wear-his-heart-on-his-sleeve type. He's been easily open with me about what he wants out of me since day one. So if he's not talking about this, it must be something huge.

I gaze at myself in my antique floor length mirror and feel

positively glowing. What does Theo say? *Shine*. Yes, I am actually freaking shining right now! For the first time in my life, I've made a dress that I know wouldn't look any better on anyone else.

The delicate rosette fabric is showcased fabulously on the large tea-length skirt I made. It's full and wavy with a sheen that makes the ivory look like the palest of pinks. It compliments my skin tone better than anything I've ever worn.

For the top half of the dress, I added a bit of edge—true Leslie style. I designed a buttery chocolate brown leather busier. It's strapless with a sweetheart neckline and fits me like a second skin.

Finley loaned me a fabulous mahogany jeweled clutch she had already and it fit with everything perfectly. Nothing else. No jewelry, no nothing. Just this dress.

The stylist at the salon did a really dewy, fresh-faced makeup application on me. That no-makeup look I could never manage to do on my own. My pink lip gloss is the only splash of color on me but it all works together perfectly.

I clack down the stairs in my nude platform pumps, ready for Theo to show up anytime. I stroll into the kitchen to find Brody and Finley snacking. Both of their jaws drop as they take in my dress.

"Oh my God," Finley says. "I knew the dress was perfect. But with the hair and makeup, it's like a dream!"

The stylist curled my auburn hair into soft tendrils and pinned back one half behind my ear with a bobby pin. She covered the pins by double knotting pieces of my hair over top. It was a really trendy look that I hoped I could replicate sometime.

"I know, right? And look…my skirt is so big I can do this all night and no one will even know it!" I say, turning my behind to them and twerking.

"That's perfect!" Finely squeals. "What about your Roger Rabbit? Does your dress hide that one?"

I tsk seriously, "'Fraid not…that one is pretty obvious. Same goes for my moonwalk."

"And your Dougie."

"And my Walk Like an Egyptian."

"The Macarena is surely out," Finley says, pinging back in perfect synch.

"Yeah…and the running man, rodeo…"

"Your classic dice roll…your cabbage patch."

"My diva power squat."

Finley and I stare at each other completely straight faced and silent…both enrolled in an imaginary game of chicken, waiting for the other to crack.

"*The fucking Macarena,*" I say, finally, and bust out laughing. She joins me with her own infectious giggles.

"I have serious concerns about what goes on in you two's heads," Brody states deadpan, staring at us with a serious look of concern.

That only makes Finley and I erupt into full-on belly laughs.

"Classic meet-the-parents moves, babe!" Finely roars with laughter and I dab at my cheeks, gently wiping away my happy tears, mindful of my makeup.

We all turn casually as we hear a throat clear from behind us. Theo is standing there gazing seriously at us with a shimmer in his eyes that makes my heart skip a beat. He remains completely motionless. I have a brief moment of panic when I think he's doing that breath-holding thing again. But then he groans softly—relaxing my nerves.

"I don't…I can't…you look…" he stammers.

I chuckle and walk over to him smoothly, kissing him on his cheek and pulling him away from Brody and Finley's prying eyes. I love my roommates but I don't need them present for every little event in my life. I pull Theo outside and into the concealed patio area.

"Leslie," he starts, but I interrupt him.

"Sorry, we were just being dumb," I chuckle softly, feeling like I have to explain the ridiculous scene he walked in on.

"You were being the most beautiful woman I've ever seen, Leslie." His face is shining with pure adoration—and something more. Something that makes me nervous and flustered. Quickly wanting to get the focus off of me and back on Theo, I smooth my hands down his shoulders and arms.

"This suit, Theo. Oh my God. I feel like we're going to the cool kids' prom." I rub my hands over him, walking around to inspect further.

Earlier in the week he asked me to go tux shopping with him. I went a bit overboard convincing him to do something a little different than the traditional black tux. My instincts were spot on. He's fitted to the nines in a slim-fitted suit that looks black at first glance, but in the right lighting, you can see a dark chocolate textured sheen to it. It's sexy as fuck. His tie is that same dark chocolate and lies smoothly over a vibrant blue button-down tailored shirt. His ivory pocket square, tie clip, and glasses make him look like he just stepped out of a GQ photoshoot.

"I don't know how you just keep getting more beautiful, Leslie," he says, seriously, dropping feather-light kisses on each of my cheeks and then my shoulders.

I half-smile at him. "Pot, meet kettle." He chuckles softly. "God, we're a sexy couple," I say playfully.

"I'm glad you're finally starting to learn. Well…that you're sexy, I mean. I'm just the lucky bastard that gets to call you mine."

"For now. As long as you play your cards right." I smile and see a fleeting look of anxiety mar his face. I kiss him deeply, swirling away any anxious thoughts his mind was running off with.

CHAPTER THIRTY-TWO

Theo pulls up to a very grand and incredibly maintained Gothic architecture building. He stops on a carpeted valet area and I watch him shoo away the valet driver in order to open my door himself.

He folds my hand in his and leads me through the large lobby and into a beautiful ballroom. It's got a great vibe—Victorian meets modern chic. One whole wall is covered in several huge modern murals and the tables are all white linens, white flowers, and white place settings.

I see a wall of silent auction items and see several of Theo's pieces displayed grandly with colored up-lighting. I make a mental note to bid on something. I need something made by my man's bare hands.

Theo grips my hand harder than necessary and I look at him curiously. Why does he look so nervous all of a sudden?

"My mum is over there. Let's go say hi." He pulls me over to where a robust woman in a long sparkly gown stands talking to someone with a headset on.

"Mum," Theo says, softly kissing her on the cheek.

"Theo." She says it proudly. Her mouth grins with pride and she looks at me bright-eyed. "You're Leslie, I hear."

"You hear right." I smile and she comes in and hugs me.

"This is my mother, Winnie Clarke."

"Nice to meet you, Mrs. Clarke."

"Winnie, please," she says, releasing me from her embrace and clasping her hands over her mouth as she looks back and forth between me and Theo. "We've heard all about you, love. So, so happy to..." she stops herself, suddenly overcome with emotion.

"Come now, Mum. You said tonight would be a happy occasion," Theo says curtly. I scowl at him. I feel like I want to snuggle right up with Winnie for a good cuddle.

She clears her throat and straightens herself, both mentally and physically. "Yes, of course. *Happy* is right. We are just very happy to see you, my dear. You are simply stunning."

Her mouth pulls into a genuine smile but her eyes look tight and strained. Sad almost. They are that same light brown as Theo's and remind me of what his looked like when I first met him at Shay Nightclub.

"I'm going to take Leslie to get a drink," Theo says coolly. He grasps my elbow and leads me away. I look back at his mother apologetically and she waves me off congenially.

"Why were you so rude to your mother just now?" I hiss as he grabs us two champagnes from a passing server.

"I wasn't," he says flatly, taking a swig of his drink.

I stare at him incredulously for a second. He looks at my expression and rolls his eyes.

"She promised she'd be good tonight," he states cryptically.

"What do you mean by that? Why wouldn't she be good?"

"Leslie, can we stop talking about my mother, please?" He seems exasperated and I'm about to fire more questions at him when we're suddenly interrupted by a skinny blonde.

"Hi," she says, meekly, with a small wave.

"Hiya, Daph!" Theo hands me his champagne and picks the small girl up into a big hug, lifting her feet off the ground. She looks embarrassed by his grand gesture and tucks her long blonde hair behind both of her ears.

"You're Leslie, yeah?" She looks at me with wide, brown eyes. She couldn't be more than eighteen.

"You must be Theo's sister, Daphney?" I ask excitedly noticing the slight resemblance between the two.

She nods nervously.

"Hi! So nice to meet you!" I hug her excitedly, feeling like meeting her makes me closer to Theo somehow. She looks momentarily shocked and nervous.

"Daphney, Leslie. Leslie, Daphney," Theo says in a clipped tone looking somewhat nervous and edgy.

"Mum said you guys had arrived."

"Yeah, just popped over here for a drink." Theo looks around the room like he's searching for someone. Daphney looks down at her hands, looking sweet and somewhat awkward as to what to say next.

"I have to run to the bathroom to powder my nose. Do you want to come with me, Daphney?" I ask and her eyes flash with surprise.

"Um...yeah, sure. Maybe?" She looks to Theo for approval.

"You don't need your big brother's permission. Come on." I grab her hand and pull her away from Theo who looks slightly uncomfortable. Honestly, what is it with him introducing me to his family?

"Your dress is...wow," Daphney says, looking at me through the huge vanity mirror in the plush ladies restroom. "Did you make it? Theo says you make stuff."

"Yeah, I make *stuff*." I giggle and wink at her, hoping she doesn't feel bad if I tease her a bit. "I did make this one actually. I even impressed myself with how it turned out!"

"That's so cool you make clothes. Theo makes furniture. I still don't know what I want to do. I'm just working for my dad."

"I didn't know what I wanted to do at eighteen either."

"I'm nineteen," she replies glumly.

"Oh, I'm sorry. I thought Theo said you just graduated."

"I did. I'm old for my grade. I...um...had to resit my GCSEs."

She stops herself midsentence. She had to repeat? That takes me off guard. I know I just met her but she seems very bright and well mannered.

"Sorry...I shouldn't have said that," she says, her eyes cast downward.

"Why not?"

She shakes her head quickly. "It's nothing...so, you do camera bags too?"

"Yes, I do. That's just as fun as dresses actually. Do you enjoy working with your dad?" I'm prying now. I feel the urge to dig deeper.

"It's okay, I suppose."

After a heavy moment of silence, she says, "So, you and Theo are happy together?"

"Yeah, we're happy. Why do you ask? Don't we look happy?" I'm smiling at her but I'm concerned Theo is giving them the impression we're not doing well.

"It's not that. We've just never seen him with anyone like you before. At least, not for the past few years."

"Like me?"

She looks horrified. "Oh God, no! I didn't mean it like that! I'm so...you're wonderful. Perfect really. It wasn't. I wasn't..."

I giggle at her nerves. "Daphney, you'll learn soon enough that I'm a smartass." I wink and she smiles, looking relieved. "Best to try and play along...more fun that way." She giggles cutely and I can already tell I'm going to like her. She reminds me of Theo.

When we come out, Theo is standing outside the door, looking nervous.

"Waiting for us?" I ask as he pulls me into his side.

"Just checking on how you two are getting on," he fixes a look at Daphney and she shrinks in her cute little silver dress.

"I'll see you later, Leslie," she says softly and scurries away.

"My dad wants to meet you. Come." Theo pulls me by the elbow and I jerk it out of his hand.

"What is your problem?"

"What do you mean?"

"You've transformed into a crabby jerk ever since we got here. Where's the sweet, sexy Theo that kissed the life out of me on my patio?"

He looks at me like he wants to argue but then bites his tongue, seemingly thinking better of it.

"This night is just hard for me, that's all."

"Why?"

"My family and I…well, it's hard to explain. I'm sorry. I don't mean to hurt your feelings. I just…I hate this charity and the cause and I'd rather just get you home and back in my bed where I can get you naked and fuck you sideways."

I ignore the fucking part of his statement because I'm certain he's doing it on purpose to distract me.

"If you hate this charity so much, why did you ask me to come?"

"I was just trying to make my mum happy."

"Then maybe you should start acting happy."

"I'll be happy when we leave, alright? Can we please just get on with it? My dad wants to meet you."

"Well, only because you asked *so nicely*."

He gives me a chaste kiss on the temple and leads me over to where his mother, Winnie, and his father, Richard, are sitting.

London Bound

"Leslie. A pleasure," Richard says politely, shaking my hand. He's a heavier-set version of Theo with a white goatee.

"Likewise. You've got quite the Superman of a son here," I say, trying to loosen everyone up with a little joke. Maybe a little story about Theo and me.

"Superman?" Winnie asks in question.

I start to respond to her question but Theo stalls me in my tracks.

"Don't mind Leslie, Mum. She likes to joke a lot."

It's like he could have slapped me in the face just now. He's always claimed to love my sparkle—my *shine*. What the fuck is his problem now? His mom looks wounded and I smile softly at her, physically resisting the urge to nut-punch Theo as hard as I can. I didn't sign up for a night out with a brooding jerk who's seemingly keeping secrets from me.

"They'll be serving dinner soon. Shall we go sit?" Richard asks, eyeing everyone cautiously like he's desperate to keep the peace. I feel terrible for how Theo is behaving. His mom's eyes already looked sad and strained earlier in the night and now his dad looks nervous. Surely they don't deserve this kind of rudeness from him!

We arrive at our large round table and I'm seated next to Theo. I glance over to the empty seat by me, wondering who it's saved for.

"Don't worry everyone. The brother is here!" Hayden peals loudly over the top of everyone's chitchat, making me jump slightly. Everyone stops talking and looks up at Hayden, who's swaying slightly.

"You literally can't throw this party without me!"

I frown briefly, wondering what that's all about. It seems like a poor joke considering the cause. Surely he's not a suicide survivor. Hayden's tux is rumpled and his hair is disheveled. He looks like he's been drinking for days, not hours. I look over to Theo with a quizzical expression and he shakes me off like there's nothing to worry about. I'm beginning to feel a lot more than just frustrated with how little I actually know about his family—and maybe even Theo.

"Hayden, my boy. Please sit down," Richard says firmly.

"Righto, Daddio!" Hayden plops down hard into his seat.

Theo leans over and whispers in my ear, "Don't talk to Hayden too much. He's obviously pissed. He wasn't even supposed to be here tonight."

I scowl at him for being rude once again but our conversation is stifled when the MC begins talking into the overhead mic to announce that the bidding starts on some of the donated items before dinner is served. Winnie hops up suddenly.

"Theo, we're auctioning off one of your pieces first. Would you be a dear and help your old mum get it up to the stage? It'd be nice to have you up there to represent it."

Theo frowns briefly at her and then looks to me. I smile brightly at him. Begrudgingly, he gets up and follows his mother to the side of the stage.

"Fancy seeing you here, Leslie. And Theo too for that matter," Hayden slurs into my ear. He stinks strongly of stale beer and cigarettes.

"Happy to help the cause," I say, feeling awkward. God, what does one even say in scenarios like this?

"What a cause it is, eh? Truly a great cause." He mocks a smile and grabs the bottle of wine from the center of the table and pours himself a drink. Theo's dad scowls at him but doesn't say anything. I chance a glance at Daphney who's watching Hayden nervously.

"Theo's never come to this gig before. You must be having a positive effect on him."

"I think he did it more for his mother than anything else," I reply, feeling a little defensive. Theo most certainly didn't do any of this for me.

"Oh, yes, Theo is always the good son. And now he's got you to continue reminding us all how bloody perfect he is." I flinch at his mean remark.

"I assure you, I'm no prize. And I'm certainly not perfect."

Hayden looks at me quizzically, trying to figure me out. I return his eye contact because I will not feel bullied in this situation. I don't know what the hell is going on here, but I don't appreciate the vulgarity of his tone.

"So, you've got some skeletons in *your* closet too, eh, Leslie?" I look nervously at Richard and Daphney and they appear not to have overheard. Hayden holds his wineglass up to me in a toast and I cut him a nasty glare. He shrugs and clinks the empty glass sitting in front of me.

"Why wouldn't you want your brother to be happy?" I ask, feeling deep down, that seems to be the issue here.

He does that mean-smile thing again and looks at me pointedly. "You still don't know!"

"Know what?" I hiss.

He chuckles and chugs down his entire glass of wine in one fell swoop, refusing to look at me. But I know what he's referring to.

Marisa. Perhaps I was a fool to come here tonight. Meeting the family is shining a huge, beaming light on how little Theo and I truly know about each other. If Marisa was so important to Theo and he's not telling me about her, maybe he's not truly over her. He said it had been three years since he'd been intimate with anyone, which must mean this woman fucked him up good.

I feel my shield rising slowly up over my entire body. Maybe I'm not what I thought I was to him. He's the one that pushed for more with me, but he's the one holding back now. Maybe I was a fool for thinking this thing with Theo would last.

Anger begins bubbling beneath my skin as I think more and more about the signs that Theo has been holding back from me since day one. Sure, I've been holding back from him too, but this, all of this is turning into a mess of secrets now. I just wanted to live my life in peace without relying on anyone but myself.

The MC announces one of Theo's pieces. It's a half-round buffet table that was carved out of driftwood. It's got a signature grey coloring to it and it's simply stunning.

"We're going to start the bidding at one thousand pounds, can I get one thousand," the announcer's voice continues as various people in the crowd begin bidding. Shit, I hadn't intended on spending that much on one of his pieces, but screw it—I'm not letting Theo bulldoze over me anymore.

I raise my hand high. "Thank you miss, we have twenty-five hundred, can I get three thousand…three thousand, anyone?" He pauses one more moment. "Sold! To…" he looks at me questioningly, waiting for me to announce my name.

Before I can think better of it…before my mind can tell my temper to shut the fuck up…I say loudly, *"Marisa!"*

CHAPTER THIRTY-THREE

A sick expression roils over Theo's face from up on stage as he clearly hears me give 'Marisa' as my name to the MC. He looks positively ill. I suddenly, completely, utterly regret saying what I just said. I glance at the table and everyone is staring at me in dead silence. Richard looks like he's about to blow a gasket and Daphney looks like she's about to be sick. Hayden breaks the tense silence with a hearty laugh.

"That. Was. Something, Leslie!" he continues, bellowing out a huge belly laugh and refills his glass and downs it in one sip again. Theo's family all remain silent, watching Hayden with a look of dread. Hayden grabs the bottle of wine and his chair scrapes loudly as he stands. "Darling family…always good to see you." He bows dramatically and stumbles away, running into the backs of people's chairs as he walks out of the ballroom.

Daphney lets out a quiet sob and I look over at her in utter shock as my mouth hangs open. Feeling his presence closing in quickly, I glance up and Theo is thundering toward me looking murderous, with Winnie close behind.

"Can I see you for a moment," he hisses in my ear and stands back, waiting for me to lead the way. I rise slowly, glancing briefly at Winnie as she nears us. Her eyes look heartbroken and horrified all at once.

Theo grasps my elbow firmly in his hands and I suddenly feel like a child getting taken to detention. I rip my arm free and he gaps at me incredulously. I stomp off toward the exit, not looking back. I'm not the one keeping the fucking secrets here! I will not be made to feel like the one in the wrong right now!

I throw the doors open and he follows me into the plush lobby, letting them slam shut behind him. It's deserted and I'm thankful for that. I have a feeling what's about to go down right now isn't going to be pretty.

"Mind telling me what the fuck you're up to?" Theo asks, his voice echoing off the high arched ceiling, his lips set into a hard line.

"I could ask the same thing of you!" I reply back snottily.

"Whatever for?"

"Who is Marisa, Theo? Why are you keeping secrets?" I ask, feeling ridiculous for having to utter the name again. Surely it's obvious that's what all of this is about.

"How do you even know anything about her?" His teeth are clenched and the veins in his neck protrude angrily.

"Your brother was very forthcoming. Too bad it's the wrong Clarke opening up to me!"

"Why are you fucking talking to my brother, Leslie?" he howls loudly, putting his hands on the back of his neck and crouching over like he's in pain.

"I'm glad I have! This Marisa girl seems to be a hot button for you. It makes me wonder what the hell you're doing with me! Your family all seems to know about her. I'm the one in the dark here! Maybe you should give her a call and see if she's still interested." He shoots himself up straight again and stares at me thunderously.

"Don't *fucking* talk about shite you know nothing about!" he shouts so loudly I flinch and take three steps back. I swear the grand chandelier rattles at the deafening volume. He swerves hard, fists clenched tightly at his sides. He reaches the large concrete wall and punches it furiously.

My eyes instantly well with tears and my whole body starts to quake. The familiarity of this scene is too much. Way too much. My flight or fight mode is here and she is demanding me to choose and choose quickly.

"Theo," I say softly, feeling my heart break at the finality of what's unfolding. He doesn't even look at me as he presses his forehead against the wall, his shoulders rising and falling rapidly.

"You're ruining me, Leslie." His voice is guttural and pained. I could cry at the sound of it. "I had everything inside, locked away. Now you're just shoving your way in without a thought. It's too much." He continues panting heavily against the wall, his hunched frame looking broken and defeated.

"I seem to remember you doing the initial shoving, Theo," I say flatly, completely devoid of emotion. I feel myself disconnecting and floating up into the rafters, watching down on our spectacle with pursed lips of disappointment.

Fight or flight, Leslie. Now! You didn't want any of this anyway!

Theo sucks in one more large breath and holds it high and tight, like I've seen him do before. I take my window of opportunity and turn and run out the grand lobby doors. As I burst out into the cool, night air, I could scream with relief when I see a row of cabs waiting at the curb. I jump in, telling the driver to go quickly and we take off around the bend.

I glance back at the door and see Theo's frame running down the pavement in our direction, but we turn the corner and he's gone in a flash. I throw my back against the seat and cry. Hard.

"You alright, love?" The cabbie asks, looking over his shoulder, clearly concerned. "D'ya need a hospital?"

"No," I croak. "Just take me home. Brixton."

I bite my fist trying to contain the urge to sob at the top of my lungs. Theo's right, this *is* too much. For Theo and for me. Why did I think he could be special? Why did I let him in? This is exactly everything I never wanted. This is exactly everything I've been trying to stay away from for five whole years. Nothing is worth this pain slicing through my heart right now. Nothing.

I'm not enough. I was never enough. I should have known. This is so similar to everything I grew up around. I pull my legs up to my chest to hug them for strength. This familiar feeling of inferiority is crippling. All those nights with Theo, all those words, all that chasing. It's never been about me. It's been about getting over Marisa.

I gave Theo Clarke a piece of what very little I had to give and now he's left me with less than nothing.

We pull up outside my house and I cry even harder as my eyes land on our bright purple door and green climbing ivy. This is my safety. This is my home. My family. This is all I need. Nothing more.

I run inside and through the living room straight down the hall for Brody and Finley's door. I bang on it loudly.

"Finley," I cry, not even attempting to mask my emotional state.

Brody swings the door open, his eyes wide and wary as he takes in my mess of a face.

"Lez?" he says, questioningly, and pulls me into his chest, hugging me hard. "Are you alright?" I cry hard into him, willing the strength to return to my emotions so I can speak. "I need you to tell me, Leslie. What's happened? I need to know *now*." His tone is menacing. I pull back and wipe my nose on the back of my hand.

"Nothing for you to do anything about, Brody. I just need my best friend."

"She's in the tub. Go right in." I nod silently and walk toward their closed en suite bathroom door, my chest heaving still with sobs.

"Leslie. Are you *sure* I don't need to do anything—absolutely sure? Because honestly, I'd really rather do something than nothing in this moment." Brody's kind face breaks me. My face screws up into an ugly cry at his loving offer of protection and I run back across the room, smashing into his chest again. He bands his arms tightly around me, murmuring into my hair. "Shhh, Leslie. Shhh…you're okay. You're okay. We are always here for you. You know that, right?"

I sniff loudly and pull back. I bark out a depressed laugh at the absurdity of my actions. Brody silently brushes a tear off my cheek, smiling down at me sadly. He head-nods toward the door and I follow his direction.

I walk in and Finley is shoulders deep in their Jacuzzi tub with earbuds in. She must hear me because her eyes flutter open and turn to saucers as she sees me. Sitting up quickly, she splashes water all over the floor.

"Leslie, what? Oh my God! What?"

"I'm okay, Finny...I just need you," I cry hard and she gestures for me to come over to the tub. I perch myself on the edge.

"I want to hug you but I don't want to ruin your dress."

"It's ruined for me anyway."

"No, Leslie! No! What happened?" She stands and grabs the towel on the shelf nearby, then steps gently out of the tub, wet bubbles cascading down her legs and onto the floor. Once she's secured the towel tightly around her chest, she perches on the side of the tub next, wrapping one arm around me.

"I don't even know, Fin. I just know he doesn't want me anymore." I cry even harder as I say the words out loud for the first time.

"How do you know that, Leslie?"

"There's someone else, Fin. It's this big secret that he won't tell me."

"That's crazy. I've seen the way he looks at you. There is no way he's ever looked at anyone else like that. That's a one-time-only kind of love."

"Love? Oh please, Fin. He doesn't love me. He just liked me—and now that's over. There's no way someone like him can love someone like me."

"Leslie," she says, grabbing my cheeks in her hands and pinching me until it's painful. I gape directly into her round eyes. "You stop that, right now! That man loves you like Brody loves me. *He loves you.*" She releases her tight grip and grabs my hand in hers. The pruneyness gives me the shivers.

"You didn't see him tonight. He was aggressive and angry and scary. It's all just gotten to be too much for me, Finley. I never wanted any of this to begin with."

"And why is that?"

I shrug my shoulders, feeling the weight of the world pressing down on them.

"The cracks, Leslie. You're keeping something from me. I know it." I crumple over and my shoulders shake with silent sobs. "What is it, Lez? What have you not told me?"

I shake my head, "I didn't want to ruin your thoughts of them."

"Of who, Lez? I am so lost right now!"

"My parents."

"What does any of this have to do with them?"

I sigh heavily and attempt to compose myself. "This was one crack I never wanted to tell anyone. I've just been too ashamed." She remains silent, watching me with fifty different emotions fleeting across her face.

"My dad." I swallow hard as those two words echo off the bathroom walls. I lean my elbows on my knees, staring at the floor, knowing that I won't be able to get through this if I look at her. "It started as small things. I barely noticed them when I was younger. I used to just think my dad was really busy and stuff." I sniff and wipe my nose on the back of my hand.

"Mom told me and Tom that she had a medical condition that made her bruise easily. She said all she would have to do is snap her bra too hard and she could bruise. It didn't seem strange to us as kids—it just seemed normal! We didn't know any better. And I think for the most part, the bruises were well concealed. I shudder to think what bruises we never saw."

"Leslie, are you telling me your dad abused your mother?" I swallow hard and nod without looking at her. "Why would you be ashamed of that?"

My face pinches tightly at the pain in my heart. "I just let it happen, Finley! I knew what was going on and I never said anything! I never did anything! I never even acknowledged it to my own mother. I was scared. Yeah, I was a kid, but Jesus! It was my mom! And I just let her…" I sob loudly, a strange guttural sound filling the room.

"Oh my God, Leslie."

"I know. I should have done something, told someone. Anything!" My mind attempts to flash back to the one time I did try to do something. But my shield shoves that memory back into the dark depths of my brain. I can't tell Finley that part—not yet. It's too raw. I'm still so ashamed. I don't think my heart can handle that trip down memory lane after everything that's happened tonight.

"Stop. Stop it right now." She grabs my face hard again and turns it to look into her eyes. I cry harder when I see the sympathy smeared all over her features. It's too much. "Leslie," she cries softly, pulling me into a hug. I hug her back and wail harder than I've wailed in a long time. We both sit there holding each other and crying for what feels like ages when she finally pulls away and says, "How have you been living with this for so long and not told *me*? I thought we told each other everything! We're best friends, Leslie!"

"It was easier to just ignore it. I think I always acted like the funny girl because I figured if people were too busy laughing, they wouldn't be able to see through me. I don't know…it's how I've coped, I guess."

"I feel like I don't even know you anymore," she says softly.

"I'm still me, Fin! I'm not going to change now that you know this about me. Being funny and upbeat is me. It's who I am. It's how I've lived my entire life. And despite being completely ashamed by not doing more for my mom when I could have, I still like me for the most part. But I don't like this part of me, this secret that I've been living with. I hate it, in fact. It's why I didn't want to get involved with Theo—or any man for that matter. You can't hide those dark parts of your soul from someone you're in love with."

"Are you in love with him?"

"No. No. He was scary tonight."

"You were scared of him?"

"Yes! He punched a wall and shouted and…"

"Were you scared he'd hit you? Like your dad hit your mom?" she asks me, looking gravely serious.

I flinch at the way she says the words so cavalierly. And I immediately want to jump to Theo's defense. Why is that? Why am I so quick to want to defend him? Was I scared of Theo tonight? Not really. No. Not of the violence. I think I was more afraid of the emotions bubbling below the surface. Could they really be love?

"I don't know Theo like you do, Lez. But every time I've seen him, the one thing that that man has in truck loads…is passion. He's passionate, Leslie. About you!" I roll my eyes. "I'm serious. Indifference in a man is nothing. Passion is everything! And you have to stop looking at yourself so negatively! You are not less of a person because of what your father did. You were a child."

I nod silently, allowing her words to marinate into something that feels better than shame.

"Look at everything Theo did just to get you to date him! That is not something a timid, weak man like your father would have the balls to do. His passion is all for you, honey. I think if you let him in, you'll be able to accept his love and not be so afraid."

I think seriously about her words. Could Theo really love me? Am I ready for that love? Seeing him get so worked up triggered something in me and sent me running in the other direction—surely that can't be good. But is his ferocity truly just passion—for me? None of this explains who the hell Marisa is!

"He's keeping things from me, Finley."

"Like what?"

"I don't know for sure, but it's something from his past. Something major."

"Honey, if you guys haven't even told each other you're in love, then I think you're still entitled to some secrets." I scowl, not liking that answer yet unable to dispute it. This Marisa girl seems important somehow, based on the things Hayden has said. I need to know why this is such a hot button issue for Theo.

"What if it's too late? What if I've ruined everything, Fin?" I cringe, thinking back to the moment I told the MC that my name was Marisa. Theo's entire family were all so visibly shaken by me saying that. How could I ever return to them, expecting to be accepted after behaving so catty and immature?

"You fight, Leslie. You fight for Theo like he fought for you."

I swallow hard, feeling a strange sense of urgency punch through me. I'm not scared of Theo. I'm scared of *losing* Theo! I'm not ready to lose him. Not yet. I never thought I'd find a man that would break down all of my walls, and he has. This can't be over.

I look up at Fin and she's smiling proudly at me. "Go."

CHAPTER THIRTY-FOUR

As I pull up in front of Theo's flat, I feel a strange foreboding envelop over me. I'm not sure how Theo will accept me after what I've done and after I ran from him. Running from him in the past wasn't something he took well, and I fear that after all we've shared it could cause permanent damage this time.

I pay the cabbie and punch the code into Theo's concealed garage door. As it rises I see a light flicker off from within Theo's shop. Theo's car is still gone, so I'm confused with who would be in his shop at this hour. Maybe he got drunk after I left and took a cab home?

I glance into his shop through the window on the door and all appears dark, but something urges me to check Hayden's office. I walk quietly into the shop, listening for voices from behind Hayden's office door.

I press my ear up to the door and hear a heavy pant and fast whooshes of air being blown out over and over. Wanting to see it with my own eyes, I twist the handle and open the door slowly, my pupils adjusting to the dim lighting in the room.

Nothing can prepare me for the image before my eyes. Nothing can prepare me for the horror that beseeches me.

Crumpled over his legs in a ball on the edge of the tiny loveseat, is Hayden. His head rises as he looks up at me with a haunted expression. My eyes flash around the room to figure out what's the matter. It's then that I see it.

A huge, lake-sized puddle of blood all over the floor.

A loud clanking reverberates in the room as the gleam of a round saw blade catches in the low lighting. It's covered in blood. Hayden pants quickly and holds his hands to his chest, looking forward.

"You shouldn't be here." His voice is harsh and cutting. "You're too…"

His body tips forward suddenly and he flies forward to the ground, catching his head on the corner of the desk before landing.

"Hayden!" I cry, running to him as he falls. I skid on my knees to a stop beside him on the cold blood-covered floor. I roll him to his back so his head lies on my lap and he blinks up slowly, gazing at the ceiling. The wound from where his head hit the desk starts seeping bright, angry blood. "Oh my God, Hayden!" I repeat, unsure what else to do in this moment.

"I'm sorry, Leslie," he utters in a struggled whisper, his eyes fluttering open and looking up at me with pitiful tears.

"Nothing to be sorry for, Hayden. I'm sorry," I cry out, feeling like an utter fool of helplessness. The wound on his head begins seeping more and more blood, so I grab the edge of my skirt strewn out around me. I bite my lip and press it to his wound, attempting to slow the increased bleeding.

I look down at Hayden's wrists to survey the other damage. They too are still bleeding, but not nearly as much as they must have been originally to draw that much blood. His eyes flutter open and closed as he appears to drift in and out of consciousness. I reach out and grab his hands to hold them tightly down against his chest. My knees and shoes scrape harshly over the top of the sawdust on the blood-covered flooring.

My chin begins wobbling uncontrollably. "Why, Hayden?" I cry out, full-on bawling at this point. I am not equipped to handle a scene like this. What do I even do? I search quickly for my phone and see it sitting back by the door all the way across the room.

"It's just too much. It's all just too much," he answers, and his face crumples into a harsh cry. I immediately wish I didn't ask the question.

"I gotta call 999 Hayden, okay? Okay? You're gonna be okay. We're gonna fix this." I slide his head off of my lap and crawl on my hands and knees over to my purse. They're shaking so uncontrollably that I stumble over the numbers several times before getting it right. I call using speakerphone and set the phone down on the desk. My phone is smeared in blood, causing me to look at my hands. I'm horrified by the image of them covered in blood. I look around the entire scene, alarmed at the massive amounts of blood everywhere. "There's still time," I add, for myself as much as Hayden.

The operator comes on and I don't even know what I'm saying to her. I think I tell her the address for Theo's flat, but I can't be sure. I can't even be sure it was a woman on the other end of the line. All I'm sure of is Theo's brother…on my lap…covered in blood. He stares blankly at the ceiling, tears trickling down his temples and into his hairline. He whispers he's sorry repeatedly. I keep shushing him and assuring him it's going to be okay.

I blink and the paramedics are barreling into the office with bags and equipment. One paramedic places his hands gently on my shoulders and lifts me to my feet while two others huddle around Hayden. He leads me through the shop and out to the garage where the swirling light of the ambulance spins around and around. The lights make my head spin and I drop down to my knees feeling suddenly woozy.

"Miss, are you injured?" the man asks, crouching in front of me trying to get my eye contact on him. I can't seem to focus on his face or his voice. All I can focus on is the thumping of my heart in my chest cavity. It's as if I can feel every valve, vessel, and vein retract and contract with a sickening gushing sensation.

"Miss…are you alright?" the voice asks again. I hear the screech of tires, snapping me out of my internal pulse. Suddenly, I see Theo barreling toward me.

"Christ, Leslie! What happened?" He squats down next to me and goes to wrap his arm around me but he's prevented.

"Sir, you're going to have to step back, I'm assessing her for injuries."

"Fuck! Where's all the blood coming from?"

"Sir, we're trying to get to the bottom of it."

"Leslie, where are you hurt, baby? Please. Tell him."

"Not me," I say in a small whisper.

"What do you mean?" Theo asks, sounding confused.

"Your brother." I swallow hard and feel a wetness streaming down my face as I stare at a groove in the concrete floor. I dab at my face, finding that I'm full-on crying. My hands, face, and dress are covered in dirt and blood—and now, wet tears. I finally am able to look over at Theo and focus on his features. His jaw drops in shock as he realizes his brother is injured. He turns around and dashes into his shop.

"So, you're not injured anywhere?" the paramedic asks once Theo is out of sight.

"No. It's not my blood."

"Thank goodness for that." He wraps me in a scratchy wool blanket, rubbing my arms reassuringly. A moment later the paramedics are gliding a stretcher out of the doorway, right past me.

"Hayden. God, Hayden," Theo says, walking alongside the stretcher. Hayden's face looks pale and chalky. He's blinking, but his vision looks unfocused. Theo watches them load his brother into the back. I hear him ask them what hospital and say he'll be there shortly.

As Theo watches the ambulance pull away, I find I'm still sitting on the same spot on the floor in the dark garage. I haven't moved since the paramedic ushered me out here. Theo strides over to me and lifts me up in his arms without hesitation. I hold onto him, but feel stiff and unsure of what's going on right now. He opens his passenger side door and guides me in, then jogs around to the driver's side.

"Buckle up, please." I buckle and we drive in deathly silence for what feels like hours, but in reality is probably just seconds. Suddenly, a sob erupts from Theo.

"Theo," I say, but he just cries harder at my scratchy voice. "Theo, please! Pull over. You're scaring me." Just as I say that, we pass a small parking ramp illuminated in yellow lighting. He whips in and slams the car in park, throws his door open, and jumps out taking long, fast strides away from the vehicle.

He grips a round concrete beam and screams at the top of his lungs, followed by a million different expletives. His voice carries deafeningly loud inside the parking ramp. He then coughs out a harsh cry as his shoulders shake manically. I jump out from my seat and run over to him.

He turns when he hears me approaching. "Leslie, God." He rushes over and meets me halfway, wrapping his arms around my waist and lifting me in a tight hug. We stay that way, completely still for a moment while all the tension, anger, and fear radiate between us. His chest heaves with soft cries and I stroke my hand down the back of his short hair, uttering gentle shhhs in his ear. He sets me down onto my feet and looks desperately into my eyes, feasting on every single tiny feature.

"When I walked in, I thought…I thought…" he stops mid-sentence and grips my hands tightly in his. He presses his forehead to mine and releases a shaky breath.

"I'm okay," I croak, trying to soothe his anxiety.

"Then you said it was Hayden and my heart dropped. I thought he was dead. When I came in and he was lying there, blinking…his eyes open…and alive…I couldn't even breathe."

I stifle a sob thinking back to all that blood and the terrified expression on Hayden's face. "Is he going to make it?" I croak, feeling panicky.

He strokes my cheek gently. "The paramedics think he'll be okay. He was still conscious when they left and they said that's a good sign."

I exhale heavily, feeling a huge weight lift. "Why would he do that tonight of all nights?"

Theo bites his tongue off to the side and looks down. Finally he murmurs, "This isn't the first time Hayden's done something like this." The comment stuns me and then all the puzzle pieces of the family's affiliation with the suicide benefit click into place. "We should get going though." He kisses my forehead chastely. "We can talk more after I check on Hayden."

I nod quickly and we get back into his car and he takes my blood-dried hand in his, completely oblivious to the mess I am on the outside.

"I'll take you home, but I can't stay. I need to get to the hospital."

"Why are you taking me home?" I ask, feeling like I'm being cast aside. He looks over at me in confusion. "I care too, Theo!" His jaw drops slightly and a frown mars his features. "Unless…" I start, and then look back out the window.

"Unless what?"

"Unless you don't want me there. After everything tonight…"

"Leslie, I want you everywhere. Always." I suck in a quick breath, his words are blanketing the open wounds inside my heart.

"I'm sorry about tonight, Theo. I don't need to know who Marisa is. I don't care anymore. I care about you. You don't have to tell me anything."

"Leslie," he says, exhaling heavily and pinching his eyes together in pain.

"No, really, Theo. I don't need to know. You don't want to tell me and I need to respect that. I care about you enough to respect that."

"You don't know because I don't want you to know. Not because I'm keeping a secret from you," he snaps slightly and looks out the side window as if warring with himself. "It's horrific and traumatic as fuck. Not dissimilar from tonight."

I remain silent, not sure how to respond to that.

"You finally brought light back into my life, Leslie. The last thing I want to do is drag you into this fucking darkness." He slams his hand on the wheel, frustration rippling down his limbs.

"Pot. Meet kettle." He frowns at my comment. "I was in darkness before you, too, Theo. Darkness is life. We can't avoid it forever." I cringe at my words and wish I could take them back because they make me the biggest hypocrite ever.

He glances at me, his eyes shiny with residual tears. "You're right. I will tell you, Leslie. You need to know. But please know that this was never about you." He kisses my hands and pinches every fingertip softly as if reminding himself that I'm real and not a figment of his imagination. "Are you sure you want to come to the hospital?"

"Yes."

"Okay. We'll talk after." He kisses my hand briefly, and then exhales with relief? Happiness? I can't tell.

CHAPTER THIRTY-FIVE

We arrive at the hospital and a nurse tells Theo they are treating his brother and we should sit in the waiting room. Theo strolls back over to where I'm hiding, embarrassed by the state of my dress. He guides me into the small, private waiting area and proceeds to call his parents and Liam. I slip into a nearby bathroom to wash my hands and face. Looking at my face in the mirror, I barely recognize myself—I look like I've been through hell and back. I sob quietly for a moment, trying to get it all out so I can be strong in front of Theo.

I decide to call Finley and explain what happened so I can get a grip on myself somewhat. She immediately offers to bring me some clean clothes, which I'm immensely grateful for. My beautiful dress is now, in fact, very ruined. I hope Ameerah isn't too upset. I'm sure once I explain things to her she'll understand.

Before Theo's family arrives, he tells me all about how this is Hayden's third attempt at suicide. The first two times involved pills, booze, and reckless driving—landing him in the hospital for weeks. It's terrifying to think about. For Hayden to choose tonight of all nights to attempt a suicide must have been a real cry for help. I shudder every time I picture that horrific scene. It's an image that will live with me until the day I die.

Richard, Winnie, and Daphney arrive moments later. Winnie takes in the sight of me and blubbers loudly in the hallways and pulls me down into a hug. Her robust chest is soft and warm—I find myself crying at the maternal contact I hadn't realized I've been so dearly missing.

She pulls back and eyes me seriously. "I hear we still have our son tonight because of you," she blurts out, still sobbing, and my face twists with emotions. "Come now, honey. I'm sorry. I didn't mean to make you cry."

"I'm sorry about earlier tonight. That scene I caused. I didn't mean it." She shakes her head dismissively at me. "This is all my fault," I cry into her arms, feeling the weight of the world on top of me.

"Hush now, darling. This is no one's fault. This is a sad, awful situation and I can't imagine what would have happened to Hayden if you hadn't arrived when you did. Don't you apologize to me ever again, do you hear me?"

"Thank you," I smile sadly. I don't deserve her forgiveness but I'll take it.

"What you've given our Theo—and now our Hayden—it's we who should be saying thank you, Leslie. Thank you for saving…" she stops herself before she loses it again. Theo's dad, Richard, comes over and smiles kindly at me, taking his wife's hand.

"Words can't explain, Leslie," he says stoically, a brief look of sentiment cast over his face. He half-smiles and leads Winnie over to the waiting room chairs.

Finley shows up a moment later with a duffle bag in tow. "Hey," she croons sadly at me.

"Hey." I get up from the waiting area to hug her. Theo does the same and I'm momentarily touched by his gesture and how at ease he is in this whole situation.

"I packed you a couple different things. I didn't know what you wanted to wear. Also a toothbrush, and shampoo, and a hairdryer, and…"

"You went a little overboard."

"Yeah," she smiles dumbly. "If you need anything—anything at all—text, call, carrier pigeon…I got you, okay? You too, Theo."

"Thanks, Finley," he says softly.

"Stealing my job?" Liam's voice cuts into our conversation. We all turn to look at him in surprise. "Hi guys," he briefly takes in the state of my dress but smiles kindly at me like he doesn't notice. "Now Finley, you can't be overly helpful or I won't have anything to do and then I'll feel like a prat."

She chuckles and looks at Liam fondly. "Okay, we can share the duties."

"Fair enough," he grins and winks at her.

"I'll see you later, k?" Finley says, turning back to me and hugging me tightly. I'm hesitant to let her go but Theo's reassuring hand on my back gives me the courage.

Winnie, Richard, Daphney, Liam, Theo, and I are all waiting impatiently for some information. It's horribly quiet and awkward. To have someone in the hospital for self-inflected wounds changes what you hope for. Of course we all want Hayden to be okay physically, but I think the majority of us are sitting here stunned by how truly injured he is mentally and what we all could have done to see the signs sooner. The physical stuff is just a direct reflection of it all.

A short, curvy brunette with sleeve tattoos comes running into the waiting room, looking flustered and out of breath. "Winnie…Daph texted me. I hope it's okay I came by."

"Rey! Oh, honey…" Winnie flops into another fit of sobs as they hug. Liam breathes loudly right next to me and looks pointedly at Theo.

"I forgot that Daph would have texted her," Theo whispers urgently across my body toward Liam, who is seated on my opposite side.

Liam shakes his head dismissively and stands up. Theo rises quickly, placing a soothing hand on his shoulder.

"I'm sorry, mate. I want to be here for you…but I can't." Liam swallows hard, glancing at Rey again. "I just can't."

"Liam," Theo starts, trying to get his attention.

Rey looks over at the sound of his voice and she's frozen in place at the sight of Liam. They exchange a heated look and she politely breaks away from Winnie.

She hurries over to us looking down at her shoes as she walks. She's obviously extremely nervous and uncomfortable about something.

"Liam," she starts, but he starts walking out of the waiting room and down the hall. He pauses briefly, looking back at her, his eyes casting downward more than into her eyes.

"I hope your *friend* is okay. I'll leave you all to it," Liam says, then twirls on his heal, exiting the waiting area.

Rey looks to me and everything feels horribly awkward. Her beautiful grey eyes look desperate and torn. She flashes a quick ashamed look to Theo and then walks nervously back over to Winnie and Daphney.

I watch her the whole time and can tell she's itching to follow Liam.

Who is this girl?

Suddenly, Rey says, "Can I just…I'll be right back, yeah? Right back!" she shouts quickly, jogging away from everyone and in the direction Liam just went.

"Who was that?" I ask Theo quietly. "She sounded American."

"She is, I think. I don't know her that well. She's Hayden's friend. Well…yeah, Hayden's friend, I think." He looks uncomfortable, shifting in his chair.

That sounds oddly cryptic. "Possibly girlfriend?" I ask, feeling surprised that Hayden has a girlfriend after the things he said about Theo and me.

Theo shakes his head dismissively. "No, just friends."

I try to press for more information but I don't want to seem insensitive to the real situation at hand. A tearful-looking Rey returns a short while later and sits dutifully by Winnie and Daphney.

After waiting for nearly two hours, a doctor finally comes in telling us that they ran some tests on Hayden and had to do a blood transfusion. I swallow hard as Winnie eyes the state of my blood-covered skirt again.

The doctor then informs Winnie and Richard that they are requiring Hayden be kept on a seventy-two-hour psychiatric hold. I step back to give the family some space. They don't need an outsider hearing all of this. I just met them all tonight for goodness' sake.

Theo looks at me questioningly. I shake my head dismissively, hoping he knows that I'm okay, I'm just trying to be respectful. Theo listens intently to the doctor and then chats briefly with his parents. They all nod and look over at me anxiously. I feel immediately nervous and uncomfortable when Theo comes striding back over to me.

"Hayden wants to see you," Theo says broodingly, the veins in his neck ticking compulsively.

"Me? Whatever for?"

He shakes his head. "I don't know, but he's quite adamant. Says he won't comply with the psych ward until he does. The social worker that's been in to see him thinks it's a good idea." He takes his glasses off in exasperation. "I'll understand if you don't want to see him. You've been through a lot tonight."

"I don't even know what to say!" The thought of facing Hayden again after the last time I saw him scares the life out of me.

"Don't worry, Leslie. I'll tell them no. It's what I think is best for you, but my mum said I had to at least ask."

"Your mom wants me to do it?"

"My mum is desperate for Hayden to get better. She'll understand, don't worry." He leans in and kisses my temple and strides back toward his family.

Why would Hayden want to see me? What could he possibly have to say to me? If it's to apologize, he's totally off the mark. He has nothing to apologize for! I can't do this. This is way over the mark for a new girlfriend. I've just met his family for crying out loud!

"I'll do it," I blurt out.

"Now, now. Leslie, love, you don't have to," Winnie reassures, rushing over to me and hugging me tightly. "Just look at the state of you. Of course you shouldn't. You've been through too much. I'm so sorry. I'm just feeling overwrought."

"These are just clothes. That's Hayden," I say simply. Winnie's chin trembles and she looks away with painful tears slicing down her cheeks. "Please let me do this, Winnie," I say, one more time, for good measure. She wobbles out a pathetic nod and Theo looks at me with a look I can't quite comprehend. Anxiety? Pride?

I pop into the bathroom and clean myself up first, changing out of my ratty dress and into some of the clothes Finley brought me. The last thing I want to do is remind Hayden what a horrific scene we both witnessed. A nurse leads Theo and me through the double door entry into the emergency area. We arrive outside Hayden's door and I suddenly feel raked with nerves.

"I'm going to be sick," I say, unable to look at Theo's face.

"You don't have to do this, Leslie. Really."

I shake my head. This is too important to ignore.

"I want to come in with you. Let me ask him again, maybe he'll reconsider."

"No," I say, placing my hand on his chest. "I'm okay," I say, suddenly feeling a burst of courage and lightly brushing my lips against his. His pained look softens as he takes me in.

"I'll be standing right here. Please, Leslie, if you need me…"

"I got this," I smile at him courageously.

"I know you do. You're strong. I…" he stops himself before finishing. "I'll see you when you're done."

I nod and place my trembling hand on the door. As I stroll in, I take in a very small-looking Hayden in bed. What is it with hospital beds making regular-sized people suddenly look so small and frail? He's dressed in a white hospital gown, matching his ghostly-colored skin. I take a quick peak at his bandaged wrists and look away nervously as his eyes flutter open when he hears the door close behind me.

"Leslie, you came," he croaks, his voice raw and scratchy.

"Yeah..." I say, eyeing the gauze and tape on his forehead. Red blood seeps through the other side.

"I didn't think you would after...well, after everything I've put you through."

"What did you put me through?"

"Well, first, harassing you that night I was drunk—and then tonight." A haunted look fleets over his features and I shake him off like it's no big deal. Even though it is a really big deal.

"Look, that was scary as shit tonight, I'm not going to lie. But you have nothing to apologize for, Hayden. Really."

"I didn't just want to apologize to you," he starts, but I remain silent, waiting on baited breath. "I want you to know that Marisa isn't who you think she is—who I've let you believe she is. You need to hear my brother out." He swallows hard. "I've been living with this darkness inside of me. One I can't seem to get a handle on. Our whole family has. Three years ago, things changed for all of us, dramatically. We've all been suffering. Me more than the others, apparently. But even stoic Theo has been a shell of a person, right along with the rest of us."

He pauses and coughs and flinches like he's in pain, but continues anyway.

"Then Theo brought you down the stairs that one day as if he didn't have a care in the world. He was laughing! I'd never seen him look like that. Not since before. He looked so…so…so *light*. I'm ashamed to say, it made me angry. Really angry. Here I am, living in hell and he's gone and got himself a floozy girlfriend." He cringes. "Sorry."

"It's okay…" I say, urging him to continue.

"Tonight—at the benefit—seeing you two there, together again…it was like…all that pressure, all that weight, all that pain came crashing back down on top of me. I got this terrified feeling that I was getting left behind…forgotten. So if that's the case, then it wouldn't matter if I was gone."

He touches his bandaged wrists gently, his face screwed up in pain. "Then you walked into my office and you looked…just so…innocent. Alarmed. Caring. And you don't even bloody well know me! I realize how stupid I've been, blaming everyone but myself for my problems and my issues, Leslie. My brother Theo…he's, he's a good man. He's a great brother."

"I'm getting that," I reply softly.

"Good. You need to know I was just jealous and stupid. Theo deserves to find happiness. He deserves you. And I am so very sorry for what you walked in on tonight."

"I'm glad I did, Hayden!" I say, feeling my eyes well with tears. "You have a waiting room full of family that loves you. Needs you. Wants you. Not everyone has that."

"I know. Or at least, I'm trying to get there. I want happiness for all of them. I want them to move on and stop being dragged backwards. If only they could all laugh again. None of us have laughed in ages. Even Theo. Until you two came down the stairs that one day, I hadn't heard him laugh in three years."

"I'm sure they want that too, Hayden. But with you here to join them."

"I know. I know this now. I know that I can help them get there if I can just get better." He clears his throat, looking away uncomfortably.

"I'm just glad you're okay, Hayden."

"I'm not okay yet, but I want to be. And that's the first time I've said those words in quite some time. I have you to thank for giving me the chance to."

"I don't deserve your thanks, Hayden. I'm not perfect. Far from it." I feel overcome suddenly by anxiety over my own issues. Here is Hayden, finally facing his head on, and I can't even stomach the idea of telling Theo my own shit!

As I go to exit his room he calls to me one more time. "Theo will tell you about her, Leslie. It's just got to be on his own time. Be patient. Please."

"Okay, Hayden."

CHAPTER THIRTY-SIX

I come out smiling but Theo looks immediately distressed at my tear residue.

"I'm okay, I promise."

"You sure?" I nod. "Good, let me take you home. Please?"

We bid our goodbyes to Theo's family. They are staying in a hotel near the hospital to say their goodbyes to Hayden tomorrow before he checks into the psyche ward.

Theo is quiet the entire drive. When we arrive at his house, he silently takes my hand and leads me into his flat and into his master bath. He flips on the shower and removes his glasses and all of his clothes, silently gazing at me the entire time. He strides over to me and pulls my t-shirt over my head and undoes the string on my cotton pants, pulling them down as he does. We're both standing before each other completely naked and silent, the shower steam swirling around us.

He grasps my hand again and leads me into his glass walk-in shower. He proceeds to tilt my head back into the water and watches me quietly. Leaning in and pausing, he breathes heavily against my skin before dropping feather-light kisses along my neck, collarbone, and shoulders. I bring my head back down and stare deeply into his eyes. I'm trying to figure him out but the raw vulnerability that stares back at me brings tears to my eyes.

He bites his tongue to the side and grabs the soap, squirting some into a sponge. He turns me away from him and begins washing me, reverently—gently and protectively covering every inch of me with the soapy bubbles. It's overwhelming. The intimacy of it all—it's all too much. Tears bubble up and fall down my wet cheeks.

Theo feels my shoulders shuddering beneath his hand and he turns me around to face him again. His pale brown eyes flash quickly between my green ones. As if consciously choosing to use actions instead of words, he tilts my head sideways and presses his lips to mine. He moves us back so the water is pouring down over our faces and between our mouths. It's a waterfall of lips, tears, tongues, and ragged breaths. Feeling everything he's telling me without words, I pour every single tear and ounce of angst I have into this kiss. All my fear, anxiety, pain, grief…all of it is swirling deeply within this soul-shattering kiss.

He pushes me back against the wall and pulls my legs up onto his hips as our kiss grows frenzied and desperate. He slides into me in one languid push and holds himself there, just letting our bodies connect in the most carnal and natural way.

He stops kissing me and looks deeply into my eyes. The vulnerability there on display for me to see—to accept—to love. I can feel it. I can touch it. Every single part of him—physically, emotionally, he's offering it to me. It's all I can do to accept it all.

Can I possibly love this man?

His lips crash down on mine again and he thrusts into me repeatedly with a harsh groan, exchanging my reverie for lust as he expertly takes me into his erotic world.

CHAPTER THIRTY-SEVEN

I roll over to feel the side of the bed and my eyes fly open when it's cold and empty. I squint at the early morning dusk seeping in through the large window in Theo's bedroom. I then see a naked silhouette sitting on the edge of the bed, staring off into the distance.

"Theo? What is it? Is everything alright?" I glance at the clock and see it's only five in the morning.

"Will you take a drive with me?" he asks, his eyes looking back at me in a strange calm. "Please?" He looks at me expectantly.

"Sure. Now?"

"Yeah, is that okay?"

"Of course," I answer. It's obvious he's been thinking about this for quite some time and my curiosity is definitely peaked.

We both dress comfortably and drive for over an hour outside of London. What I experienced in Theo's shower last night was more than I ever expected this all to be. Are we on the precipice of something more? Am I ready for that? Is it what I want after everything I've been trying so desperately hard to avoid for so many years? After last night, I would go anywhere with this beautiful man.

Finally, Theo turns down a long gravel lane in the rural areas of Essex. He stops the car at the very top of a wide hill. The morning sun casts a golden glow on a beautiful property spread out before us. A grand Victorian style house shimmers in the golden sun with a white stucco siding and cream trim. It's beautiful. Perfectly symmetrical with mirrored round windows on either side of the doorway. It has grandeur about it but with country modest. I look over at Theo and see his hands clenching the wheel tightly. His neck veins pulse and I see the anxiety building again. It's like I can feel his pain growing inside the car. How can a beautiful home like this resurrect such a reaction?

"Hey," I say softly, breaking whatever inner turmoil he's got building inside of him. "What's that over there?" I ask, pointing to a large piece of wood hanging from a rope on a huge weeping willow tree.

He tears his gaze away from the house and he follows my line of sight and shrugs. "We used to swing on that," he mumbles, almost incoherently.

"So, this is your family's home?"

"Yeah, for now. They are getting ready to sell it though." His tone is clipped and tight.

Feeling like whatever he's getting ready to tell me is too hard for him right now, I think lightening the mood might help. "Will you push me?" I turn my bright green eyes on him and give him a beaming smile.

He looks at me and I see his hardened features soften ever so slightly at my innocent expression. His lips form a small line of a smile. "Sure."

We get out of the car and head over to the tree. Theo looks so casual and at ease in his loose cargo shorts and grey pullover. But I can tell he's anything but.

"So what's the deal—you straddle it…or stand on it?" I ask, trying to lighten the mood.

He fixes a bemused expression on me. "Take your pick. I'll push you."

I nod and make my way over to the tree. "I prefer straddling."

"I'm aware," he adds flatly.

I fix a harsh, indignant stare on him and he chuckles softly. I shoulder past him, letting my arm hit his. Then I very unglamorously tuck my cotton dress between my legs and jump onto the makeshift swing. Theo pushes me and I take in the breathtaking view of the large rolling hills spread out before us.

"It's beautiful here," I say, hoping to break the silence and get him talking.

"It used to be."

I lower my feet and drag myself to a stop, swerving around to look up at him.

"It's beautiful," I state again, with a firm expression that he reads loud and clear.

He shakes his head and looks away, walking over to the edge of the hill that is in direct line of the house. I hop off the swing and join him as he sits down on the ground with his legs bent and his arms draped around them.

Knowing that he's battling something, I sidle up next to him and grab his arm. The familiar scent of his cologne sends the butterflies off again. It's amazing how just his scent attracts me. This is not even close to the time nor place to be thinking about sex. But after the stressful night we had, with his brother and our fight, then our very intimate shower, my emotions are all over the place.

"You don't have to tell me if you don't want to," I offer softly, feeling his shoulder tense and harden against my cheek.

He shakes his head. "I don't even want to tell myself. It's like—if I don't talk about it, it might not have happened. I have moments in my day-to-day life when I feel like it never happened. I can actually fool myself into believing that it was all a horrible dream."

I remain silent, waiting patiently for him to continue. "It was easy to forget about for a little while when I met you." I nod, feeling the weight of the world resting on his shoulders. "I was never *not* going to tell you. I just wasn't ready to shatter this thing that we have. It feels so important. Do you feel it too?" He looks at me nervously.

I nod in agreement, feeling anxiety rise in my chest at my admission.

"Hayden calls it all a darkness. What we've been living in for the past three years. But it was so much worse than just darkness, Leslie. It was a fucking nightmare with a gag down your throat. That day…" he stops and juts his jaw out and takes a deep breath in and holds it. His body frozen and tense as he brings a shaky hand up over his glasses.

My heart breaks at the site. He's holding his breath again. It must be some weird defense mechanism he uses when he feels intense pain.

"Stop, Theo. Please!" I cry out suddenly when the blotches resurface.

A loud rush escapes his mouth and he looks over at me confusedly. His determined expression turns horrified as he takes in the tears streaming down my face. "Leslie, I'm sorry. I don't even realize I'm doing it sometimes!"

His hands come up to cradle my face and I close my eyes and feel his thumbs wipe away the tears. I'm stunned slightly by my emotional outburst. I pull my face out of his hands and shake my head, looking down the hill at the house. "I hate when you do that. I just want that on the record." My voice quakes and I bite my lip, feeling ashamed that I'm turning this into something about me.

"I'm sorry," he replies softly. "Why are you crying?"

"I don't know why I'm crying. I just…when you do that…it feels like…I don't know. Like I could…" I shake my head, unwilling to finish my thought. How did this all happen so fast? How did this man become so completely everything to me?

He wraps his arm around my back and pulls my head down onto his chest. I feel the rise and fall of his lungs and feel instantly comforted. "I'm sorry. I'll stop. I won't do it anymore," he murmurs while dropping kisses into my hair.

"Why do you do it?" I ask, feeling like I know already but wanting him to explain it.

He shrugs beneath me and silence stretches out for what seems like an eternity.

"It started after Marisa died. Actually, the day she died." My throat closes up and I lift my head so I can look into his pale brown eyes. He gazes down at the house and gets a faraway look in his eyes. "You know, the thing I can't forget, the thing that still wakes me in the middle of the night?" He looks at me like he wants me to guess, but I remain silent. "It's my mum's screams."

He looks back down at the house and I will myself to hold it together so he can get through this. "She screamed over and over. She wouldn't stop screaming. She'd try to speak at times, to tell us what to do next, to tell us to go find Dad, but she could never finish a sentence without screaming." He shakes his head, a look of disgust smearing over his features. "I'd never heard my mother scream my entire life. The woman wasn't scared of anything. We've had field mice in the house before and even that wouldn't make her scream. She's a tough old bird."

I scoot in closer to him and wrap my hands around his arm as he continues.

"Marisa's my sister, Leslie. She's just two years younger than me. She was my best friend in the whole world." His voice quakes and he purses his lips together firmly.

"We came home together for the weekend. Hayden was still living at home 'cause he didn't want to do university. Mum and Dad were always taking the piss out of him for that, but I think they thought he'd change his mind eventually. Daphney was still in school."

"Marisa and I would come home together from London on the weekends a lot. It's such a laugh when our whole family is together. And being out in the county feels great when you've been cooped up in the city."

A pained look fleets across his face and he takes a deep breath in and lets it out quickly. "We grew up riding quads, hunting, fishing, lots of outdoorsy stuff. Mum and Dad have over fifteen acres here, so growing up we were always running off and exploring."

"It sounds amazing," I offer, trying to show my support.

He gives me a sad smile. "Freak accident. That's all I heard anyone saying at the funeral. Old wrinkly types walking all over our damn house saying what a tragedy it was. What a fluke it was. Shouldn't have happened. Much too young. Fucking tossers…the lot of them. They don't have a fucking clue what went down that day."

"Hayden had Marisa on the back of his quad and I had Daphney. We had all been out for a couple hours down by the stream just mucking about. Marisa was whining about having to pee and Hayden was winding her up and telling her she needed to pee in the grass 'cause he wasn't going to take her back to the house." He clears his throat. "Marisa got her way as she always did and she and Hayden took off back toward the house. A few moments after they left, Daphney said that she needed to pee too." He chuckles softly.

"They couldn't have been more than five minutes ahead of us. As Daph and I pulled up to the house, I saw Hayden just doing laps round and round the house by himself, seemingly killing time until Marisa came back out."

He clears his throat harshly, pulling from the depths of himself to continue.

"Hayden and I always joked a lot. I think being both boys, we knew we could be hardest on each other. Anyway, as we approached the house, Hayden was coming 'round and I shouted something daft at him. Something rude about what a shite driver he was. That's when it happened. He turned around to mouth off to me, and then…" his voice cracks and he drops his head down between his bent legs, using his arms to shield his face from me. He pants heavily for a few moments.

"I saw the whole bloody fucking scene." His voice is muffled and I shake the pain off myself to be there for him. I rub his back encouragingly. He looks up suddenly and tears stain his cheeks and nose.

"Right as Hayden glanced back toward us, Marisa came 'round the corner of the house and stepped right in front of him. He struck her and her body flung toward the house. He jerked the wheel in reaction and his quad rolled, throwing him from it."

"Oh my God, Theo."

He shakes his head disbelievingly and swallows hard. "Everybody asked us how fast he was going but none of us knew. It couldn't have been that fast, but the way their bodies flew made it seem like he was driving a fucking race car instead of a quad."

"Daphney screamed and I slammed the brakes in shock. I stood there and held my breath waiting to see movement from either of them but both of them just laid there. Then my mum came round the corner and that's when all hell broke loose. That's when the real screaming started. She was screaming words but I couldn't understand anything. I had to pry Daphney's hands off of my waist to get to my mum. To help her or something. Daphney's grip on me was so hard. So strong."

He chokes out a cry and continues, "I didn't know why mum was screaming. I knew it was a bloody awful accident but death didn't even register on my radar. I couldn't understand why Mum was losing it so bloody awful."

"I ran straight to Hayden first because he was closest. Mum was kneeled over Marisa, so I thought she could get her sorted. Hayden had just started to come to when I reached him, but his leg was so obviously broken I had to look away. He looked…I don't know, just like, blank I guess. Like he had no clue where he was or that his leg was broken."

"But the entire time, my mum continued screaming these blood-curdling, earth-shattering screams. She screamed and screamed and screamed. I left Hayden to tend to my mum because…in that moment…she seemed to be the one that needed the most help."

My jaw drops in horror as I picture the scene Theo is describing. Tears now run freely down my face, matching the tears running down Theo's. He's staring down toward the house stiff as a board.

"I couldn't even help my mum though. I took one look at Marisa in my mum's arms and I knew she was dead. Her body was completely slack. Lifeless. I just dropped to my knees and held my breath, willing the screaming to stop…willing the whole bloody scene to stop. Everything. I don't know how long I was kneeling there without breathing but it must have been a while because when I heard Daphney approach, I shot up to stop her from seeing Marisa and I was so lightheaded I fell down. I remember seeing spots in my vision. My mind was whirling and I grabbed Daphney and yelled for her to go get Dad. I think that's what my mum was screaming. I don't know though. I called 999 but I have no recollection of it. I don't remember what I said to the operator, I don't remember any of it."

"Theo." My voice breaks through his trance and he looks at me, almost surprised I was still there. "Sorry doesn't even begin to cover it."

"Don't say sorry, Leslie. Not you. Anyone but you. Sorry is the shite that the rest of the world says to us. The crap about it being a freak accident. Sorry for your loss. It's terrible. So sorry. You can't say those words to me, Leslie. Please. I'm begging you. Promise you'll never say sorry."

I nod, my chin trembling at the urgency behind his request. I can't imagine that day. This beautiful family being ripped apart in the blink of an eye.

His expression sobers suddenly as he gazes down towards the house. "If Marisa would have fallen just a half a foot either way, she would still be alive. Her neck hit just perfectly."

Silence creeps in between the two of us as the horror of his words sink in.

"Why didn't you want to share any of this with me?" I ask quietly, not wanting to push him too hard but needing to know more.

"Isn't it obvious?" he asks incredulously. "It's horrifying, Leslie! And damning! It's damning to live with this tragic past. This tragic mark on your story of life that you could have easily prevented. You don't need this shite on you too!"

"Why is it damning for you?"

"It's my bloody fault!" he howls loudly. "And don't try to tell me it's not. If I wouldn't have distracted Hayden, then Marisa would still be alive and Hayden wouldn't be slitting his fucking wrists!" His voice is laced with aggression. Guttural. "That whole day has had a ripple effect on my family that is bloody endless. We are so fucked. I don't know how you're not running for the hills yet."

"Theo!" I say, turning his angry gaze back to me. "Look, I'm not going to tell you it's not your fault. Just like I'm not going to tell you sorry. Only you can come to those resolutions on your own. But Jesus! You have to let me say something!"

He looks at me curiously, clearly emotionally frazzled after reliving it all again.

"Regardless of the whys, or the hows, or the causes, it happened and it sucks. But…I don't know…we found each other despite it all!" I smile pathetically and he scowls, trying to wrap his brain around the meaning behind my words. "I know that sounds terrible because you'd love to go back in time and bring your sister back. I'd love that for you too. But maybe just try focusing on what you and I have been given." I grab his clenched hand, twinning my fingers through his. I stare at our hands seriously for a moment, letting these thoughts marinate for just a tad longer. I swallow hard at the realization of the serious commitment I'm making to this man after everything I've been through with the one man in my life who's supposed to protect me.

"I agree with you, Theo. What we have between us…is important. And who knows if we would have even found it without all that you've been through." I exhale heavily, feeling like I've just admitted way more than even I knew I was feeling.

He glances down at our hands as well and then looks forward at the house again, biting his tongue in deep thought.

"I would have liked to see a life with both of you in it," he murmurs and then smiles sadly. My heart bleeds at the innocence of that statement. He looks like he's about to say something more, but then shakes it off and clears his throat gruffly. "And now, this house that we grew up in haunts every one of my dreams. Just looking at it now. It's all I can picture."

"That's why your parents are selling it?" I ask tentatively.

He nods. "They can't live here anymore without seeing Marisa everywhere and having that tragic day replay in their minds."

I nod and look down at the beautiful home. It's so perfectly situated. It doesn't even remotely resemble a place that would host a horrible nightmare for an entire family. I almost feel sorry for it. I know it's not a person and feeling sorry for an inanimate object is silly, but fuck it. I do. This beautiful house appears to hold way more beauty than it does horror.

"I want to see it." I stand up and brush the butt of my dress off.

Theo looks up at me quizzically. "Did you not hear anything I just said?"

"I did. It's terrible. I still want to see it. I want to see where you grew up. Can you handle it, you think?"

He stands up and eyes me cautiously. "'Course I can handle it. I just…I just…"

"Let's go then," I grab his hand and pull him back toward the car. He looks visibly shaken and uncomfortable, his face red and blotchy from the salty tears.

"Please? Show me around?" I ask sweetly. He half-smiles, looking a bit more like the Theo I'm used to.

CHAPTER THIRTY-EIGHT

He drives the car down the steep gravel road and pulls through a large open gate and around a raised landscaped flowerbed that sits high up on the rocks in the center of the circular driveway. He parks right in front of the pale blue double-door entry. He looks nervous, but I see the tiniest flicker of excitement in his eyes.

"Are your parents home?"

"Not for a bit. They're still seeing Hayden off."

"Let's do this then!" I sing merrily.

We get out of the car and I notice a huge five-car garage perpendicular to the house. Jeez, Theo's family has money, but the house doesn't scream it out loudly. It's a quintessential old English home that looks lived in, but well cared for.

Theo holds my hand tightly as he grabs the hidden key from beneath a clay toad. He opens the doors and I smile, taking in the home that Theo grew up in. The foyer is large and airy with lots of bright natural light shining off of the modern slate-grey tile.

"The house is from the 1800s but my parents have done updating. Several generations of Clarke's have lived here. I was a boy when we moved out here after my grandparents moved into the village."

"It's beautiful," I say, taking in the modest staircase leading upstairs. "Were all the Clarke generations in the furniture business?"

"No, not all. It was my great grandfather that started it."

"And you're continuing it," I smile proudly.

"In a way," he shrugs. "Not the distribution center though. I think Daphney might be in line for that. Speaking of which, you're not paying for that table of mine."

"What do you mean? It was for charity!" I reply incredulously, throwing my hands on my hips.

"I'll donate, don't worry."

"We'll see about that. Stop being so bossy and show me around!"

"Pot. Kettle," he murmurs, grabbing my hand tightly. He leads me down the hallway into a large and beautifully updated kitchen. It's all white granite and knotty pine cabinets. The wallpaper is an olive-green sheen with a texture. I drag my hand along it as I mosey around.

"This is the wallpaper I think your eyes look like sometimes," he says, looking slightly sheepish and stuffing his hands into his front pockets. Gosh, that conversation we had about my eyes feels like so long ago! So much has happened.

He looks so nervous and uneasy in his own home. I hate it. I smile sweetly and bite my lip, willing away the cuteness of his face so I can find the nerve to walk over and kiss him. Surely I shouldn't still feel nervous around someone who's kissed nearly every inch of my body. But God, sometimes he's so freaking hot that I can't help but feel anxious! I walk toward him and his eyes flutter with a brief look of discomfort. I ignore it and muster up my balls of steel. I grab the front of his shirt and pull him into me, taking his lips tenderly with mine. He returns the kiss delicately at first, until his libido takes over and his hands come up and clasp my face. He pushes his kiss forward with equal passion and just when I think we're breaching the point of no return, I pull away.

"Show me more," I say breathily. He gives me a lopsided smile and leads me out of the kitchen, looking slightly more relaxed.

He takes me around the rest of the house and I get a feel for Winnie's quirky, old-fashioned style—which I kind of dig. It's a hodgepodge of oddly upholstered furniture with random collectibles, wallpaper patterns, and some eccentric items. I make note to ask her about those later if I'm ever back here again. It's cool in its own unique style. The best part is that the whole house just feels comfortable and lived in. It makes me wonder what it would have been like to grow up here with loving and nurturing parents, like Theo's seem to be.

"This was a playroom when we were kids. It's just storage now," Theo says nervously, gesturing toward one of the doors we pass on the second floor.

I raise my eyebrows. "Well? What are ya waiting for, buster?" I ask, stopping in front of the door.

"Buster?" he asks quizzically, turning around and crossing his thick forearms across his chest.

"Yeah, buster, buddy, big boy, butchie, badass, Belved…" Theo's lips slam into mine, silencing my very awesome tirade of various endearments that start with the letter B.

He breaks the kiss with a chuckle and I smile up at him. "You like those endearments, do you? I'll make a mental note of that."

He winks and pecks me on the lips once more. "Were you just going to call me Belvedere?" he asks, looking confused. He walks past me and grabs the doorknob.

"I was. Good guess! You really do get me." I beam proudly at him. "Look it up in the Urban Dictionary. You won't believe all the crazy definitions for it!"

"I think I prefer Superman." He bites his tongue and I have to stop myself from kissing the beautiful twinkle in his eyes.

He opens the door and I take in the large expanse of the room. It has three large bay windows with sheer white valances. Several totes and boxes line one whole wall, along with bookshelves full of antique toys and books. A tiny school desk sits up by the window and I walk over to inspect it and check out the view. I smirk at the image of a young Theo playing school here.

"It's pretty much just storage now. Mum says she can't bear to throw out our toys in case any of us ever give her grandbabies. Maris…" he stops speaking suddenly, his face flushing with red.

"Marisa? Marisa what?"

He shakes his head dismissively attempting to brush it all away. "Do you not talk about her, Theo? Like, at all?" He shakes his head sadly. "That seems miserable."

"It is. Just like this house," he says with a heavy sigh and joins me, leaning his large frame against the window frame. I wrap my hands around his waist, pressing my ear against his chest. His heart thunders inside and it makes my own heart hurt. This haunted-house feeling he is portraying is so tragic.

"Theo, look around…how can this place haunt you?" I ask, looking out the window overlooking the back of the property. A narrow creek runs straight through the wild pasture and a flock of ducks meander near it. It's like you can see love poured into every facet of this place.

His lips form a hard line of sadness. "I see my sister everywhere here. We were best friends, Leslie. We shared everything with each other. I…I just can't bear it here anymore." He scowls broodingly out the window.

"Theo, stop. Look at me." He turns his eyes to me, glistening with unshed tears. They look pained. Desperate. He's so clearly aching for all he's lost. Not just his sister but his home, his family, his upbringing. In his eyes, he's lost it all. But there's still so much that he's refusing see. "You can't let the ugly win over the beautiful. The beautiful is here Theo, in this house. The memories of your sister. This playroom. That stream. Your family. It's all beautiful. Can't you see you that?"

He blinks quickly, attempting to rein in his tears and I hate it. I hate that he's trying to hide himself from me. When one slips out and down his cheek, I grab his face and kiss the trail of the tear all the way from the hollow of his eye down to his scruffy jawline. When I pull back and look into his eyes again, something shifts. Something in his expression, his demeanor, his stance. All of it. It feels monumental and it makes me nervous as hell.

"*You* are beautiful, Leslie." He tucks a stray auburn lock behind my ear tenderly and moves my bangs off to the side, like he always does. "Your light, your smile, your playfulness." I roll my eyes and look down, feeling horribly uncomfortable with all these compliments. This man is Superman, how does he even see me?

He crooks his finger under my chin forcing me to look him in the eyes. "I mean it. I never stopped chasing you because you are the light to my darkness. The one thing that just shines in my life. You make it all less horrible, Leslie. You…are worth *every single millimeter* I ran to catch you." He swallows hard, glancing out the window briefly and then swings his gaze back to me, his expression turns urgent. "I said last night that it was all too much, that I was overwhelmed. I need you to know that I am overwhelmed—but only because I've been wanting to tell you something for a while now, but I didn't want to scare you."

"Theo…" I start.

"I am in love with you, Leslie," he says, strongly, and with conviction—halting my words and looking desperately into my terrified eyes. I can't bear the vulnerability he's portraying, so I look out the window. This is all just so—again. He turns my chin to look at him. I can no longer hide the tears running freely down my face.

"I love you, Leslie. I would chase you through a romantic cleanse any day to tell you that. To tell you that you are the one thing in my life that came along and made me feel like I wasn't by myself anymore. You pulled me into your shine—your sparkle." He smiles sweetly. "I love you. So much."

I let out a strange puff of a cry and my face screws up with the emotions I'm failing miserably at hiding. "This is so hard for me to hear, Theo," I cry heavily, casting my gaze down again.

"Why?"

"I don't deserve it!"

"Of course you do. You deserve it all."

My heart crumbles beneath his words. He doesn't even know. He doesn't know what I've come from and I can't stomach the idea of ruining this moment right now.

"I've never felt this before. I've never heard anyone say it like you just did. You just put it all out there and I believe you! And it scares me that I believe you."

"It scares you to believe me?"

"Yes!"

"But why?"

"Because it can't be real! It's too much. It all can't possibly be for me. This feels like a dream."

"Why can't it be our dream? Together? Why can't it be our dream coming true? Accept this, Leslie. I need you to. Please. *Please…love me.*"

"Oh God, are you kidding?" I bark out an unattractive laugh. "Of course I do!" I sniff loudly, batting away my ridiculous tears. "I've never loved a single person more. It's freaking obvious, isn't it?"

"No," he laughs happily.

"Welp, I do. I love you, Theo. Dammit anyway. I didn't want to, but you just barreled in. I didn't stand a chance."

The gleam in his eyes is contagious. "God I love you."

"I love you," I say, again, getting more of a feel for the words.

He strokes my cheeks with his thumbs. "So much," he murmurs in a rushed tone as he connects our lips in a hungry, all-consuming kiss. It's amazing how one word can change the passion behind a kiss and make it so much more. No longer too much, but just enough.

CHAPTER THIRTY-NINE

"Oh stop looking so damn proud of yourself," I say, shoving his chest playfully as he holds himself over the top of me.

"What do you mean?" he asks in mock indignation.

"You're all pleased because I screamed *I love you* during sex. It's really unattractive to gloat, you know. You could just let us savor the moment or something."

"Oh, I'm savoring that one forever, Leslie Lincoln," he says, thrusting his still-situated situation inside of me slightly. It's definitely lost the shock factor now that we've both finished, but it still revs my engines for round two. "And I'm not gloating," he adds and then chuckles as I stare at him in horror.

"Liar!"

"Okay, I'm totally gloating."

He slides off of me and lies on his side, languidly dragging his fingers over my flat stomach. When our kiss turned a bit inappropriate for a children's playroom, we sloppily kissed and stripped all the way down the hallway toward Theo's bedroom. All the childlike qualities in his room are gone now. His mother has redone it into a beautiful guest bedroom.

I gesture above my head to the long antique mirror hung as a headboard on the bed. "Is your mom a bit of a perv?" I ask in blatant curiosity.

He chuckles, "Yeah, I know. We all gave her crap when she put it up. Marisa actually called Mum a Madame for a whole weekend." He laughs slightly and then stops, looking uncomfortable.

"It'll get easier," I say, stroking his face with my hand. "So what about this tattoo? I have a feeling it means something but you've always been a bit cryptic," I ask, stroking the back of his arm across the Gaelic letters.

"It means sister. I got it the day of the funeral actually. It was impulsive but I was just so angry at everyone being so daft at the funeral. I had to get out and do something that felt real."

"It's beautiful. I love it." I sit up and kiss it softly and he pulls me down to his lips.

"I love you," he murmurs against my mouth, his eyes twinkling at me. "I've been waiting for this for a while now."

"What? Shagging me in your bedroom with that pervy mirror so you can watch yourself? Don't let that Superman title I've given you go to your head," I say, smiling indignantly.

"That and the other stuff. I've had *that word* on the tip of my tongue for quite some time."

"What do you mean? Love? You've loved me for a while and haven't said it?"

"Yeah, I told you I didn't want to spook you. You spook easily, Leslie."

"I do not spook easily," I say, dragging the sheet up over my naked chest and thinking about how I totally spook easily.

"You do, but it's okay. I think I know how to handle it now." He kisses me chastely on my stomach over the top of the white sheet and lays his head on my belly. I lightly scratch my fingers through his short buzzed hair.

"So, how long?"

"How long what?"

Oh, he's going to be cheeky now?

"How long have you been holding that little four-letter word in?"

He straightens his head off my belly and looks at me in challenge. "Since that night you were in your pajamas."

"Which night?"

"The cheetah footie ones. The ones you were wearing that night you were going to watch a movie with your roommates. When Liam and I showed up."

"You didn't love me then! That was so long ago!" He shrugs. "I was so horrible to you," I say softly, feeling ashamed.

"Yeah, I saw that night playing out a lot differently."

"I'm so sorry," I offer, not sure what else to say.

"It's okay. This moment right here was worth it all."

"It was pretty perfect here," I giggle, cozying deeper into the bed. Then it dawns on me. "Hey! We made a new memory here!" His happy expression morphs into discomfort. "Don't over think this, Theo. We had sex in this beautiful house, in the room you grew up in. We said I love you to each other for the first time. You cannot take that specialness away from us."

Just then a rumble shakes the walls slightly, interrupting our moment.

"Oh shite! That's the garage! My family's back. Hurry!" he says, jumping out of bed, gloriously naked.

"Theo! My freaking dress is in the playroom!"

"So are my shorts, shite. C'mon, let's hurry. We can't get caught in my bedroom."

"What's going to happen if we get caught?" I ask, feeling scared shitless.

"My mother is a bit conservative. We called her the Queen of England growing up."

"Oh, fuuuck!"

Theo cracks open his bedroom door and motions me to follow behind him. We pad down the hallway and he stops to pick up my bra.

"I think this belongs to you."

"Shut up, you cheeky bastard. *Move*!"

We walk a few more steps and he grabs his shorts up off the floor. Jesus, we left a fucking breadcrumb of clothes throughout the entire second floor. I hear a creak and my eyes snap up to look over Theo's shoulder and I collide with Theo's mother, *Winnie*.

Oh fuuuuuck.

"Mum!" Theo says, standing up straight, holding his shorts over his front and tucking me in behind him with his free hand.

"Theo! What on earth?"

"Laundry, Mum. Just doing some laundry."

"Naked? You do laundry naked, do ye? I never! Theo Clarke,

this is above and beyond…" she grows eerily silent as Theo trembles under my hands. I peak around him to see what's happening and he erupts into a full-on belly laugh.

"Laughing! Now you're laughing?" Theo continues roaring in laughter and I bite my lip and sneak a peek at his mom. "Leslie, is that you behind there?"

My silent laughter that I've been doing so good to conceal bursts out of me. "Yes, Mrs. Clarke."

"Oh! I'm Mrs. Clarke now, am I? You two have been caught with your trousers down, and you think it's time to be formal. This is so ghastly, Theo. I am just so disappointed."

Theo continues shaking with laughter and I clamp my hand over my mouth, trying to find some semblance of strength to be respectful while standing butt naked with my bra in one hand, clinging to her naked son with the other.

"I'm really sorry, Winnie!" I cry and laugh even harder.

"I think you might need to call me Mrs. Clarke from now on, Leslie. You two…find your clothes and get your arses downstairs. NOW!" she barks out harshly and swivels on her heels and goes back down the stairs.

"I am mortified," I say with a horribly unconvincing giggle.

"I am too. But I love it," Theo says, turning and walking backwards, pulling me down the hallway. The smile on his face is positively infectious. I can't help but smile back up at him. "And I love you," he adds, yanking me into him and kissing me deeply, stumbling our naked butts through the doorway.

"Another memory!" I guffaw and he silences my smart mouth with a smacking kiss.

CHAPTER FORTY

After a horribly awkward homemade breakfast on the patio with Winnie, Richard, Daphney, and Theo, Winnie is finally looking me in the eyes again. I do my best to answer Richard's kind questions about my job and my move to London. I successfully dodge questions about my family, but I can feel Winnie's hard eyes on me the entire time.

Daphney chats animatedly through the majority of the meal. She seems like a different girl than the one I met at the charity ball. She's lighter—happier in her own environment. Or perhaps she's just happier having some of her family back home. I can't tell.

Eventually, Winnie tells Theo that Hayden willingly signed up for a thirty-day treatment facility instead of doing the seventy-two-hour hospital hold. She said it was a great facility that came highly recommended from the counselor they spoke with this morning.

"I'm just grateful for a break from all the worry," she says with a forlorn look on her face.

Theo's dad clears his throat. "A break is nice, but I'll be ready to have him home again…on the mend I hope." He looks down at his plate awkwardly.

"Take a walk with me, would you, Leslie?" Winnie asks suddenly, taking all of us off guard.

I nod, glancing over to Theo, who looks nervous but smiles at me reassuringly.

"Let me just run these in," I say, getting up to take my dishes into the house. Daphney follows closely behind and eyes me seriously as I scrape the plate clean into the trash.

"Something on your mind, Daphney?"

"I just can really see it." Her skinny frame twists slightly as she surveys me skeptically.

"See what?" I ask, tucking my hair nervously behind my ears.

"How you make Theo so happy."

That stops me in my tracks. "What do you mean?"

"I don't know," she says, and shrugs her shoulders. "Something about you, though. I can see it. I'm glad you're here, Leslie." She smiles one more time and turns to head back out to the patio.

Well, that was…nice?

A moment later, I'm walking with Winnie in a heavily wooded area off to the side of their garage. A small path is carved through it as if they do a lot of walking over here. She leads me into a hidden gazebo that looks like it was plucked out of on an English Cottage magazine.

We both sit and I feel nervous and unsure of what Winnie wants to say to me. I'm sure it has something to do with me saying Marisa's name at the charity last night.

"Relax, Leslie. I'm not going to scold you. You're an adult. And you're actually clothed right now, so it's not my place."

I half-smile at her and turn to face her.

"I am sorry about saying Marisa's name though. I want you to know that."

"I know, love. And I'd be lying if I said I didn't think Theo made a grave error in judgment inviting you into his life."

Her statement slams into me like a dagger to the heart. "I'm so sorry, Mrs. Clarke. I didn't know. I am horrified at my behavior. Really. I was so stupid."

"Call me Winnie, dear. I've seen you in the buff for goodness' sake." I smile awkwardly. "Losing a daughter is the truest tragedy a person can face, Leslie. No parent should have to bury a child. It's just not right."

"I know. I know and I'm sorry. Theo only just told me."

"Please stop saying sorry," she says, looking forward stoically with her hands clasped behind her back. "After Marisa's death, I needed something to latch onto. A duty to fulfill. A way to turn a negative into a positive. To try to help someone else. There's no *cause* to raise money for what happened to my Marisa." Her voice catches in her throat and she clears it quickly to continue. "So when Hayden began struggling, my mission became clear."

"I've been so consumed with Hayden that I've not noticed how hurt the rest of my family has been. But…seeing Theo laugh like that in the hallway today. It…it…" her voice wobbles and her eyes well with tears. She stops walking to look straight into my eyes. "It made me realize that I haven't heard that sound in so long. Much, much too long. I've buried my head in the sand and called it a cause, and that is so wrong."

"You were doing the best you could," I say, rubbing her arm. The affection snaps something inside of her and she pulls me into a hug.

"Thank you. Thank you for finding my boy and loving him when I should have been doing better. You do love him, don't you, dear?" she asks, pulling away and looking at me with sad watery eyes.

"More than anything," I say, meaning it with all my heart.

She smiles. "I thought so. While I can tell that you have no respect for people's house rules, I can definitely see a shift in my son." She brushes my bangs out of my eyes just as a loving mother would to her daughter. "And that change is for the better."

"You have a beautiful family. I envy it," I say, my voice wavering.

"You envy us?"

"I do. It's not this easy for some families."

"I don't know what about all of this is easy."

"Just that, you have each other. Flaws and all, you still have each other. That love is beautiful to see."

She stares at me skeptically with a sideways glance. "You seem quite easy to love, my dear."

I swallow hard, willing the pain away. Now is not the time. As if taking mercy on me, Winnie changes the subject.

"Now, let's have a quick chat about being appropriate in my

house and then I'll release you back to my brooding son who's pacing back and forth over there. Do you see him?"

I squint and giggle at the sight of Theo fidgeting by the house, looking nervous and worried. Good Lord, his mother isn't that bad!

"Come back up for dinner sometime soon, Theo. Please?" He nods silently. She looks over to me, "Leslie. Dinner…please?" Winnie asks, hugging us both by Theo's car in the driveway. Richard and Daphney are standing on either side of her, grinning knowingly.

"Dinner sounds great," I reply. "Is the dress code casual…or optional, maybe?" I ask cheekily. Theo and his entire family gape at me incredulously. It's Winnie's peals of laughter that break the awkward tension.

"Was that too soon?" I ask, laughing along with everyone.

"Yes!" Winnie says, seriously, and then starts laughing again. "Oh goodness, love. Theo, take this poor girl home before I enroll her in etiquette school!"

We drive away and I look back at Theo's smiling family waving to us from their beautiful home.

CHAPTER FORTY-ONE

"So…I have to go to China," I say, looking up from my computer to Theo stretched out on my daybed.

"What? Why?" He looks indignant and offended.

"Stop! Look at your cute face right now, all grumpy. This is my job, this is what I do." I shrug my shoulders.

It's been nearly a month since Hayden's incident. Theo and I have been out to visit his parents twice since the first encounter. I can already see a lightness forming around them all again and it makes me feel happy that I get to bear witness to his family's healing. They all were so warm and welcoming both times we've been out there. And their house has an essence to it that can't be explained. It feels so comforting.

Winnie told Theo just last week that they were putting the sale of the house on hold for now. I think since the home has been in the family for generations, it was a difficult struggle for them to sell it anyway. The fact that things seem to be improving amongst all of them made it a no-brainer to put the sale on hold. I could tell Theo was happy with that change of plan.

Although, Hayden gets out of his facility soon and that has everyone's nerves on edge. I know they all just want to see him happy again and at peace. And after my chat with Hayden at the hospital, I'm hopeful that when he comes out and sees his family doing better, it'll help him heal as well.

The family connection the Clarke's have is just not something I ever grew up with. My dad was always busy working. When I got older, he always nagged on me about my chosen major in college. Apparently, he didn't see any way I could make a living with a textile and design degree. I resented my mother for never standing up for me…or herself. The one time I did try to stick up for her, it ended so horribly that I still feel ill at the memory of it all.

"I don't want you to go," Theo mumbles gloomily, snapping me out of a terrible memory.

I stand up and make my way over to him on the bed, cozying up beside him. "Sorry, Superman. You'll have to fly solo for a week."

"Jesus! A week? This is terrible news. Terrible news indeed." He takes off his glasses and pinches the bridge of his nose.

"Think of how great reunion sex will be!" I smile saucily, grabbing his glasses and setting them on the end table. "You better give me something to remember you by. I don't want to get hotdog out of hibernation."

"Me neither! Hotdog isn't hibernating as far as I'm concerned. He is well and dead."

"You better not have done anything to my hotdog," I growl as I crawl on top of him, straddling him.

"I've got plenty to keep you occupied, stuff your bloody hotdog," he growls back and grabs my sides roughly, switching places with me.

I giggle up at the twinkle in his eyes and let him prove his point for the next hour.

"Lezbo! You owe me a lunch!" Frank croons at me as I brush my teeth in the bathroom.

"Lunch?"

"I haven't seen you in ages! You've been in Loversville properly ignoring your best mate."

"Frank! We just had family flick night last night! And we did it last week too!"

"I know…but I don't like sharing you with those arseholes."

"By arseholes, do you mean our roommates?" I ask, raising my eyebrows at him in alarm.

"Yeah, they're a bore, Lezzie. I just want you and me time."

"Okay, Frank…tell you what. How about I work from home today? Give me a couple hours to finish a few things and then we can go see Ameerah and Umar. Sound good?"

"I suppose. Let's do alfresco lunch somewhere too. It's bloody gorgeous out."

"Two gingers eating in the sun? I don't know," I tsk disapprovingly.

"You're hardly a true ginge'. But I'll keep you anyway," he winks.

London Bound

A few hours later, Frank and I walk together over to Fab's—dress in tow. After the Hayden incident, my beautiful dress was trashed quite a bit. Ameerah demanded I bring it in to her to look at and that was the last I saw of my masterpiece. I'm bringing her a replacement dress I've been working on for the past month, excited to surprise her. It's beautiful, but it still doesn't hit the level of my leather and rosette number.

"Leslie, child! Just the girl I wanted to see!" Ameerah coos, stepping through the beads. "Whatchu got there?" she asks, gesturing toward the garment bag in my hands.

"I've just finished up a replacement dress for your window. I know it's not the same fabric, but it was the least I could do."

"Honey, I told you I didn't care 'bout that dress. I just care about you. Why don't you listen?"

"I told her the same thing, Ame. Our Lezbo is a bit obnoxious, isn't she?"

"Yes, but she's got a kind heart. And...I have a feeling you're going to be really happy in a moment."

"Why?" I ask as she disappears behind the beads for a minute and reemerges again with my leather rosette dress in hand.

"What is that?" I ask, feeling shocked.

"It's your dress!" she smiles proudly.

"What did you do?"

"It's a dye technique my mother taught me. What do you think?"

I walk over to her and my jaw hangs open as I take in the cool red swirly colors she's dyed all over the cream rosette skirting.

"It was too pretty to just throw in the trash."

"It's even cooler now, will you show me how you did it?"

"Of course, child! Always!" She smiles at me proudly.

"You should put it up in the window!" I say brightly.

"Naaa, I was thinkin' you needed to keep this one for home. You okay with that?"

"Ameerah, the fabric was very expensive."

"When you throw that much passion into a simple dress, it belongs to you. You keep it. I won't take no for an answer."

"Thank you!" I say, looking up at her smiling dark-skinned face. She smiles back at me, looking like a proud momma bear gazing down at her cub.

"I'm bored," Frank's obnoxious voice cuts over our special moment. "I'm going next door to look at porn."

The bell rings and Ameerah and I chuckle at Frank's blatant honesty.

LB

"I'm done, Frank. You want to go get lunch?"

"Hang on a tic Lez, you gotta see this! This vibrator from the fifties looks like a bloody hairdryer with a hair brush on the end!"

I glance over Frank's shoulder and cringe, "Oh my God! That looks terrible! Why would they do that?"

"For pleasure, of course!" Frank answers deadpan.

"That does not look pleasurable." I glance up at Umar watching us with mirth. "How are ya Umar, ol' buddy, ol' pal?"

"Good, Leslie. How are you? Haven't seen you in a while."

"The bitch is in love, Umar. Can you fucking believe it?" Frank interjects gloomily.

"Bitter much?" I reply and Frank rolls his eyes. "Let's go get some lunch." Frank sighs dramatically and waves a theatrical goodbye to Umar.

We find a cozy café down the street with patio seating on the sidewalk. Once the waitress delivers our drinks, I lay into Frank.

"What's happening with Billy the Kid?"

"What?" Frank asks, looking down and grabbing a chip out of the starter we ordered to share.

"You know what I'm talking about. Your cowboy lover. The one you showed your bedazzler skills to. The one you've had over three times in the last month. That's a record for you, Frank!"

Frank looks down quizzically, furrowing his red eyebrows. I smile at his crazy frizzy hair sticking around every which way, smashed under his white beret.

"Oh him. I think it's time to toss him to the curb."

"Why?"

"He keeps calling and coming 'round uninvited. I don't get it."

"What's not to get? He obviously likes you."

"Please," he scoffs.

"Please what, Mr. Sour Puss? Why are you being so grumpy about all of this?"

"You should know better than anyone, Lezzie," he mumbles.

"What is that supposed to mean?"

"Look, I'm not going to lay all my shite bare to some random bloke. The same way you haven't laid all your shite bare with Theo." He frowns at me seriously. "You and I both know you're not being completely honest with him."

"Honest with him about what?"

"About whatever issues you've run away from in America."

My blood runs cold. "Did Finley tell you?"

"No! Though I'm quite offended now to discover that she knows and I don't!"

"How do you know then?"

"It doesn't take a genius to spot a wounded soldier, Lezbo. I knew the day I met you that you were running from something. You were living in a bloody hostel for crying out loud."

I remain silent, not really knowing how to respond.

"Look, you don't have to tell me. I don't need to know. I just need to know that you're okay and I can see that you are with Theo. He loves you…crazy neuroses and all. I just hope you're being completely honest with him. He was honest with you, after all. No relationship can survive on secrets. "

I feel horribly nauseous at Frank's stern expression right now. Frank never gets serious, so for him to give me this speech must mean he has serious concerns. And he's right. I haven't been honest with Theo. I haven't even been entirely honest with Finley! I only told her part of the story because the rest is just too painful to relive.

Now I find myself completely in love with Theo—all of my protective armor down. I've only just started to feel safe with our situation.

"Since when did honesty become so high up on your ethics chart?" I mumble into my drink.

"Leslie, as soon as love gets involved, honesty is always the best policy."

CHAPTER FORTY-TWO

I'm leaving for China in two days and Theo refuses to let me out of his sight. I sneak out of my bed, careful not to wake him and make my way to the bathroom to pee and take my pill. I really and truly need to go in to the office today! I have to stop letting this sexy man in his sexy glasses pull me away from my job! And I still haven't found the right time to open up to Theo about my family. How will my Superman handle it all?

I brush my teeth and fill my cup with water to take my pill. I frown slightly as I pop the last of this pack into my palm. My period still hasn't shown up. Is this the right packet? Seems strange. Maybe I need to get off of these and try something else. Surely it's not normal to skip a period.

I swallow hard trying to bury the imminent dread creeping over my body. I can't be pregnant. I can't be pregnant. I'm on the damn pill. This is nothing like that. I make a mental note to get into my doctor again, it's been a couple years since my last appointment, so it's time anyway.

I head downstairs for some coffee, feeling slightly nervous about my messed-up cycle. "Hey Julie," I say, finding her eating cereal in the kitchen booth. She nods silently looking back down at her magazine.

I grab a mug and dump a bucket of milk into the cup before topping it off with a dash of coffee. I blow on it for a moment, tentatively taking a sip while deep in thought.

"Hey Julie," I say, again. "Random question. You're on the pill, right?"

"Yeah, why?" she asks, looking up from her reading.

"Do you ever not get your period?"

"Um...no, not really. Why, did you not get yours?" She looks nervous as her eyes widen fractionally.

"No...I got it, it was just really light."

"Oh, yeah...that happens to me too." She waves me off like I'm crazy.

"Okay, thanks!" I say brightly, filling a second mug for Theo.

I dash back upstairs and feel a horrible sinking feeling in my gut because I was only halfway honest with Julie. What I'm not telling her is the fact that it was last month when my period was light. And by light, I mean, just barely spotting. This month...it's a complete no show. This can't be good.

Theo is up and slipping on his jeans as I walk in the room with our coffees. "Hey you." He smiles lazily, scratching the top of his head.

"Hey yourself," I reply, drinking in his shirtless form standing gloriously beside my dress model. He always looks so manly in my girlie room.

"Cheers," he says as I hand him his cup. "You okay?" he asks, squinting slightly at my eyes.

I'm unnerved by his intuitiveness. "Yeah, I'm fine! Why wouldn't I be?" I reply, my voice hitting a nervous pitch.

He stares at me seriously and then sets his mug down and walks over to me.

"Are you thinking about how much you're going to miss me when you're gone?"

"Hmm?" I reply, my thoughts running away.

"Because I am going to miss you…like crazy." He leans down and drops a tender kiss on my lips, his breath fresh and minty from just brushing his teeth.

"I um, have to go to the office today, so…" I start, trying to extricate myself from his arms.

"Me too," he says quietly, still eyeing me carefully and refusing to break his hold around my waist.

"Well…I best get ready. I'll see you later, 'kay?" I struggle to look into his beautiful brown eyes. If I look at him, he'll know something's up, and I don't even know what's up yet so there's no need to even talk about it.

"Okay," he says, looking somewhat apprehensive. "You good?"

"Great!" I reply enthusiastically, finally breaking free from his embrace.

I'm great. I know I'm great. Please let me be great.

I make an appointment at the clinic as soon as I get to work. I leave for China soon and I need to figure out what the heck is going on with me before I leave.

Two days later, with trembling hands, I sit as the lab tech takes a vile of blood from my arm. She shakes the blood in the test tube and marks it with a sharpie and tosses it into a clear plastic bag with my name on it.

When I called to make the appointment it was awkward city when the nurse asked me if there was any chance I might be pregnant. I hemmed and hawed for an agonizing twenty seconds unable to find the words I so greatly feared. The nurse could read between the lines and said the doctor would do a lab test on me so we knew the answer by the time of my appointment.

"We'll send this off for rapid results. The doctor will have them by the time of your appointment this morning," the tech says, looking like it's just any other Tuesday and she doesn't hold the fate of my future in that tiny vile.

I nod silently and get up on shaky legs and make my way to the doctor's office. I lied to Theo this morning and told him I had to run into the office for something before my flight leaves at noon today. I tried to get an appointment yesterday, but this was the only time they had available because of a cancellation. My appointment with the doctor isn't for another hour and a half, but I sure as shit can't go back home and wait. So I'll just sit here in the waiting room, hoping they have mercy on me and call me back early.

Two hours later, I'm ushered into a small exam room by a nurse. She leaves me by saying the doctor will be with me soon. I grip my hands in my lap so hard that white imprints of my fingers show every time I release them.

A short while later, the doctor comes in, looking perfectly at ease in her navy scrubs and light brown hair tied neatly back in a low ponytail. She's young. Too young. She can't possibly know what the matter with my period is.

"Well, it's as I suspected, Leslie. You're pregnant," she says, looking at me seriously.

I say nothing.

"I would guess a couple months along already, based on the high elevation of your HCG."

I continue to say nothing.

She sits down on the wheelie stool and scoots closer to me, touching my arm gently.

"I take it based on your silence that this wasn't planned?"

Yep, still saying nothing.

"Leslie, you're going to have to talk to me before I can let you leave here."

I blink slowly. "I have to go to China for work today! My flight leaves in three hours."

"You're fine to travel, just don't eat anything strange while you're over there."

"Like what?"

"Raw fish—raw anything, really. Weird herbs. Just stick to normal foods."

"How did this happen? I'm on the pill," I ask, feeling cheated by something.

"Do you take your pill faithfully every day at the same time?"

Why is she looking at me sympathetically?

"Yes, well...I mean, I take it every day, but not always at the same time." In the early days with Theo, there were several days where I forgot my pills at home and didn't take them until that evening after work. Sometimes I'd even have to double up. I knew that wasn't good, but I figured if I was getting them in, I was fine.

"Well, they aren't one-hundred-percent effective and that's if you *do* take them properly. You can't vary the times you take them or they lose more of their effectiveness."

"I'm going to be sick," I croak.

"Have you been having morning sickness? You can have it any time of the day, you know."

"No! Nothing. I feel perfectly normal."

"Well, not everyone has pregnancy symptoms. You might be just one of the lucky ones."

"Lucky?" I bark out a laugh.

She half-smiles at me. "Do you want to talk options?"

"What do you mean?" I ask, frowning at her.

"Well, you have options, Leslie. If this is an unwanted pregnancy, you do have choices, but not for long."

"I don't want to talk about choices," I clip out, feeling even sicker at that idea. "I haven't been very healthy though. I'm sure I've drank alcohol since this happened—not a ton—but some. I'm not on any vitamins. I'm not doing anything good for myself!" My voice is starting to shriek.

She smiles kindly. "Are you a heavy drinker?"

"No," I shake my head firmly. Honestly, I haven't been drinking much at all since I started sleeping with Theo, so maybe I'm okay.

"Okay, don't worry. This happens a lot. You don't share a blood supply with the baby until around six weeks pregnant, so any alcohol or drug use really won't have an effect. Obviously that needs to stop now though. And I need to see you back here in two weeks for an ultrasound to determine fetal age. But I'm guessing you're at least eight weeks along."

Two months? "I've only been with him for that long," I reply flatly.

"Is he a good guy?"

"How do we ever really know?" I ask, feeling that ill feeling roll over me again. It was easy to accept Theo's love when it was just for me. Now I have to have him love a baby too?

"I suggest you take your China trip as time to think about this and decide how you feel about it before you tell him. But that's from one woman to another, not a medical professional to her patient."

I nod through a few more basic pregnancy instructions and the nurse comes in to give me a sample pack of vitamins so I don't have to go to the drugstore before my flight leaves.

I ride the Tube back to the office—my mind whirling constantly with all the new information. God, I'm twenty-six years old! I'm too young to have children. I didn't even think I wanted children at all, and now this! And oh my God, Finley! All she wants is babies, and she can't even have them. I watched her whole world crumble last year over this. And now I have an accidental pregnancy. This could ruin our friendship. Completely and utterly ruin it. I could lose everything all at once. Theo. Finley. Would Frank let me still live with him if I have a baby? Oh my God, my life has just been completely unhinged.

I step off the Tube and head toward my office, feeling completely overwhelmed at the idea of facing Theo. He's supposed to pick me up soon at my office to take me to the airport. How am I going to act around him? How will I be able to hide this from him? Maybe I can talk him out of giving me a ride.

I stand outside the fire exit at my office and pull my phone out. My hands are shaking like crazy.

"Lez! What are you doing here? You're supposed to be on your way to China!" Vilma calls down through the window.

"My flight doesn't leave for three hours, Vilma. Can I get some privacy please?"

"Christ! What's eating you?" she says and disappears back inside. I cringe at her reaction, feeling like an utter bitch, but not willing to take any of it back.

I click *call* on Theo's name and he picks up after two rings.

"Are you calling for an early pickup?" he drawls in a husky tone.

"Huh? What?" I ask, taken off guard.

He chuckles softly. "I thought maybe you were going to duck out of work early to surprise me so we could have a little rendezvous before I take you to the airport," he croons into the phone.

"God, is sex all you think about?" I snap.

"No, 'course not. It was just a joke. What's got your lack of panties in such a bunch?"

"Nothing, Theo. I just…I don't need a ride to the airport anymore."

"What do you mean?" he asks, his tone clearly annoyed.

"I'm taking the Tube. It'll be faster not dealing with the traffic."

"Alright, then I'll come to your office and ride the Tube over there with you."

"That doesn't make any damn sense, Theo. I'll just see you when I get back."

"Leslie."

"What?"

"What are you doing?"

"Nothing…I just…this…this…Theo!" I flail my hands in the air dramatically. "It's…it's all just horribly unnecessary."

"What exactly are you referring to? You're going to have to be more specific."

"I'm feeling smothered, alright? We're together every night. You can't even let me take myself to the airport? I used to do this stuff all by myself once upon a time you know. I didn't need you to do all this for me!"

"Smothered." The line is eerily quiet. "Right then. Well, I wouldn't want you to feel smothered. Enjoy your trip."

"Theo…" I start, but he hangs up and I pant heavily at the sensation of being hung up on. My hand flies to my mouth and I quickly dash into my office, running to the bathroom, effectively emptying the contents of my stomach into the toilet.

Perfect timing.

CHAPTER FORTY-THREE

It's nearly midnight when I land in Hong Kong and I feel exhausted. I take an airport shuttle straight to my hotel. As soon as I get into my room, I drop my bags on the floor, strip down naked, crawl into the large, king-sized bed, and cry like I've never cried before. I've been holding in my shit for as long as possible and I can't hold it in a second more.

The morning light streams in brightly through the wide-open hotel windows. I never even closed the damn curtains when I came in last night. That's how delirious I was. My face feels tight and dry from crying myself to sleep, and my mouth is parched as hell.

I wrap myself in the sheet and mosey over to the window looking down the huge skyscraper building. Hong Kong is up and moving, already busily going about their business without a care in the world. And here I am...pregnant and alone.

Pregnant. How? How can I be pregnant? I don't even feel any different. Aside from puking yesterday, I haven't noticed a thing. Maybe my breasts have been tenderer—but I thought that was because my period was coming.

I touch my stomach to see if I feel anything different, a sob erupts out of nowhere. How can this be happening? What if this is all too much for Theo? Could I do it on my own? Or worse, what if he's a terrible father, like mine?

After blowing my nose and wiping my fresh tears, I decide there's no way I can work today, feeling like I'm feeling right now. Our Hong Kong office gal and interpreter, Midge, would think I was mental coming in looking like I do. I don't have to head to the factories until later this week, so today shouldn't be an issue.

I find my phone inside my purse and power it up, realizing I never even turned it back on after the flight yesterday. As the boot up completes, a slew of notifications start pinging over and over and over. They are all from Theo, wondering if I got here safely. They start off innocent enough and then turn into panicked and worried. I pull up his contact and connect the call immediately.

"Leslie!" Theo cries into the phone. "Are you alright?"

"Yes, I'm sorry. I forgot to turn my phone back on after the flight and I fell asleep in my hotel room."

"Christ, Leslie!" he admonishes. "Do you know how worried I've been?"

"I'm fine. Why were you so worried?"

"You tell me I'm smothering you and then run away to a foreign country. I'm fucking…*right here, mate.*"

"What are you doing?" I ask, wondering who he's talking to.

"I'm here."

"Here where?"

"Outside your hotel."

My stomach drops. "You're in Hong Kong? Theo! Why?"

"Millimeters, Leslie."

"Flying to bloody Hong Kong is a lot more than chasing me around London, Theo."

"Look, I just need to see you. I can't explain it Leslie, but I need to see you and then if you really want space..." he pauses momentarily, breathing heavily into the phone, "I'll give it to you."

I say nothing.

"Please, Leslie."

"I'm in room 2720."

"I'm in the elevator."

A moment later I've pulled on a tank and shorts and have just finished brushing my teeth when I hear a knock at my door. I look briefly at my stomach in the mirror and still can't see anything. I sigh heavily and open it.

Without a word, Theo barrels in the door, crashing into me and pressing me against the wall—assaulting my lips with his. I fight it at first, trying to turn away, but I can already feel my arousal building as his firm, rippled body presses into mine.

"Leslie," he cries, sounding pained. He kisses me again and when I still don't respond as passionately, he hooks his finger into my mouth and lets it linger. Instinctively, my lips close around the girth of his digit and I suck. Hard. Both of our eyes flash in heady desire and we slam our lips together in a wanton, bruising kiss. He breaks the kiss and moves down my neck to my collarbone and shoulder.

"Theo!" I cry as he quickly slips his hand down my shorts and inside of me, feverishly working me into a hard and fast frenzy. His other hand is wrapped tightly around my waist, holding me close to him so I can feel every inch of his excitement along my side.

"You can't run from me, Leslie. I love you. Please." His voice is coarse and mournful. It tears through my shield and clamps tightly around my heart.

"I love you too," I cry, and tears fly out of my eyes. I grab his face and connect our lips again so he can't see me crying. They stream down my cheeks and intermingle between our lips, tasting salty and sad. He pulls away from me, looking desolate.

"Please, Leslie, what is it? What's happened?"

I shake my head, "Just make love to me, Theo. Please?" His eyes rove over my face, searching for answers that I'm not ready to give him. He relents and pulls my tank over my head, gazing ardently down at my bare chest. He bends over and takes one of my nipples into his mouth and I cry out loudly. They are so sensitive. This is…this is too much!

"Theo," I say, tipping over the edge in less than ten seconds. He looks up at me just as shocked as I am that I just came off of nipple stimulation alone. I aggressively grab the hem of his t-shirt and yank it up over his head. My eyes and hands feast on every perfectly sculpted muscle on his chest and abdomen.

He wraps his arms low on my waist and lifts me up so his face is nestled between my breasts as he carries me over to the bed. He lays me down gently on my back and grabs my shorts and slips them down my legs, then moves to push his jeans down.

He slowly spreads my legs open and crawls up to rest between them, all the while gazing into my eyes—reverently, but with glimpses of pain.

"Leslie, I thought we were past the running stage," he groans, running his nose along my neck and jaw.

I shake my head, unwilling to reply to that and trying desperately to focus solely on my raging arousal.

"I've told you I love you. I know you love me. I can't have you running from me whenever something spooks you." He slowly pushes himself into me, inch by glorious inch, not giving me his full length.

"You have to tell me what it is so I can help you, Leslie. We can work through things better together." Finally he pushes all the way in and I let out a high-pitched groan of delight at the feverish ecstasy of him so deep inside of me.

"Please, Theo," I say, wrapping my legs around his hips and urging him to move inside of me. He continues staring at me, obviously relishing at my discomfort and the control he has in this moment.

"Promise you won't push me away, Leslie."

"Okay," I gasp as he wriggles his hips ever so slightly.

"I need to hear you say it."

"I won't push you away."

"And you won't run."

"I won't run, Theo!" I snap at him. "You're probably going to be the one to run from me anyhow."

He looks completely taken off guard. "Leslie, don't you know anything? I'll never run from you. I'll fight for you…forever. I've never loved anyone the way I've loved you. I want to love you forever."

"Forever is a long time, Theo. You'll get tired of me." My chin wobbles at that thought.

"Dammit, Leslie!" he barks incredulously. "Stop saying that! I'll never tire of you! I want to marry you!"

My chin stills.

"You…you want to…" I feel stunned and overwhelmed and too scared to say the word aloud.

"Yes, I want to marry you. But this was not how I planned on asking you." He looks down between us incredulously. "I'm fucking balls deep here, Lez!"

A manic giggle escapes from somewhere deep inside all of my pain and insecurities and Theo's eyes soften at the sound. He sighs heavily, resting his forehead against mine. "I love you," he whispers against my lips.

"I love you more," I whisper, feeling another tear slip down my temple.

"No bloody way." And with that he begins rocking into me at a feverish pace that has both of us reaching our climax together.

CHAPTER FORTY-FOUR

"I need to tell you something," I say as Theo comes strolling out of the bathroom in nothing but his white boxer briefs and glasses.

God, those fucking glasses.

"Okay," he says, looking seriously at me like he was expecting this.

"Okay," I repeat, sitting up and propping my back against the headboard, my legs folding up against my chest. For some reason balling myself up and squeezing my legs to my chest makes breathing easier.

"You said you wanted to marry me," I start and stop as Theo blanches.

"Leslie. I didn't mean to say that just then." He sits down on the bed, reaching for me and I pull away from his touch. "I just…you got me so frazzled and nervous. You ran off to Hong Kong without a care for my feelings and I felt panicky."

"So you didn't mean it?"

"Christ, no! I meant every bloody word!"

"What? Theo, you're confusing the shit out of me."

"I meant everything. I do want to marry you, Leslie. But you deserve so much more than that for a proposal. You deserve the world. You deserve a fucking helicopter ride, or a hot air balloon proposal, or a sign on a plane in the sky."

"I guess now would be a good time to tell you I'm afraid of heights."

He chuckles softly and reaches for my hand again and I let him take it this time.

"I just mean I want our life to be perfect. You deserve perfect, Leslie."

"What if it's not perfect?" I ask, biting my lip and pulling my hand out of his to rub my shins nervously.

He swallows hard, looking gravely into my eyes. "I mean, I guess if you look at my family you can see that I obviously know how to handle the imperfect. The point is I want to give you everything."

"Kids?"

"Kids?" He looks off to the side confused and dismissive. "Yeah, I'd love to have babies with you, Leslie. You'd make a great mum."

"You really think so?" I ask, my voice thick with emotion.

"I don't think, Leslie. I know. You have the biggest heart. Christ, I've loved you from nearly the first moment I saw you. I didn't believe in that kind of love until you came into my life. If we have children, they won't stand a chance and neither will I."

"Theo," I cry, losing my control entirely. I lunge into his arms and hug him hard, crying like I cried last night. His body is firm and rigid, radiating anxiety.

"Leslie, please. This is *killing* me," he whispers, slowly stroking my auburn hair down the back of my head.

I pull away from him and look down at his chest. He pushes my hair away from my wet cheeks as I pant out three huge breaths.

"I'm pregnant, Theo."

His hand stills alongside my face and he takes in a breath and holds it.

"No Theo! You said you wouldn't!" I cry, shoving him in his chest and leaping out of the bed. He exhales quickly and takes a deep breath of air, looking dazed and confused.

"I'm sorry! I didn't think. Fuck, Leslie, please!"

I grab my shorts up off the floor and pull them up roughly. "This is fucking great, Theo. I tell you I'm pregnant and you have a damn panic attack."

He rushes over to me, grabbing my wrists.

"That's not what that was, Leslie! Please." I find my tank top by the door and pull it down over my head. "You've just shocked me. I never…I never thought…"

"Never thought what? Finish!" I cry loudly, my hands clasp tightly around the back of my neck.

"I thought you were breaking up with me, Leslie! Fuck!" he booms, turning away from me and striding over to the window. He scratches his buzzed hair aggressively and rotates back to me, throwing his arms out dramatically. "You were going on and on about not being perfect and I thought you were going to tell me you were done with me and all of that was goodbye sex. And shite! Then you said you were pregnant and I had this flash of our future together and it was so...and I was...I was...I don't know! Overcome I guess!"

"Overcome in a good way, or overcome in a bad way?" I ask, perching my hands on my hips, feeling infuriated.

"Christ, just give me a second. I just found out the woman I love with everything I have is going to have my child. This is...this is..."

"What?" I ask, crossing my arms tightly over my chest.

"It's fucking fantastic!"

"Fantastic?"

"Yes, Leslie. I don't know how many times you're going to have to hear me say I love you for it to sink in. But Jesus, picturing you as a mum is about the most beautiful thing I could ever imagine."

A sob erupts as his words blanket me in affection.

"I'm so sorry for mucking this up, Leslie. I didn't realize. I didn't even think. I'm so bloody happy, the only way I could be happier is if you were in my arms right now."

I run over and collide with him as he lifts me up off the floor.

"We have to get this right, Theo," I cry against his shoulder.

"Of course, love."

"No, I mean it. This baby has to have it good from us. We can't mess this up."

He sets me down pushing my bangs away from my eyes. "Why

would we mess it up?"

I shake my head. "You don't know, Theo. I've not told you because I've spent the last five years running from it. Similar to how you didn't want to talk about Marisa. But I want to tell you. I want to tell you everything and be completely honest so we don't mess this up." I finish clutching my hands to my stomach. The gesture feels strange but natural somehow.

"I had been living in London less than a year. It was in the very recent wake of me telling my parents I was dropping out of college and moving to London. They were decidedly upset and argued with me over the phone, but there was little they could do. I had made up my mind.

I called one night to try to, at the very least, mend some fences with my mother. Tom had just started his first year at Iowa and I wondered how my mother was doing home alone with my father."

I swallow hard and Theo senses the anxiety growing in my shoulders so he pulls me down over to the bed. We both sit on the edge and he's softly rubbing my back but I can barely feel it as my mind wanders back to my past.

"Growing up, my father was horrid. He'd make cutting remarks about my clothes, my friends, my dreams—anything he could crumble with his bare hands…he did. The worst of it was, he put on a wonderful show in front of people in town. As the only local dairy farm, the Lincoln name was well known. So I just swallowed and bit my tongue every time we were in public together and he acted like the loving father he never was.

I think that was why I always joked around and did wild things with Finley. It was my escape. My release. When I was away from my dad, I was free to be myself: Crazy Leslie. And laughing and joking around was so much easier than crying. Despite all of my hatred I had toward my father, I still loved my mom. And I was feeling tons of guilt for leaving her behind with him.

When she answered the phone, I had trouble understanding her. She sounded like she had gauze in her mouth. I pressed her about it and she said she just had a toothache. I knew something was seriously wrong. I could feel it.

I was able to catch a flight home two days later. When I came in the front door and locked eyes on her, I nearly fell over from shock. My mom was sitting at the kitchen table, applying ointment to the side of her completely swollen-shut eye. Her face was littered with small cuts and bruises yellowed from age. I hardly recognized her."

LB

"Mom," I say, my voice catching in my throat.

"Leslie! Why are you home?" she asks, looking nervously behind me.

"Mom!" I cry at the sight of her. Her tiny, frail body and greying hair look dull and lifeless.

"Stop crying. Right now. Your father will be coming in any second."

"Why, Mom? Why?" I rush over to her and drop to my knees, crying even harder because of the feeling of loss. I'm completely at a loss. My dad has struck my mother before, but nothing even closely resembling this.

"What's this? The prodigal daughter returns," a grave voice booms from behind me.

I stand up slowly, turning to look at him. He's filthy from

working outside all day, the creases on his skin more prominent than last I remember.

"Dad," I say softly, trying to find the courage inside of me that I needed to stay standing.

"Leslie. You home for good?"

"No," I let out a huff of a laugh and his face turns grave. "I came to check on mom. She doesn't look very good."

"She took quite a fall helping me with the cows."

"Fuck off," I bite out meanly. I've never spoken to my father this way. My whole life, I just nodded and smiled or avoided him at all costs. But living in London the past year has changed that. I no longer feel stuck beneath his thumb. I was my own person. An adult. I'm twenty-one and this shit has to stop.

"Come again," he says, looking at me furiously.

"You need to fuck off, Dad. You went way too far this time."

"You don't know what you're talking about, kid."

I swallow hard at the endearment—*kid*. It sends shivers down my spine.

"I'm calling the police," I say, moving past him to grab my purse. His foot flies out and catches me on the side of my knee and I fall hard to the ground.

"Thomas!" my mother cries.

I wince at the pain radiating from his swift kick. I glance over my shoulder and see him standing stock-still over the top of me. I try to push myself up off the ground and he shoves me back down with his dirty boot, hard on my back. My back aches where his boot landed.

"You'll stay down if you know what's good for you," he roars with an evil to his voice I've never heard before.

A large part of me wants to stay down, cowered in the fetal position until everything disappears. But the image of my mother's bruised face and all the bruises I've ignored as a child flash across my memory and it makes me sick. I try to push myself up again.

He leans over and grips the back of my neck with his hand and squeezes hard. The tips of his fingers dig into the sides of my throat, restricting my airway some.

"Leslie!" my mother hisses. "Just stay down."

Just when I start to get nervous and panicky for more air, his grip loosens slightly. "You think you're tough now? Better than us?" he says spitefully.

I bite down on my tongue and quickly attempt to push myself up again. He lets me this time, but once I am on my feet, he shoves me hard away from him by my neck.

Feeling determined still, I reach to grab my purse off the table and he yanks my arm roughly to face him. Pain slices across my face as he backhands me and sends me halfway across the small kitchen. I manage to stay on my feet, but flinch as I feel the nick of his wedding ring catch the ridge of my cheekbone. The pain is minimal at first. I mostly feel shock and confusion over the feel of my brain being rattled in a way I have never felt before. Then bursts of pain shoot outward beneath the skin of my cheek in a fiery rage.

"Thomas, please!" my mother cries again, coming to stand between me and him, holding her hands out protectively. I clutch my face as my eyes well with tears. The sting of the salty tear running down my tender cheek smarts and I bite my lip, trying desperately to mask my emotions.

"Leslie, you need to go," my mom utters wobbly, turning around, grabbing my arms and leading me to the door.

"Mom, come with me," I cry. She shakes her head quickly and avoids eye contact. "Mom!" I cry again, trying to get her to look at me, trying to find any fraction of a piece of the mother I grew up with all those years.

"Leslie, stop it. You chose your life. I chose mine. You need to go. I'm asking you to leave!" Her face looks serious and panicky.

"Mom," I huff, as I feel her drift away from me before my very eyes. "Please?"

She shakes her head no. "You go, Leslie. You make your own life. I'll be just fine." She pushes me out onto the deck and closes the door in my face, without so much as a glance back.

"That was the moment I knew. I would never have a relationship with my parents again. Marshall sure as hell wasn't home anymore. And I would never let a man control me the way my father controlled my mother."

I clear my throat loudly trying to compose myself enough to continue. I shrug my shoulders sadly as Theo cradles my head to his chest and strokes my hair over and over, his hands trembling.

"I went and hung out with Finley at college for a couple days after my mom kicked me out. I just went completely wild. Fin had no idea. I did what I always do. I put up a shield and masked all my pain with humor. Tom called me a couple days later and told me to come back home because he thought we could talk some sense into Mom if we were together and Dad was out of the house. No matter what we said to her, she wouldn't listen. She wouldn't involve the police. She wouldn't leave him."

"So I flew back to London and didn't talk to her for almost two years. Tom updated me on them here and there. I still couldn't bring myself to call her. She emails now—occasionally. It's strained, but it's something, I guess." I pull away from Theo's chest to look him in the eyes for the first time since I started telling him my story. His pale brown eyes are wide and glossy and his face is covered in pity.

"Thinking about that moment I left my mother with him will haunt me forever. I've been living with so much shame for not doing more to help her. I could have called the cops that night. He assaulted me too. I was an adult. But I didn't and it still makes me sick to my stomach that I did nothing. I just left!" My voice cracks at the end.

"You can't force your mum to do anything, Leslie," Theo says, looking at me seriously.

"Doesn't change the shame. It's still there. I think it'll always be there for me in some small way."

"Christ, Leslie. I'm so…I'm so…"

"Don't say sorry," I say, pulling away from him a bit more. "Remember, Theo? You told me I couldn't say that to you. Same rules apply."

"Fuck me, I want to find your dad and pummel him." His vein muscles bulge as he looks away.

"My mom allowed herself to live under his thumb and rely on him for everything. It was the ultimate betrayal having her push me out the door when I was just trying to love her." I shake my tears away and sniff loudly, clearing my throat. "Then I just tried to quit caring about them at all and focus on my friends and my job—they were safe for me."

"You've done amazingly, Leslie. You have a great job, wonderful friends, and a home. You've created the best life for yourself despite him…them."

"I know. But I hope now you can understand—if only just a little more—why I resisted you so hard. You were so pushy Theo, and so demanding and so…well, it scared me! I made a promise to myself that I'd never let a man affect me like that."

"Christ, Leslie, I'm nothing like your father," he groans, frustratingly rubbing his hand over his head.

"I know, Theo, but I was terrified of being vulnerable to any man! I didn't want to need anyone but myself."

"It's okay to need me, Leslie. I bloody well need you!" he says, leaning forward and holding my hands tightly between his. I swallow hard, looking down at our hands and how different they look side by side.

"Leslie…you hold all the cards, surely you know that."

I smile sadly. "I want to share the cards, finally. With you." I look up at him smiling, my eye sparkling with more tears. "Fifty/fifty. Well…maybe 33/33/33."

He looks at me quizzically.

"This baby, Theo. I think I'm happy for it. I think it's our chance to really atone. Make up for all the darkness in our life with something beautiful. We can be beautiful parents, don't you think?"

He laughs adoringly at me. "Of course, Leslie. You're going to be the best mum and I am going to be crushed with more love than I'll know how to handle."

"Crushed with love?"

"Crushed with love."

"Sounds badass," I smirk and he chuckles, pulling me into him for a kiss.

"Sounds perfect," he murmurs against my lips, tenderly stroking my belly. That little touch to my stomach makes everything click into place. This man is worth needing. He's worth trusting and we're going to pull each other out of the darkness. Together. As a family.

CHAPTER FORTY-FIVE

"I'm sick with nerves, Theo."

"Don't be. She's your best mate, Leslie. She won't hate you. I know it."

We've just returned from the doctor's office and had our first ultrasound. We saw our baby. *Our baby!* I'm no expert, but I'm pretty sure as far as ultrasounds go, we knocked ours out of the park. Surely not all parents can say their babies danced during their first scan. Our baby didn't just dance…she had moves! Or he, I suppose, but I'm convinced it's a girl. Our ten-week-old little babe was putting on an epic show for its mommy and daddy and shit got really real, really fast.

Now my bubble is shattered as I sit in Theo's car, willing myself the strength to go into the house and talk to Finley.

Finley. My best friend.

I went through a horrendous time with her last year when she got her official infertility diagnosis. It crushed her. It nearly ruined her and Brody forever. She did not handle it well and now her best friend that she ran to for solace is going to drop this bomb on her.

I'm such a jerk!

I wrench the door open and barely even say goodbye to Theo. I can't be troubled with pleasantries. I need to talk to my best friend.

I push open our purple door and my eyes land on Finley as she comes bouncing down the stairs.

"Hey! I was just looking for you in your room. Where you been?"

I swallow hard. "Let's chat."

"Cool, come to my room, I want your help picking out what to wear tonight. Brody is taking me on this Jack the Ripper walking tour and I have no damn clue what to wear to something like that!"

I laugh dumbly and follow her to her bedroom.

"Where's Brody?" I ask, looking around nervously.

"Working at the new job! He's loving it," she says, walking into their walk-in closet and shouting out at me as she rifles through her clothes. "He says restoring historical buildings is a whole new world he never would have had an opportunity with back in the states. I'm so happy. Moving out here was such a big deal for us, ye know? It was such a leap of faith with Brody not having a job, but it's all working out! It's meant to be!"

"Finley," I interrupt her supposed monologue, joining her in her huge closet.

"What?" she says, looking quizzically at me. "What's wrong, Lez?"

"Can we sit?" I ask and she nods and starts to walk out but stops in her tracks when I plop my butt down and sit crisscross on the floor in the middle of her closet.

"I need to tell you something, Finley. I'm so scared because it's something I am very happy about—but I don't know if you will be."

"What is it?" she asks, sounding startled and mirroring my seated position, touching my knees encouragingly.

"It was an accident Fin and that only makes it all worse. But I want you to know that if I could make this okay for you…if I could fix any of it for you…I'd do it. I'd do anything for you, Finley, do you know that?"

"Yes, Lezzie, I know! Please tell me. You're freaking me out."

"I'm pregnant," I say, dropping my chin and eyeing her carefully.

Her mouth opens in a perfect O and she blinks dazedly for a moment.

"It just happened. I fucked up on my birth control. I didn't take them when I should have. We've had an ultrasound just today and I'm ten weeks and I'm freaking out because you're my best friend and I know how bad you want this and how hard you tried and—"

"Leslie!" Finley snaps and I shut my mouth instantly. "You said you're happy about this?"

I nod silently.

"Then there is nothing more to say, you idiot!" she cries, holding my arms and looking at me seriously. I let out a huge puff of shaky air and smile sadly at her.

"After everything with last year and you and Brody…I just…I

didn't want to hurt you, Finley. The very last thing I wanted to do was hurt you. I've been sick with nerves at the idea of telling you this!"

"Leslie," she groans. "I don't want your pity. That's the very last thing I want. Do you know how terrible it feels to be pitied for something you can't control?"

I look at her strong, stoic face and my chin begins to wobble.

"I wasn't trying to pity you," I say in a choked whisper.

"Being afraid to tell me something you're happy about because you're sorry that I can't have that same happiness, is pity, Leslie. I don't deserve that."

"I'm sorry," I say weakly.

"I know you are. You just don't understand. But you need to know that I'm going to be okay here. Yes, it sucks that I've wanted children for so long and I can't have them. I'm still processing those feeling. But I've got Brody by my side and he is everything I need in life. Just him. I am perfectly fulfilled by his love and his love alone."

I nod wobbly at her.

"I don't know what our future holds for children. I have no clue and I don't really want to even think about that for a while. The world is our oyster right now and we live in a brand new country with all new experiences. No pity for me, Leslie. Ever."

"Okay. No pity," I say seriously and we both laugh pathetically at each other.

"And honestly Leslie, if it was going to be easy and miraculous for anyone, anyone in the whole wide world, I would choose you! You're going to make the most wonderful mother."

"You really think so? I'm kind of a moron a lot," I say on a strange strangled crying laugh and Finley smiles at me adorably.

"You are…but that's what's going to make you such an awesome mom. That kid is going to have the best life. And for the moments where you're really acting like a moron, she…or he…will have Auntie Finley to run to."

"I would just love that, Finny," I say and she pulls me in for an awkward hug over the top of our legs.

"God, we're going to have to clean up our potty mouths!" she groans.

"Oh fuck, we have loads of time for that," I say and we both erupt into a fit of giggles.

An hour later, Brody walks into the bedroom shouting for Finley.

"In here, babe!" Finley calls from where we're both laid out flat on the floor of her closet.

"Frank was looking for you two," Brody says from the doorway, looking down on us completely at ease with this strange place we've chosen to gab for over an hour.

I hear Frank before I see him. "Is that my Lezzie, Fin-Fin?"

"Yep, they're right here," Brody says, thumbing over our way.

Frank's tall lanky frame pops right in next to Brody. He looks hilarious all skinny and trendy, with bright frizzy hair standing next to tall, broad, Brawny-Man Brody. They are quite the pair.

"Are you two having a cuddle without me? I thought we talked about that!" Frank cries, looking near tears.

"C'mon over here, Frank and Beans," I say, opening my arms to him. He comes barreling into the closet and nuzzles up next to me, wrapping his skinny arm around my tiny belly. I still have to tell Frank and I'm already looking forward to whatever crazy reaction he'll have.

"So, what are you guys doing?" Brody asks, leaning his tall frame against the doorway.

Finley shrugs. "Girl talk. Lots to be thankful for, ye know, babe?"

His eyes twinkle lovingly at her. "You should see it from my view."

"Get a room!" I groan. Frank and I erupt into giggles. A lot to be thankful for is right. Things here look pretty damn bright at the moment.

THE EPILOGUE

"Well, who's going to be the Godparent? If you chose Finny over me—I swear, Leslie!"

"Frank!" I scream, stepping out of the bathroom after the most painful pee of my life. "Now is so not the time!" I groan loudly, feeling another contraction slamming down on me.

"Frank, come on, mate! I need to get her back out the door. We only stopped here because Leslie demanded I grab her cheetah onesie."

"I'll be able to fit into it once this basketball comes out!" I cry.

Theo wraps his arm protectively around me, murmuring expletives about the fucking onesie.

"Take these, too!" Finley cries, running out from the living room with Brody close on her heels. She hands me a pair of cheetah print slippers. "I got these for you for the hospital. You know…for the pushing part." She thrusts her fists up victoriously and smiles proudly. "Keep your feet warm!"

"Finley!" I groan. "You're so sweet."

"If fucking slippers get factored into the Godparent selection, I will murder someone."

"FRANK!" We all shout simultaneously.

"Okay, we gotta go. We'll call you as soon as I pop this baby out!" I say as Theo ushers me out the door.

"Team Girl!" Finley cries.

"Team Boy!" Frank cries.

"Good luck guys," Brody says, and they all stand teary-eyed in front of the purple door, waving Theo and I off down the road and to the hospital.

LB

"One more push should do it, Leslie!" my doctor says, grabbing some gauze and doing God knows what down there. I sure as hell ain't looking to find out. "You ready?"

"Theo!" I cry, feeling suddenly panicky and looking up at him urgently as he clenches my fist below his chin.

"Fuck, Theo. What if we were wrong? What if we should have gotten married! What if being engaged isn't enough? We don't want to give this kid a complex. We shouldn't have waited until after the birth. We should have done it before like your mother wanted us to! Winnie knows everything! Dammit! We should have listened to Winnie!"

"Leslie, it's fine. We'll be married before this baby even has its first birthday," he says, dropping a kiss into my damp hair.

"And Theo! Listen! If it's a girl," I swallow hard, feeling tired and out of breath. "We have to treat her like a princess."

"I know, baby."

"I'm serious! We have to support her no matter what her dreams are, no matter how fucked up and dumb they might sound to us. Shit, she might want to join the circus, Theo! We have to tell her that sounds tits cool, right?"

"I don't know about tits cool, but yes, something positive. Got it."

"And if it's a boy, we have to make sure he respects women." Theo nods seriously at me. "Like, not just respects them because he thinks he has to or he's trying to get into her knickers or something, but because he wants to, because he thinks women are worthy of that kind of respect. Theo, he needs to cherish them!"

"We'll teach him, Leslie. We'll make sure."

"But we have to just love them too, Theo. We have to let this boy or girl be loved and adored for who they are, and not let them ever feel like we're forcing them to be a certain way, okay?" I'm bawling uncontrollably now, a painful knot hard in my throat.

Theo presses his forehead firmly to mine and my eyes flutter—screwing closed tightly.

"We'll get this one right, Leslie. We will."

I open my eyes and nod up at him, tears streaking down my cheeks. I look back at the doctor. "Okay," I say, giving her permission to continue.

"Okay, Leslie. And PUUUUUUSH!"

"It's my lot in life to be surrounded by beautiful women," Frank says, cooing softly at the pink bundle swaddled tightly in my arms.

"Not a bad gig, eh Frank?" Finley says, smiling happily from the other side of my bed, our baby's hand wrapped tightly around her index finger. She gets tears in her eyes every time she looks at me, but I can tell they are happy tears. Deliriously happy tears.

"Why can't we know her name?" Brody asks, standing at the foot of my bed looking down at all of us proudly.

"We're waiting for my parents, they just texted saying they're on their way up," Theo says, lying next to me, one arm wrapped behind me and the other arm holding our baby's other hand.

A moment later, Theo's entire family comes shuffling into our little hospital room and everyone squeezes together to get a look at our beautiful baby girl. Winnie and Richard's eyes are both overflowing with tears and Daphney looks like a kid seeing Santa for the first time.

"Oh, baby!" Winnie says, coming close and hugging our little family in one big embrace, her soft chest mushing down on top of our little girl. She cries out loudly and Winnie pulls back, mortified. We all laugh at the sound of our baby's sweet little voice.

"You want to hold her?" I ask and she nods eagerly, taking our already sleeping baby in her arms like an old pro, swaying her gently.

Hayden shuffles forward to get a closer look and I smile brightly at him.

"Uh, here," he says, awkwardly handing me a wooden box. "I made this. It's supposed to be like a keepsake box or something. I don't know what you put in it. Baby stuff, I guess," he says and smiles sheepishly.

"It's beautiful, Hayden," I say, running my hands over the intricate design etched into the wood. "I didn't know you made stuff too!"

He shrugs, "Nothing as cool as Theo's stuff."

"Not true," Theo says. "Hayden's got a really delicate touch that I've never been able to master."

Hayden smiles, looking embarrassed. "She's beautiful, guys. Let's hope she has Leslie's smile," Hayden says, half grinning at me.

"Well," Winnie says, interrupting my quiet moment with Hayden. "The time is now. You've kept us all in the dark for long enough. Let's hear it. What's our little angel's name?"

Theo's eyes turn to mine I give him a small nod of approval. He clears his throat nervously.

"Her name is…Marisa. Winifred. Clarke."

Theo's mom's breath stutters, and her eyes well and dump tears down her face. "Marisa?" she cries, completely losing it, shaking the baby slightly with her quiet sobs. Theo's Dad, Richard, wraps his arms around her, enclosing Winnie and Marisa in a steadying embrace.

"It's a fine name. It'll feel good saying it more often again," he says, his eyes shining with tears too. He leans over, dropping a soft kiss on Marisa's pink hat-covered head.

"Here, love, you take her back before I really lose it," Winnie says, weepily passing our sweet Marisa back to me.

"Bloody beautiful name," Frank croaks and my eyes grow wide as I see tears flowing freely down his face.

"Not you too!" I say, looking at a crying Finley in Brody's arms.

"Oh piss off, Lez…this is the best day ever," she says with a wobble.

"Best day ever," Theo whispers into my hair, dropping a kiss on my head.

I look down, adoringly, stroking Marisa's soft pink cheeks, feeling a bit overcome myself. How is this kind of instant love possible? We've only just met! I gaze up into Theo's twinkling eyes. This man somehow loved me from the beginning—issues and all. And now he's looking at me with even more adoration than I ever thought possible. I didn't know I could love him anymore, but bloody hell, I do! I love him so much more.

This baby gave me that. Our little Marisa. Theo chased me and opened my heart up in ways I never thought I could ever open it up to any man. He brought me out of my darkness and I brought him out of his. And now we have this beautiful beam of light nestled safely between us in this hospital bed. This life I've got in store for me looks pretty bright indeed.

Best. Day. Ever.

THE END

If you enjoyed this book,
please consider taking the time to post a review.
Reviews are extremely helpful to authors
and there is no better way to thank them for their hard work.

THE ACKNOWLEDGEMENTS

Man, it's hard to believe this is my fourth book already! In some ways it feels like I've been writing forever, and in other ways it's like I've just begun! My one-year writing anniversary is coming up and it makes me feel grateful for how much my world has grown.

For starters, I've gained so many new friends across the pond! Visiting the UK for the first time in April was a serious full circle moment for me. I think I must be psychic because I just knew I was going to love it there and it did not disappoint. You lovely Brits welcomed me with open arms. You not only loved my books, but you loved me…obnoxious American and all. I can't thank you enough for making London truly the most magical place on Earth.

Big fat thanks to my creative sounding boards…my editor, Heather Banta, my author bestie, Sarah J Pepper, and my sister, Abby Wheeler. You three talk to me about my characters like they are real people. You are tough on me when you need to be and you help push me past those points where I want to bash my head against the wall. Drinks are on me next time…as soon as my concussion heals.

To my beta readers and proofers: It takes a lot of people to get a book to print. You need a lot of eyeballs to catch things that you're too close to see anymore. You all helped make this release one of my smoothest! Thanks for being gentle with me and handling all of my writer insecurities with patience.

To book bloggers and my London Lovers…Just, thank you! Thank you for making this fun. Thank you for being eager to share. Eager to read. Eager to cheer. It's just so damn awesome.

Thanks to Rock Star PR & Lit for working hard with me on this release!

A special thanks to Stephanie Rose for opening up to me about a very sensitive subject matter that she's dedicated her life to helping others fight through. Your candid and very personal insight helped me shed honest light on a deeply tragic journey that so many people suffer through.

I always have to thank my husband. Man, my husband. He puts up with a lot from me. I've accepted the fact that I cannot estimate the length of time "book stuff" takes me. So when I say I'm going to be home in an hour, and I'm still gone two-to-three hours later, the fact that he still loves me regardless is a beautiful thing. He's adjusted to this new world of mine and even though it's incredibly hard, he's with me through it all.

My daughter, Lolo. She changes with every book release and I love documenting something about her in the acknowledgments. Right now, she loves to tell me I'm her best friend. That fills me with such immense joy and love that I could burst on the spot. She was my first dream come true and these books are my second. Not many people can have two dreams come true. I hope we're always best friends, you little miracle! But even if we're not, I will always love you. And I will always hug you until it hurts…just a little.

My angels. My six sky-babies. My six precious beings that weren't here long enough for me to read to. I love you all more than words can say. When I see you in heaven someday, I will read you books until you can't take them anymore. I will tell you I love you until you can't believe I still have a voice. I will sing songs to you until you fall asleep in my arms…the one place that I've yet to hold you. For now though, I will continue holding you in my heart and thanking you every day for the inspiration to follow my dreams.

With love always, your mommy.

FOR MORE ABOUT THE AUTHOR

www.amydawsauthor.com

www.facebook.com/amydawsauthor

www.twitter.com/amydawsauthor

Check out more novels in the London Lovers Series, available at all major retailers!

#1 Becoming Us

#2 A Broken Us

#3 London Bound

#4 Not The One   coming soon

Also, a Memoir by Amy Daws:

Chasing Hope

A mother's story of loss, heartbreak, and the miracle of hope.

Sign up for the Amy Daws newsletter to stay informed of official release date announcements!

www.amydawsauthor.com/news

Made in the USA
Coppell, TX
09 February 2024